SLOW BURN

Also by Victor Kelleher

For young people

Forbidden Paths of Thual
The Hunting of Shadroth
Master of the Grove
Papio
The Green Piper
Taronga
The Makers
Baily's Bones
The Red King
Brother Night
Del-Del
To the Dark Tower
Where the Whales Sing
Parkland
Earthsong
Fire Dancer

For adults

Voices from the River
The Traveller
The Beast of Heaven
Em's Story
Wintering
Micky Darlin'
Storyman

VICTOR KELLEHER

SLOW BURN

VIKING

Viking
Penguin Books Australia Ltd
487 Maroondah Highway, PO Box 257
Ringwood, Victoria 3134, Australia
Penguin Books Ltd
Harmondsworth, Middlesex, England
Viking Penguin, A Division of Penguin Books USA Inc.
375 Hudson Street, New York, New York 10014, USA
Penguin Books Canada Limited
10 Alcorn Avenue, Toronto, Ontario, Canada M4V 3B2
Penguin Books (N.Z.) Ltd
Cnr Rosedale and Airborne Roads, Albany, New Zealand

First published by Penguin Books Australia, 1997
10 9 8 7 6 5 4 3 2 1
Copyright © Victor Kelleher, 1997

Typeset in 12/15 Times by Midland Typesetters, Maryborough, Victoria
Made and printed in Australia by Australian Print Group, Maryborough, Victoria

National Library of Australia
Cataloguing-in-Publication data:

Kelleher, Victor, 1939– .
Slow burn.

ISBN 0 670 87799 9.

I. Title.
A823.3

This project has been assisted by the Commonwealth Government through the Australia
Council, its arts funding and advisory body.

1 Beginnings

Say what you like, there aren't any real beginnings. That's what I've come to believe anyway. Everything's connected, sort of twisted together, like a whole lot of tangled lines. If we want beginnings we have to choose them. We have to pick out one thread from all the tangle and say, 'This is where things got started', or, 'My life would have followed a different course if such and such hadn't happened'. We have a kind of story then, or at least the start of one.

Personally I find that really hard to do – to choose a starting point I mean. Whenever I look back to those early days at home, for instance, I just feel confused. I know that if certain things had been different, then none of the bad stuff – what Mal refers to as the 'conflicts' – would have taken place. The trouble is, I honestly can't isolate a moment in time when everything changed for the worse. There's no single event I can heap the blame onto. Like I said before, it's all a tangle.

So be warned: don't go looking here for clear-cut beginnings. I ran out of once-upon-a-times long ago. The best I can do is write down some of the things that stick in my memory and leave you to make the choice – you, the person reading these words, whoever you turn out to be. That way maybe this'll become your story, too. Or as much yours as mine, because nobody can really lay claim to a story. Some people, unlucky ones like my mother, never even get to claim the story of their own lives.

The day Mum received the news, she didn't come home until early evening. She admitted afterwards that she spent most of the afternoon sitting on her own in a coffee shop. 'Thinking time,' she called it.

I was only fifteen then, not much more than a kid. I knew more or less what was going on, but it hadn't really sunk in. It was all 'out there' still, slightly unreal, the way things often are when you're young.

For Cath it must have been much harder. She's my older sister, by nearly three years, and at close on eighteen she'd already woken up to the real world. She'd guessed that the worst things don't necessarily happen to someone else.

'What did they say?' she demanded the moment Mum walked in the door, as though it was *her* test results she was asking for.

I expected Mum to blurt it all out, good or bad, because that's what I'd have done in her position; but she wasn't going to be rushed. She made a cup of tea first. Then, instead of giving us the news we'd been hanging out for all afternoon, she started talking about the past. In particular, about her childhood in a small country town, where her father had worked on the local asbestos mine.

He later died of asbestosis, by the way, like a lot of those old guys. I suppose you could call that a part of our family mythology because it happened before I was born. 'My Gramps died of rotten lungs,' I used to brag to the other kids in primary school. Like so many bits of information I'd grown up with, it didn't seem to mean a lot.

Anyway, I thought I knew everything about those early days. I'd heard Mum carrying on about them a hundred times before. 'Here she goes again,' Cath and I would say with a groan, and we'd roll our eyes up into our heads and pretend to faint.

That evening, though, it was different, and not just because of what Mum said. There was also the way she looked. Focused – that's the only way to describe her face as she talked. Her voice the same. Nothing dreamy or faraway about her at all. Listening to her, you'd have thought she was describing something that had happened only a day or two earlier.

'I was the eldest of five kids,' she told us, 'and when the fifth baby arrived the house was bursting at the seams. To make more space Dad closed in the front veranda and converted the kitchen and dining room into bedrooms. That was the usual thing in those days, how most of the old houses came to lose their verandas. And as the eldest child, the built-in veranda fell to me. It wasn't much wider than a corridor really, just a makeshift space with a fibro outer wall and a row of old casement windows.'

'Mum, please . . .' Cath interrupted, but Mum shushed her by firming the line of her lips.

'There was a kitchen of sorts at one end of the veranda,' she went on, 'and my bedroom at the other, with the front door in between. It may not sound much to you, but the fact is I loved it out there. In the mornings the sun would come streaming in, and I'd lie in bed in the warm and watch Dad get ready for work.

'He'd start by shaking out his overalls – the same pair he wore all week – flicking them so hard the dust would fly free and whirl around in the sunlight. Like snow, that's how I remember it, and Dad in the middle of it all, putting his overalls back on and kissing Mum goodbye.'

She paused for a second or two, and Cath let out this sort of breathy sigh; but by then I was looking only at Mum.

'It was asbestos dust of course,' she added as a kind of afterthought, her voice more matter-of-fact than ever. 'I daresay you guessed that already. If I close my eyes I can see it still. It had a feathery, delicate look. Quite beautiful, the way it danced and twirled in the sun, especially when the outer door swished shut. As a kid I always thought of it as the part of himself my dad left behind.'

She stopped, and I noticed then that Cath had started to cry. Real quiet, secretive almost, her shoulders hunched up around her chin. She was making little sobbing noises that she muffled with her hands, so it was a bit like listening to someone crying in another room.

She jerked her head away when Mum reached towards her; but Mum wouldn't take no for an answer.

'I'm sorry, love,' she whispered, stroking Cath's hair with the back of her hand. 'I'm really, really sorry.'

As if it was her fault. As if she was the one to blame. I think that was what got to me most of all.

@ @ @

She must have told Dad the truth straight off, because that night he got much drunker than usual. He was as bad as I'd ever seen him. By ten o'clock he'd begun roaring around the house and we had to lock the doors of our rooms; by midnight he was out on the front lawn shouting at the sky, a lot of crazy stuff about how God had let him down.

He finally passed out on the back veranda, and he was still there the next morning, sprawled on the old couch. You could hear him groaning to himself in his sleep; and when I peeked between the blinds his face looked terrible in the early light. Kind of old-young and ruined.

As things turned out, that was the last time I ever saw him. During the day, while the rest of us were at work or school, he packed up his gear and left. Just like that. No goodbyes or anything. Not even a note to Mum.

'Good riddance,' Cath said when we checked his cupboards and found them empty.

I think more than anything else she felt relieved, but not me. I was so mad I couldn't get any words out.

'He's weak, that's all,' Mum said sadly. 'This is the only way he can cope.'

Apologising for him, too. Even for him.

◎　　◎　　◎

When the letter arrived from the Company's lawyer I didn't understand it at first. It sounded so stiff and official, like one of those Government documents that don't seem to apply to anyone, alive or dead.

'They're saying they can't award me compensation,' Mum explained. 'I didn't actually work on the mine, so I'm not their responsibility.'

There was a whole lot more in the letter than that. Technical details mostly, complicated stuff about 'multiple causal factors' and 'the random incidence of similar disorders in the population at large'. But it was just so many words. The more you studied them, the less they meant. Basically Mum was right: what it came down to was the Company's refusal to accept any blame.

Even Cath was incensed, and after Mum she's the most forgiving person I've ever met.

'We'll fight them!' she said, both fists bunched, her normally pale cheeks stained a bright pink.

'What with?' Mum answered helplessly. 'My single parent's benefit won't go very far in the law courts.'

Cath had no real answer to that. The best she could do was wander around the house muttering vaguely about how she was going to *make* them pay.

As for me, all I wanted was to hurt someone – Mum, Dad, my long-dead Gramps, the nameless lawyer who had written

5

the letter, anyone – but mainly Dad, for having run out on us.

'Yeah, we'll make them pay,' I agreed, echoing Cath's words, but meaning something entirely different.

'Hush!' Mum said. 'That's stupid talk. It won't get you anywhere.'

Yet for once she was wrong. Because somehow it managed to bring me all the way to where I am now. To this fortress-style camp high above the coast, with forest all around, and the distant sound of a creek murmuring up through the dark.

It's not much, I admit, and it can't last. According to Mal, a few days is about all the time they'll give us. Maybe less. Still, it's better than being written off in some standard lawyer's letter; and then, months later, being consigned to a sterile bed in a city hospital where you're hardly more than a number.

Anything's better than that.

⊚　　⊚　　⊚

Our very first demo was Cath's idea. It must have been quite a while later because by then Mum had already had a stay or two in hospital.

'We have to make a stand somewhere,' Cath insisted, and dragged me along. To a march against uranium mining which finished up with a whole bunch of us picketing the company offices.

I can't say any of it did much for me. Not then. The picketing part I really hated: all that useless violence which didn't seem to achieve a thing. Probably the only reason I mention it here is because it's where I first met Mal.

I didn't know him from Adam at that stage. He just happened to be standing beside me when the police closed in.

'Don't resist the bastards!' he muttered, and slid an arm through mine.

6

But I'm no good in those situations. I never have been. I can put up with pushing and shoving, even with the occasional sly kick or punch. God, I had to when Dad was around. What I can't stand is people getting off on having a go at you. And that's how it seemed on our first demo. Some of the cops reached for our hair when they could have grabbed an arm; and one kept up a running commentary as he dragged people off, telling them in so many words what little turds they were.

I usually start to lose it when that happens, and it was no different then. Worse maybe, because I was unprepared. Somewhere in the background I could hear Mal shouting for me to take no notice of them and to 'play dead', but I'd already lost my chance. I was too far gone. The next thing I knew I was in the back of the police wagon, feeling bruised all over.

There were plenty of other people in there with me, most of them none too thrilled at being arrested. A few, though, looked really pleased with themselves, as if they were having a good time.

One middle-aged woman kept breaking into laughter, out of sheer happiness I suppose. I reckon as far as she and her mates were concerned they'd really made it at last. They'd arrived. And looking at their gleaming faces, I wondered what on earth I was doing there. With so much shouting and screaming going on, and with the people next to me starting to chant again and pound on the metal walls of the wagon, I felt light years away from that closed-in veranda where the dust motes, according to Mum, had danced in the sun like tiny snowflakes.

I must have lost it again round about then. It was like stepping into the dark and out again, and finding myself at the other end of the wagon with my cheek pressed to the grille in the door and Mal's face only a few centimetres away, staring in at me.

'Have some self respect!' he shouted. 'Don't give them the satisfaction!'

The cops hauled him clear before he could say any more, but that was enough – short and sharp and straight to the point, which is typical of Mal.

After that it was much easier to shut out the noise; to sit quietly in the wagon beside the others and concentrate on the things that mattered. On my long-dead Gramps for one; and on Mum herself and what she might have said if she'd seen me there.

⊚　⊚　⊚

Then there was the day I stole the flowers.

I didn't plan it or anything. I just happened to be passing a garden full of roses, the gate wide open, and it seemed the most natural thing in the world to walk in off the street and pick a great big bunch for Mum. The only dumb part was going straight on to the hospital, instead of taking them home first and wrapping them in fancy paper, the kind you get in florists'. Because when Mum saw them in my arms, unwrapped, and with the ends of the stems twisted and torn, she guessed straight off where they'd come from.

'That's not how we do things in this family,' she said. 'It's not our way.'

I looked around at the bare cream walls of the public ward. Is *this* our way? I wanted to shout at her. Is *this* how we're supposed to do things? But as usual the words wouldn't come. Not when I needed them.

'It's only a bunch of flowers, Mum,' Cath said in a small voice. 'What does it matter?'

'It matters,' she answered, refusing to budge even though she was seriously ill by then and having a lot of trouble breathing. 'It makes a difference to me.'

And I longed to shout at her again; to remind her that a few lousy flowers were the least of our worries. As it was, I just threw them down beside the bed where they lay in an untidy heap, the petals spilled out across the floor.

'You'll regret that, my boy,' she said, and I did.

⑥   ⑥   ⑥

Mum was never happy about us going on demos. I visited her once the day after an anti-logging demonstration, my face badly bruised, and she couldn't hide her disapproval.

'You'll end up like your father at this rate,' she said, though to be fair it didn't come out harsh the way that may sound.

'He wasn't drunk, Mum,' Cath explained.

Mum had to catch her breath before answering. 'There are more ways of getting drunk than from a bottle,' she said at last, 'and your father explored most of them. I don't want you following in his footsteps, that's all.'

'What about your footsteps?' I asked.

'Nor mine either,' she said, but I could tell she didn't really mean that.

At heart, I'm sure she wanted us to be like her; to stay the same inside, never mind what anybody did to us. I could feel her willing it as she lay there looking at my bruised cheek. It was like – how can I explain? – like someone trying to coax an unspoken promise from you. The kind of promise you know you can never keep.

⑥   ⑥   ⑥

I don't have separate memories of our everyday visits to the hospital. Mostly they blur together, and when I try to separate one out from the rest, all I can think of is the corridor leading up to the ward. Long and creamy-white and empty.

In fact, the part about it being empty isn't strictly true, because there were always people around. Patients in dressing-gowns and visitors and nurses pushing trolleys. Empty is how I picture it all the same. And in this picture that I carry around in my head I'm walking and walking and never quite reaching the end.

Cath isn't there with me, which is really odd, and the only sound is of someone coughing. It's a stifled, apologetic sort of cough; the kind you hear in a cinema or theatre; the cough of someone who's doing their best not to disturb anyone else, and failing miserably.

I described all this to Cath once, and she said: 'You make it sound exactly like a nightmare.'

I have no quarrel with that.

◖ ◖ ◖

On our second-to-last visit I refused to go into the ward.

'What's the point?' I said, and stopped at the door. 'We can't do anything for her.'

'Jesus, Danny!' Cath protested. 'This is your *mother* you're talking about.'

As if I hadn't realised that already.

'All the more reason to stay out here,' I said.

Cath stood on tiptoes, her eyes almost on a level with my chin, and so close she seemed to be squinting.

'You get in there, you little creep!' she said in a hoarse voice that wasn't quite a whisper and wasn't a shout either.

When I still wouldn't budge she started wrestling with me in the middle of the corridor, the two of us staggering from side to side until one of the nurses forced us apart.

'Shame on you!' she said.

'No, not on me!' I shouted back at her.

She blinked, not understanding.

10

'He's upset,' Cath said quickly, and slid between us. 'It's a difficult time.'

'There *are* other patients to be considered,' the nurse reminded us, and left.

Cath still had hold of my coat, and she stood on tiptoes again and pressed her cheek alongside mine.

'Just this once,' she whispered. 'To say goodbye, that's all.'

But I wasn't having anything to do with goodbyes. I was definite about that.

'Do it for *me*,' Cath said. 'Not for her, for me. Please, Dan.'

Somehow, while she was talking, she'd managed to work us across the corridor and into the open doorway.

'Go on,' she said, pushing me from behind.

But by then there was no need for me to go in. Through the crack on the hinged side of the door I'd already seen her. She was asleep, calm and quiet for a change; and in the few seconds I stood gazing at her, the only thing I could think of was that she had no right to look so peaceful. No right at all.

Cath was still trying to urge me inside, but I'd made up my mind.

'Why does she always have to be so bloody forgiving?' I complained.

'Mum? It's her nature, I suppose.'

'Well, it's not mine,' I said, and I pulled free and ran off along the corridor.

'That's a lie, Danny,' Cath called after me. 'It's a lie and you know it.'

⊚　⊚　⊚

Maybe Cath had a point, because when I dreamed about the visit later that night, everything worked out differently.

I was standing at the entrance to Mum's ward the same as

before; and she was exactly as I remembered her, lying peaceful and still. Except this time I didn't run off. I walked in of my own free will and sat beside the bed.

'Mum,' I said. 'I've come to say goodbye.'

At the sound of my voice her eyes flicked open. She gazed straight at me and smiled.

'I knew you'd come,' she said. 'I knew it.'

She sounded so happy that I wasn't ready for what happened next. It was as if my being there and saying goodbye had triggered something. One minute she was solid and real, the next she'd begun to fade, until soon she was hardly more than a ghost. I could see the folds of the pillow through her head, the sheet under her hand.

'Mum?' I said. 'Mum!'

And I woke up, feeling guilty as hell. To a pitch-dark house that didn't seem like home any more. A house I didn't want to be in, not on my own.

Without bothering to turn on the light, I slid out of bed and padded down the hall to Cath's room. She only woke up after I'd climbed in beside her.

'You're too old for this,' she said, and clicked on the bedside lamp.

I couldn't really argue with her. It was the morning of my seventeenth birthday, which is something else I'm not likely to forget. Just the same I reached across and clicked off the light.

'Half an hour,' I pleaded, 'then I'll leave.'

I could hear her breathing in the dark, her body straight and stiff beside me.

'I can't take Mum's place, Danny,' she said after a while. 'I can never do that.'

'Shut up,' I said.

But she wouldn't be quiet, wouldn't just let me lie there safe and warm.

'Mum kept asking for you this afternoon,' she said, and I could hear in her voice that she'd started to cry. 'She kept asking where you were, and I didn't know what to say.'

Already there was a greyness in the room, from the coming dawn. I could see the curve of Cath's cheek in the light from the window, the faint shine on her wet skin. I thought: *If I close my eyes I can shut out the day.* It was how a kid thinks, but I didn't care.

'Did you hear me, Danny?' Cath said, her body still tense and stiff and half turned away.

'I heard,' I said, and felt her slacken and give in, the two of us snuggling into the dark of the bed together.

'That's all right then,' she said, which was another lie, but hers this time.

⊚   ⊚   ⊚

I didn't feel like crying the next day either. The day of our final visit to the hospital. It was as if I'd dried up and didn't have a single tear left in me.

Not Cath though. She was slumped in a chair on the other side of the bed, her face in her hands. Every time she sobbed or shuddered, the tears trickled out from between her fingers and dripped onto her lap.

I was watching Cath because I didn't want to look at Mum's face on the pillow. It had changed. It wasn't the way I wanted to remember her. It was the face of someone else entirely. Someone without a soul is all I can say.

I hadn't ever meant to look at this other person. I'd known all along it wouldn't be a good idea. Yet a few minutes earlier my eyes had strayed in the general direction of the pillow, of their own accord almost, the way eyes often do. From then on, whether I liked it or not, I had these two faces in my head;

two faces that refused to match. One full of life, the other empty.

According to Cath, that's my problem. She reckons I can't accept the fact that Mum's gone, that the dead face is now the real one.

'Let the grave have her, Danny,' she's told me often enough. 'It's what she would have wanted.'

'Is it?' That's more or less my usual answer. 'How can anyone *want* to be dead? Or to die like that especially?'

Anyway, enough said. Back to our last day at the hospital. There I was trying to pretend I hadn't seen the second face on the pillow when Cath suddenly stopped crying, wiped the tears from her eyes, and glared accusingly at me.

'What the hell's wrong with you?' she said angrily. 'Do you have a piece missing or something?'

I understood what she meant. She was asking why I hadn't collapsed into floods of tears like her.

'Maybe Mum was the one who had the piece missing,' I said, and found myself risking another quick glance at the pillow.

'Don't you bad-mouth her now,' Cath warned me, and jumped up from her chair.

But voices can be like eyes sometimes. They act like they have a life of their own, never mind what you might want them to say.

'She was as bad as Dad,' I said. 'In the end they both ran away. They didn't have the guts ...'

Cath came at me before I could finish. I tried to make it to the door, but I slipped and fell.

'Get up, you little bastard!' Cath yelled, standing over me. 'Get up, or I swear to God I'll ... I'll ...'

She didn't manage to finish either. The door flew open and one of the doctors came rushing in. I thought for a minute Cath would set about him too. She was capable of it – a bit like Dad in the old days, before the booze got him. The doctor must have realised as much because he muttered a few words of protest and soon beat a retreat. Then Cath was hauling me to my feet, dragging at my hair, my collar, anything she could reach.

She'd stopped being mad by then. All the fight had gone out of her. She'd begun crying again, her tears dripping onto me now. And when she finally had me upright, all she could do was wrap both arms around my waist and bury her face in my chest.

(That last part at least I understood: she didn't want to look at the person on the pillow any more than I did. And who can blame her?)

'What are we going to do with you, Danny?' she whispered, her face still pressed into my shirtfront.

I had to think about that one, and it wasn't easy, not with the bed only a pace or two away. So I gave up in the end, just like Mum.

'I don't know,' I said, 'but I'll think of something. I promise.'

⊚   ⊚   ⊚

I thought it would rain. I had this vague idea that it usually rained at funerals. But it blew instead, long steady gusts that bent the trees outside and howled around the crematorium like some wild beast. (That's how Mal described it afterwards.)

A bunch of Mum's rellies had come down from Brisbane for the service, second cousins and great aunts and uncles we barely knew. A few even insisted on making speeches. I can't say I listened much. I didn't listen later either, at the house, where they stood around eating sandwiches and cakes and drinking tea.

Eating and drinking, for God's sake! Filling their faces on a day like that!

And all the talk. Roomfuls of it. With the wind the only voice that seemed to matter. Mal's wild beast stalking the crematorium and the house.

I think that was the only voice I really heard. It found a partner or echo near the end of the service when the far doors of the crematorium opened and the coffin trundled in. For a few seconds you could hear the furnace roar. Another beast, there to take her. Then the doors closed, and we were back to the talk and the tears.

I was glad she'd gone, mind you. The smell of the flowers was bad enough, but the thought of what they might be hiding was worse.

'When my number comes up,' Dad said once – he was probably drunk at the time – 'there'll be no stinking grave for yours truly. Who wants worms and maggots gnawing at their corpse? Whew!' He held his nose as though blocking out a bad smell. 'The flames can have the rubbish that's left over at the end. And welcome.'

It was the same for her. The furnace burned away the part I didn't care to think about and gave us in its place a small heap of greyish ash.

Days later Cath poured it from the urn into our cupped hands. We breathed gently on it, and the tiny ash peaks wafted away in powdery waves.

'What'll you do with your half?' Cath asked.

I tasted it with the tip of my tongue. It was gritty and bitter and tasteless all at once, but her just the same.

'I'll find somewhere for it,' I said.

'What about here?' she suggested, and threw her handful into the wind.

We were standing in the back garden at the time, the house already closed up.

'Go on,' Cath urged me. 'Why not? Get it over with.'

I nearly did. What stopped me was the story Mum told us, of the asbestos dust flying free in her bedroom-cum-veranda all those years ago.

I shook my head. 'No, I'll find a better place than this,' I said.

Cath must have thought I meant some green valley or lake or something; but what I had in mind was one of those bullet-shaped silver amulets you hang on a chain around your neck. The kind you can buy at the markets. I have mine still all these years later, warm against my chest; hard and sure when I press my hand to it. As Cath so often reminds me, I've never really let her go. On the other hand, why should I?

But I'm running on ahead of myself again, and I need to get back to the funeral. To the day that ended a whole part of our life. And also ended hers, period. No more tomorrows for her once the furnace doors had closed.

You might think those flames were hot and final enough to end all the talk as well, but no way. Even mouthfuls of cake and tea couldn't do that. Once back at the house, it went on and on. Memory lane stuff mostly. Dozens and dozens of stories about how marvellous or clever or witty or beautiful she'd been; how she'd done this and said that; and how she'd had this really wicked sense of humour that had the old aunties laughing and crying in their teacups.

And d'you know? I didn't recognise her in any of it. I didn't catch so much as a glimpse of the little girl on the veranda, watching her dad go off to work; or of the woman who lay coughing in the hospital bed for weeks on end. So where was she? The real person, I mean. And what had she lived for anyway?

I whispered those questions to Cath, and she dragged me into the pantry behind the kitchen and gave me a good shake.

'She's in *there*,' she said, tapping me hard on the forehead. 'This is the only place that matters.'

But there were lots of other things in my head too, which I didn't know how to handle. All kinds of feelings and ideas that had got hopelessly mixed up with her.

Mal was the one who sorted them out for me, but that was a bit later in the day. In the meantime, while the rellies were still around, Cath and I had to cope with this stranger who happened to have Mum's name and who everyone kept yakking on about.

Even Cath lost her cool eventually.

'Go home!' she bawled at them. 'Go away and leave us alone!'

They took that in their stride as well.

'It's the shock,' one old bloke said – Uncle Ken or Bob or something like that.

'There, there, dear,' an old auntie added, patting her. 'We understand.'

And they were off again, as if making up for the fact that they hadn't come near her while she was alive. As if Dad and his drinking had really been their reason for staying away.

By late in the afternoon Cath and I had gone past the desperate stage. We'd taken to giggling and laughing together in corners, like conspirators in some secret plot that only we knew about. And our laughter, in Cath's opinion, was what finally drove them out.

At the front door, seeing them off in the tired evening light, we had to put up with a last round of advice and tearful memories and would-be wise sayings. Then they were gone and there was only the emptiness of the house for us to deal with.

Coffin-like, that's how it felt. It could almost have belonged to anyone. With used cups and plates scattered everywhere, it

18

was more like some deserted restaurant than a place where people lived.

Cath didn't waste any time. 'Mum'd throw a fit if she saw all this,' she said, and got stuck into the clearing up.

When in doubt, keep busy, that's Cath's motto. She says it's not my motto too because men think home's a place where they get waited on. Right or wrong, I couldn't bring myself to start collecting up plates and half-chewed sandwiches, not on that evening. I left Cath to it while I wandered from room to room, trying to take in the strangeness of it all.

That's how I managed to stumble on Mal. I mean that literally, because he was sprawled on a chair in my bedroom, and I tripped over his feet in the half dark, not realising he was there.

For a few awful seconds I nearly believed in ghosts. The noise I made brought Cath running, and she's never been very keen on Mal. She reckons his character is too much like his name, though I've tried explaining how there's a lot more to him than that.

'Get him out of here,' she demanded, clicking on the overhead light. 'Today was supposed to be for family, no one else.'

Mal has these skinny shoulders which he shrugs a lot. 'My, we're really getting picky, aren't we?' he said, but he didn't stick around.

I saw him off at the front door, the same as I had the rellies. Except in Mal's case there were no tearful farewells. Quite the reverse.

'So what do you plan to do about her?' he said.

He was standing on the porch with his back turned, his face lifted to the western sky.

I didn't want to understand him, not at first.

'Her?' I said, trying to sound dumb.

He swung towards me. 'Your mother,' he said bluntly. 'The one they killed. Who else?'

And on the badly lit porch of a house I didn't call home any more, everything seemed to come into hard, bright focus. That's the only way I can explain it. All the fuzziness and confusion of the previous weeks and months seemed to disappear.

Cath, meanwhile, had crept along the passage, because suddenly she was there at my back.

'Don't listen to him, Danny,' she whispered. 'He's a creep.'

But I couldn't pretend any more. I *had* listened, and it was exactly like hearing myself speak, as though my own words and thoughts had spilled out of someone else's mouth.

I'll say this for Mal, he always knows when to press home an advantage.

'So what's the plan?' he said again. 'Or are you just going to let them get away with it?'

He didn't wait for an answer. He can be cunning when he wants to. He simply stepped off the porch and walked out into the waiting dark.

'Let him go,' Cath said.

She'd said the same about Mum, and I didn't take any notice this time either. Because I'd already worked it all out by then, deep down in myself where words don't really reach. I'd decided that nobody has to die for nothing. Nobody. Not even someone as forgiving as Mum.

2 The Journal

I thought I might have to go interstate, but when I looked up the Company in the phone book I found they have offices here in Sydney.

I went there this afternoon, for what Mal would call a recce. They're in one of the big buildings in the CBD, a towerblock of glass and stone, just as I'd imagined. I saw from the notice-board in the foyer that they have the top three floors.

I didn't go up. I stood in the foyer for an hour or so, watching people walk to and from the lifts. People in suits mostly, men and women. Any of them could have worked for the Company, they were so much alike. I wasn't prepared for that. I'd had this idea in my head that the ones from the Company would have a definite look about them. All I'd have to do was glance in their direction and I'd see in their faces who they were.

How dumb can you get!

The funny thing was, when I arrived back at the flat Cath started quizzing me.

You've been up to something, she said, you have that look!

I couldn't help laughing, which only made her more suspicious.

I know you, Danny, she said. You're not like the rest, you wear your heart on your sleeve.

I said: What about the ones who don't have a heart?

She shook her head. According to Cath there're no such people. Everyone cares about someone. Even Dad.

Maybe, I said, remembering all the faces in the foyer.

I made up my mind to go again today, and then didn't. KFC, the kids at school say, meaning chicken. And it's true. I *do* feel scared. Not of who I could find up there, hidden behind all the glass and stone, but of what I'll be letting myself in for.

Whatever you put your hand to, Mum used to say, do it with all your might. She liked to quote from the Bible, and for once I agree with her. And with it, the big B.

Whatever you put your hand to . . .!

It's a scary thought. As scary as that towerblock of theirs, with its thousands of windows for eyes.

Never mind, it'll keep.

Sept 5

Had a bust-up with Cath over wagging school.

A whole week, Danny, she said, really shocked.

So I told her how I'd left for good. I didn't have to think about it. I just knew, in the heat of the moment, that school was behind me for ever. I don't belong there any more. I'd dumped it the moment I'd walked into the Company's building.

That only made Cath madder at me. You don't have long to go! she shouted. And Mum asked you to stay on. It's what she *wanted!*

I should have kept quiet. Instead I said: Mum also wanted us to become doormats, like her.

After that things got out of hand. There were neighbours knocking on the ceiling below and on the floor above. Someone even came and banged on the door.

I put a stop to it in the end.

Dad would be proud if he could see us now, I said, and Cath didn't utter another word. She just rushed off and locked herself in her room.

I can still hear her crying as I write this. I wish I could explain everything and make her understand, but I can't. She's too like Mum.

I went again this morning. There's a high-speed lift that bypasses the lower half of the building and only stops at the upper floors. It opened directly opposite the reception desk so I didn't have time to change my mind. The receptionist hardly looked any older than I am, which helped. She was wearing a fancy suit and she had the usual manicured hands, but underneath all the glitz she was just another school dropout. I couldn't have hated her if I'd tried.

I told her I was a student doing research on mining companies, and her smile didn't slip once all the time I was talking.

You'll need to see our Mr French, she said.

While she was trying to raise him on the phone, another man arrived in the lift. In his fifties, I'd say, with grey hair and an important look about him. You could tell he was somebody just from the way the receptionist acted.

Who's this then? he said, smiling at me.

When the girl explained, he laughed and said he'd deal with it himself.

He took me along a corridor and into the biggest office I'd ever seen, with the biggest desk. A secretary followed us in, but he waved her away too.

Some grass roots contact will do me good, he told her, or something like that.

The office had windows along two whole walls, and shelves underneath for rows of fancy-looking rock samples.

What do you think? he said, and nodded towards the view. He was already rummaging in a drawer for brochures.

I went over and looked down. It was a real power trip, with half of Sydney spread out below. A million dollar view, Dad would have called it, and I knew right off that this was the man I was after.

He had an armful of brochures when I turned back.

Here, he said, these should help with the project.

I checked through them. They were all about mining for gold and nickel and silver and other metals.

Where're the ones on asbestos mining? I said. What have you done with those?

His face changed then. He came closer to how I'd imagined him.

God Almighty! he said. So that's what this is all about. I might have guessed.

I dropped the brochures at his feet and they landed in a fan-shape, like the flowers I'd thrown down next to Mum's bed at the hospital that day.

These aren't what I'm after, I said, and left.

Hey! What's your name? I could hear him shouting as I walked back along the corridor. Someone get that bloody kid's name!

His name – I'd seen it on the door – was Albright. Preston Albright. It felt a bit like those glittering rock samples on the shelves in his office. Something hard and sure to hold onto as the lift carried me down to ground level.

Sept 8

I waited across the road from the building just before lunch-time. He came out at about one, and on his own, which was surprising. I found out why a few minutes later, after I'd followed him to this Japanese restaurant. Through the window I saw him walk across to a table at the back, where a woman was already waiting. She was much younger than him and better looking. They didn't kiss, just clasped hands for a moment, but it amounted to the same thing. Their faces gave them away.

He left before she did. I stayed, and followed her this time.

26

Sitting alone on the train, she reminded me of the receptionist in his offices. Underneath all the makeup and the flashy gear, she's hardly more than a kid. Not really great looking either. Just young, which is probably what turns him on. Her flat's pretty ordinary too, in one of those cheap red-brick buildings in Marrickville. I made a note of her name on the post box, but it's not like his. There's nothing hard or bright about it.

As I came away I decided she had more in common with Mum – with us – than with him.

Sept 13

Cath says I should be ashamed, signing on for the dole when I really belong in school.

I don't *belong* anywhere, I said, which is true.

What I couldn't tell her, though it's also true, is that the dole (if I ever manage to get it!) is just a method of buying time.

And also of wasting time, because every evening it's the same. I wait in the underground carpark for him to come down, and then watch as he drives away in his big car to God knows where. I've tried the phone book and Directory Enquiries, but they don't help either. He might as well not exist outside of office hours.

Except he does. He *does*.

Sept 16

I've waited outside her flat two days running, and tonight he drove up bang on six o'clock and stayed till late.

Got you! I thought when he first arrived, but I was wrong. At midnight he climbed into his car and disappeared, same as always. The incredible vanishing man!

I didn't come home straight away. Her flat has a veranda

which somebody's built in, like Mum's when she was a kid. There's a pepper tree next to it, and I climbed up and peered through the window. I could see her sitting on the unmade bed in her dressing-gown, her face sort of blank. Not happy or miserable or even in between. Just empty.

I really hated him then. Him. The person he is.

When I eventually find out where he lives, what then? The big question.

Mal asked me the same thing the other day.

I'm not sure yet, I told him. I'll decide when the time comes.

So this is the great master plan, he said, and started laughing.

I hadn't counted on the rain, and there's no shelter near her flat, not even a shop doorway to stand in. I was soaked by the time his car arrived, and cold. The crowbar felt like a chunk of ice inside my coat, and I was shaking so much I could barely hang onto it. That wasn't just because of the cold though.

I waited a while longer, for the night to get really dark, then I waited some more. By about ten o'clock I knew I wasn't going to do anything. I tried to, I swear. I kept telling myself it was only a car, a lousy heap of metal, but it didn't make any difference. The road felt about a kilometre wide, and I couldn't get myself to cross it.

I finally gave up and trudged home through the rain.

Cath was still up watching TV when I arrived, though it was after midnight.

What time d'you call this? she said, her eyes fixed on the screen.

Bedtime, I said, and tried to sneak off to my room before she could get a good look at the state I was in.

But Cath has eyes in the back of her head when it suits her.

You look like hell, d'you know that? she called after me. Like a ghost.

Yeah, a ghost, I said. Maybe that's how I feel.

She killed the TV with the remote and swung around.

You've got it all wrong, Danny. Mum's supposed to be the ghost, not you. You can still do something with your life. You've still got choices to make.

And there it was in a nutshell. I have to admit I couldn't have put it better. Sometimes I wonder what I'd do without Cath.

Sept 21

Rain again, and cold, the car more or less in the same parking spot outside the flat, like a rerun of the other night. Except this time I kept in mind what Cath had said about ghosts and choices, and I marched straight across the street and rammed the crowbar into the gap beside the door.

It's easy to see now how I didn't really think the whole thing through, because the car alarm caught me off guard and I nearly panicked. I didn't freeze or run off, but for a while all I could do was go on heaving away on the crowbar, even though it was pretty clear I wasn't getting anywhere. Or nowhere that mattered. The main door panel buckled, the side window cracked, but the lock held. As I should have guessed it would, because he's not likely to be driving around in some piece of junk, is he? Not my Company man.

I'm not too sure what steadied me. Someone calling out maybe. Shut that bloody thing off! Past the scream of the alarm I heard the crash of a door being thrown open somewhere in the flat building. Then I was round on the other side of the

29

car, *thinking* again, using the butt end of the crowbar to smash at the passenger's side window.

It gave way after about three hits and I was in. A few seconds, that's all it took to check the glove box and find it empty. A few seconds more and I was out of there, away through the back streets of Marrickville, with nothing to show for my trouble. No address, no log book, nothing.

But I didn't care. I'd done it, that was all I could think of. I'd made the first move. I'd shown him what he could expect from now on.

I can't remember actually stopping, though I must have, because next thing I was crouched in the dark in one of the old unused dirt lanes. There was a biggish tree overhead and the smell of rain. Heavy drops kept plopping onto the ground all around me. I was soaked again, but it didn't seem to matter. The only thing that mattered was the feel of the crowbar in my hands. If it hadn't been for some dog barking away in the background, I would have shouted out loud with relief. Still, I couldn't stay quiet.

You see, I said, speaking the words softly to the dark, and the dog went wild. You see!

Later, at home, I wondered what I'd got so excited about. Then later still, when I woke up in the night, all I could remember was breaking into a car.

For what?

Sept 23

Mal says that what I need is a motorbike. He reckons he might even be able to borrow one for me if I'm serious.

I told him, I'm serious.

He gave me a doubtful look, what I think of as his I-don't-know-about-you-Danny look. He'll probably come good all the same. He usually does.

The bike's really ancient, like a leftover from Dad's generation. Maybe older. It goes though. Just. If you coax it.

What did you expect? Mal complained. A bloody BMW? That'd make you as bad as him, the bastard you're after.

Mal came around and helped me strip the motor. It wasn't hard, not with a two-stroke, but the shit we cleaned out of it! Afterwards it went a lot better. We push-started it in the lane behind the flat and it blew out a lot of smoke and then ran well. 'Sweet' was how Mal described it. He can get quite clucky over things like engines. Never about people. With them he's different.

They knew how to build these crates in the old days, he said. A bit of TLC and they keep going for ever. She'll get you there all right. Just see you make the bastard pay.

I could hear the difference in his voice right at the end. Real hard. Sometimes I wish I was as sure as Mal.

For practice, I offered Cath a ride.

What about the cops? she said. You don't have a licence.

Stuff the cops, I said.

Yeah, stuff them, she agreed, carefree for a change, and we rode out to Maroubra and sat on the beach eating ice-creams.

There were people flying kites down near the water. Old fashioned kites, not those guided-missile things that sound like F18s. One had a grinning face painted on its underside and it kept swooping overhead with this funny sighing noise.

When will things get better for us, Danny? Cath asked all of a sudden.

I pretended to look at the kites.

Soon, I said.

No, I mean it, she said. I really want to know.

The people handling the kite strings were charging up and down at the edge of the surf, shouting into the wind and laughing. One of them, a woman twice our age, stumbled and fell in the shallows. She stood up, dripping wet, laughing harder still, and you could tell she didn't care a damn.

Maybe we should take up kite flying, I said.

Although I was facing away, I could see Cath's expression from the corner of my eye.

Yeah, I thought you'd come out with something like that, she said.

Sept 30

I've decided to do it in stages.

Stage one was today. Or was supposed to be. I waited across the street from the exit to the underground parking. The perfect spot. Except when his car appeared, the bike wouldn't start. I kicked and kicked the bloody thing. By the time the engine caught, he was long gone.

Bugger Mal.

Oct 1

Second time lucky. The bike started at the first try and I followed him through the city and across the bridge.

It wasn't as easy as I'd expected, mainly because of the rush-hour traffic. Some drivers really resent motorbikes. They crowd you when you ride in the middle of the lane, and they nudge you aside if you pull over. One Volvo damn near drove me into the side of the bridge.

What with having to stay alive and also keep him in sight, I was in a sweat long before I reached the North Shore. When he turned off the freeway a few kilometres further on, I let him go.

I had to come home the long way, via Gladesville, because I'd forgotten to take money for the bridge toll. I was so pissed off, I kept thinking: that's more money he owes me. But it was all bullshit. Worse, it was the way *he* would think, because this isn't about money. It never has been, not even long ago when they sent the lawyer's letter. Especially then.

Whatever happens in the next week or two, I have to get that through to him. Somehow.

Oct 2

He didn't show today. He was probably visiting his girlfriend in Marrickville.

The child bride, I called her when I described the set-up to Mal.

The under-age whore, more like, Mal corrected me, and laughed.

It was the only time we've ever had a serious row. At one point he even threatened to take back the bike.

Just try it, I said, and he must have realised he'd gone too far because he backed off.

You're full of sentimental crap, Danny! he yelled as he was leaving. You're soft, d'you know that? A puppy dog who's playing at being a wolf.

Cath heard him from the other end of the flat.

Who wants to be a wolf anyway? she said.

Not Cath, that's for sure.

Oct 3

I picked him up at the freeway exit, just on dark. It was much easier following him on the North Shore, even in the half light.

I could have tracked him all the way if I'd wanted, but I peeled off a bit before Northbridge. I don't want him getting suspicious.

Mal's back, and I'm glad.

No hard feelings, bro, he said, and gave me his double handshake.

He also gave me a picture of a wolf he'd torn from a magazine. A beautiful animal, but fierce, staring straight at the camera with round unblinking eyes.

Make believe it's a mirror, Mal said, and grinned.

He'd brought along some beers, and I sat with him under the tree out the back while he drank them.

Have one, he said, and when I shook my head he didn't make any of his smart-arse comments about our 'family heritage' as he calls it.

You're right, was all he said. You need to keep your head clear at a time like this.

I knew then we were back on track and I could talk to him again. Though mostly I complained about how my Company man had taken to spending all his evenings in Marrickville.

Crutch time, Mal called it, which made us both laugh.

Yeah, crutch time, he repeated after the fourth or fifth beer. That could be the way to get to him, bro.

It was something I'd already thought about, but somehow it still seemed wrong. To involve the girl, I mean. If she'd stayed as the well-dressed woman in the restaurant, all grown up and sure of herself, I wouldn't have minded. But ever since the night I peered through her window and she changed into an empty-faced girl on an unmade bed, I've definitely had no quarrel with her.

So maybe Mal wasn't far short of the mark about a week ago. Maybe it's no good pretending to be a wolf when you're not.

Maybe . . .

I'll admit this much: after Mal had gone I didn't *feel* a lot like a wolf as I stumbled round in the dark picking up his empty cans. The smell of them was the worst part. It reminded me of Dad.

Oct 8

Stage three. The easiest of the lot because he only lives a few kilometres beyond where I last left him. In a house overlooking Sugarloaf Bay. (Where else?) A big place built of concrete and glass, just like the towerblock. I was glad about that. It tied everything together.

There were two cars in the garage, so I knew straight off he was married. No kids though. Or none that I could see. The house is set up on concrete pillars, with a stairway leading down to the bay, and when I crept up the stairs in the dark I could see him and his wife sitting at opposite ends of the dining room table. Not a kid in sight, and no sign of one either. All the rooms I peered into had the same neat, unlived-in look, like something out of an ideal-home-type magazine.

His wife's about his age I'd say. A bit younger maybe, but not by much, with pale hair that's grey and blond at the same time. They don't talk a lot. Mainly it was 'Pass the salt' or 'How was your day?' – that sort of stuff, polite but friendly. So she obviously doesn't know about Miss Fancy Pants in Marrickville.

That got me thinking. About what might happen if she *did* find out. That for starters.

It seemed a good idea while I was there at the house. Maybe

it was being out in the dark, spying on them, that made it seem right. You feel different about people when you start peering through windows. Kind of in control. Powerful even. Like him.

That's what worries me. The thought that this is how he feels, this is what it's like to stand in his shoes.

Later, riding back across the city, I remembered something old Purvis, our history teacher, told us at school. He was talking about the rights and wrongs of some war or other. You act like the enemy, he said, and you *are* the enemy.

Oct 9

I tried making up one of those anonymous letters you see in movies, where you cut words from newspapers and magazines and stick them onto a plain sheet of paper. It took longer than I'd expected because some of the words were hard to find.

I got about halfway down the page (as far as 'She is much younger than you') and then I chucked it in. It felt really mean.

You act like the enemy, etc.

I can almost hear Mal's disapproval, but what the hell! He can make like the bad guys if he wants.

Oct 13

I've spent the last few evenings at Sugarloaf Bay. Tonight he was off somewhere (in Marrickville probably) and she was there on her own. She's pretty sad when he's away. Most of the time she just sat in front of the TV, though she wasn't all that interested. You could tell from the way she kept glancing towards the uncurtained window. At the lights across the bay I expect. Once she looked straight at me – or at the place where I was crouched – and I held my breath and didn't move. I couldn't hear the TV, only the slap of the water on the shore below. Then she drew both hands down her cheeks and sighed and switched her gaze back to the screen.

Round about ten she fell asleep. The TV was still on and she'd lolled sideways on the couch, with her head tipped back. It was how Mum used to sit and doze in the weeks before they took her into hospital. The same look on both their faces.

But never mind how she looks, they're not the same. They never can be. And I went over and tapped on the window with my nail, loud enough to wake her.

I heard the veranda door open as I was creeping off down the stairs. She sounded puzzled more than scared.

Is that you, Preston? she called out.

Oct 15

Mal still reckons both the women are fair game. After all, as far as my Company man's concerned, they're his personal property. Things he owns. Extensions of him almost. Or so Mal says.

I asked Mal: Like his house, d'you mean?

Why not? he said.

I managed to keep a straight face.

So if I chuck a brick through his window, it'll be like chucking a brick at him. Is that the idea?

It was only meant as a joke, not serious, but Mal immediately brightened up.

Now you're talking, Danny, he said, and rubbed his hands together. You're really talking.

Oct 24

I haven't been round there for quite a while. Nor to the Marrickville place either. Mal must have guessed because yesterday morning he asked for the motorbike back.

Get stuffed, I told him.

He didn't seem to mind.

He said: Just as long as you're going through with it.

It! That's the real problem. How to decide.

Cath's no help. The very opposite in fact. This morning, for instance, she started on at me about how I lie around in bed all day.

I'm thinking, I said.

Yeah, that's what worries me, she answered. You're always dangerous when you're quiet, Dan. Even Mum knew that.

I could feel a row waiting to happen, like some ugly stranger at the door getting ready to come in. To keep him out, all I had to do was turn the lock. Instead, I lifted the latch.

Mum didn't know much, though, did she? I said. Just look at where she is now.

After that it was on, with Cath screaming at the top of her voice, telling me how screwed up I am and how I'm hell on wheels to live with.

When it comes to trading insults, Cath's always been much quicker than me. She's the really bright one in the family, let's face it. And after a while I couldn't take any more. I just couldn't.

It's the only time I've ever hit her, and I swear it'll never, *ever* happen again. I'm certain of that. I felt terrible, and so did Cath. She sat huddled on the couch for ages afterwards, crying to herself.

A bit later, when she was quiet, I managed to coax her over to the table, but I couldn't get her to eat the food I'd cooked.

I'm losing you, Danny, she said, and started to cry again. You're drifting away, and there's nothing I can do about it.

I'm here, Cath, I whispered. I'm not going anywhere.

She shook her head, not answering, refusing even to look at me.

A few days more then, I pleaded, and I think that was when I finally made up my mind. Things'll be better for us after that.

She turned towards me, her eyes all red and swollen.

No they won't, Danny. They'll be worse.

She sounded so down that I did something I'd vowed never to do again. I wished Mum alive, Dad back with us, and our old life firmly in place. For ever.

But you can't do stuff like that and get away with it. I've learned that much. It made me feel awful, nearly as bad as when I'd hit Cath.

I'm not fifteen any more, Cath, I told her. I'd wind the clock back if I could, but I can't. No one can.

She must have wondered what I was talking about. I wonder a bit myself sometimes.

Oct 30

It's all arranged. She'll be out of the house, because she always is on Wednesday afternoons. It's her day for tennis, which she never misses. And he'll be in the city as usual. At least I *hope* he will. I rang his secretary and tried to set up an appointment, to make sure he's there on the day. I told her I was an independent prospector with news that would interest him, but she wouldn't buy it.

Mr Albright is busy all afternoon, she said firmly, which didn't mean a thing. It was her way of putting me off. Still, he's just arrived back from a trip, so he's not likely to disappear for a while.

Now all that's left is the waiting. The hard part.

Nov 1

To pass the time I've started going for runs. They help me sleep, and they've also eased the tension in the flat.

d to see you doing something normal for a change,
when I staggered in after my first run.

g the bike's normal, I answered, but she shook her

You look different when you come back from those rides,
she said. This is better.

Cath treated us to a movie last night.

It's like old times, she whispered, cuddling up in the dark.

But it wasn't. The movie was about some people who have
to trek across a wintry landscape. There's one scene where
they're caught in a blizzard, and flurries of snow, like fine
white dust or powder, are blowing into their faces.

Jesus! I said, and I got up and walked out.

Cath followed a few minutes later. She didn't say anything.
Not then. She clung to my arm all the way home as though
she was scared I might flit off somewhere and lose myself like
those people in the storm.

Outside the flat, in a dark part of the street, she stopped and
took my face in both hands.

This is no good, Dan, she said. You have to learn to forget.

Forget what?

You know.

And forgive too?

Yes, that as well.

What do you take me for? I said, and tried to pull away.

Both her fists were bunched in my hair, hanging on.

This is crazy talk, Danny. There's nothing you can do about
the past. You're the one who said we can't wind the clock
back, remember?

I can stop the clock though, I told her.

She let go of me, her face pale in the shadows.

What do you mean?

You know, I said. You can guess.

No, tell me.

It was the first time I'd said it aloud: I'm going to kill the bastard. The one who did it to her.

She backed away.

This isn't you, Danny. It's someone else.

Then she left me in the street. I looked up, but with the city at my back there wasn't a star to be seen. I stayed there all the same, until I was sure Cath had gone to bed and I wouldn't have to talk about it any more.

One day to go.

Nov 4

I'll just describe what happened. I'm not proud of any of it. It's the way things worked out, that's all.

I arrived soon after midday and hid the bike in a small reserve beside the house. She came out at two, in her tennis gear, and drove off in the car. I gave her ten minutes or so, in case she'd forgotten something and had to come back, and then I crept around the house to the lower stairs, down near the jetty.

It wasn't hard getting into the house. I was pretty sure they didn't have an alarm system, so all I had to do was force a back window. The rest was easier still. I stripped the beds in the bedrooms and made separate heaps of the sheets and blankets. I did the same with the curtains in the living room, and then soaked each of the heaps with petrol. There was some petrol left over, so I trailed it between the heaps, linking them all up.

And that was it. I was ready and it still wasn't quite three o'clock.

I had a drink of water before I rang his office.

Mr Albright's a very busy man, his secretary told me – as much as to say, get off the line and stop wasting my time.

But I was ready for that.

It's about his wife, I said. An emergency.

His wife?

You could hear the difference in her voice, and less than a minute later he was on the line.

Who is this, please?

A friend, I said.

Of mine?

This was the part I'd rehearsed: No, of your wife's lover.

There was a long pause.

Her lover?

Yes, he's with her right now, back at your house. I thought you might be interested.

And I put the phone down.

It rang a few minutes later as I'd guessed it would. I let it go on for a while before picking it up.

Yes? I said, keeping my voice low so I sounded different, older.

The line went dead straight away, and after that it was a case of wait and see.

I reckoned he'd need twenty minutes to get from the city at that time of day, but in fifteen his car was outside. The front door slammed, and I heard him stalking down the passage.

Joy? he called out. Joy, are you there?

To reach the main bedroom he had to cross the living area, and I'd stationed myself behind the door. I had the noose all ready. Before he could turn, I slipped it over his shoulders and pulled it tight. He didn't go down without a struggle, but I'm much bigger than he is and I used my weight. Forcing him to his knees, I pinned him from behind while I slipped the other noose around his ankles.

He'd been swearing at me up till then. He only went quiet

when I heaved his feet back and up and tied the loose end of the rope to his wrists. Trussed like that, he could hardly move. He had to twist his head around even to see me.

What do you want? he said, and he didn't sound like a company director any more.

You, I said.

Look, if it's money you're after ...

I didn't let him finish.

Some things you can't buy with money, I told him, and stopped because he wasn't listening.

He'd smelled the petrol. You could tell from the way he lifted his head clear of the carpet and sniffed the air.

He began to yell after that, real panic-stations stuff. His face was nearly purple and drops of spit were flying in all directions. I'd meant to tell him a whole lot more – about Gramps and Mum and everything – but now there didn't seem much point. Whatever I said, he wasn't going to take it in. Not in that state. So I stuffed some tissues into his mouth to shut him up and walked over to the heap of curtains.

I let him have a good look at the matches before I struck one, and I suppose that was my mistake. Because although he went on squirming and grunting, his eyes grew kind of quiet. Watchful. Fixed on the flame.

He knew what was going to happen next, and I thought I did too. I'd let the flame drop, and that would be it. End of story.

Except it wasn't the end of anything, because my hand started to shake, real bad, and I blew the match out instead. The same thing happened with the second match, and the third, and all because of those eyes of his. Ugly eyes, that's how I remember them, bloodshot and half popping out of his head with fright. Not the sort of eyes you'd normally care much about. Yet I still couldn't do it while they were watching me.

You're going to pay! I shouted at him, the way Cath had

shouted years ago when the lawyer's letter arrived, but it didn't mean much any more. It was all bluff because he'd won. He'd beaten us.

I had this sick feeling in my gut, and I chucked the matches away and crouched down on the carpet with my back to him. I could hear him grunting behind me, but it was Cath I was listening to. *This isn't you, Danny*, she'd said, that night in the street, as though she had a crystal ball or something.

Who the bloody hell am I, then? I said aloud.

But when I turned around he had no answer for me. He looked more scared than ever, the sweat pouring down his face, his shirt and jacket all wet with it. His trousers pretty wet too, around the crutch. The poor bastard probably thought I was playing with him, getting some kicks before I finally whooshed the place.

You're not worth my trouble, I told him. D'you know that? You're nothing.

Which wasn't true, but I said it all the same, then walked out and rode off on the bike.

I rang his secretary from a pay phone.

Your Mr Albright could do with some help, I said. I'd get round to his place if I were you.

I wouldn't have minded some help myself, though not from her. Not even from Mal. Him least of all, because I didn't need Cath's crystal ball to guess what *he* would have to say.

Luckily he wasn't at home, so I just left the bike outside his flat with a note. 'Thanks for the loan.' It was easier that way. I couldn't have stood having him look at me as well. Not all in one afternoon.

Nov 5

Mal came over this evening. I saw him from the window and persuaded Cath to tell him I was sick in bed and asleep.

After he'd gone she pestered me with a lot of questions.

I don't have any answers for you, I said. I thought I did, but I don't.

Oh, we're in *that* mood, are we? she said. Pardon me for breathing.

It had to happen eventually. This evening, when Cath tried to keep Mal out, he pushed past her and came storming into my room. There was nothing for it but to tell him the truth. Everything.

I'm disappointed in you, Dan, was all he said, which was less than I'd been expecting.

Join the club, I called after him.

With Cath it wasn't quite so bad.

I've let Mum down, I said.

Stuff like that always gets her going. It's like a red rag to a bull.

Jesus, Danny! she shouted. You're such an idiot sometimes.

She rushed out, and I heard something break in the kitchen. Then she was back in the open doorway, taking long breaths to stay calm.

I told her the truest thing I could think of.

I can't help the way I feel, Cath. No one can.

She came over and sat on the side of my bed.

Yeah, I know, she said.

I think that's maybe why we stick together, Cath and I. Because underneath all the anger, she knows. She's the only one who does.

3 Letters to
Home

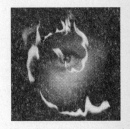

Dear Cath,

I know I should have written before. I've started quite a few letters over the past weeks, but they never seemed to get anywhere. I'm sorry about that because I expect you're worried sick by now, wondering where I've got to.

Well, I'm down in southern NSW where I came with Mal about a month back. I'll explain why in a minute. First I want you to know that I'm fine. Really well in fact. Far better than when I was in Sydney, though under the circumstances maybe that's not saying much. Still, there's nothing for you to worry about.

Now, as to why we came down here. You've guessed it – it was Mal's idea. He reckons I'd got it all wrong, and that what happened to Gramps and Mum is the same as what's happening to the whole planet. As he sees it, we can't afford to get too fired up about the suffering of a few people. Not even people we're close to, or those starving African kids you see on TV. We have to think bigger than any of that. We have to look past what he calls the 'casualties of war' and concentrate on the really big issues that affect everyone. Like the fate of the forests. 'Trees before people' is one of his favourite sayings these days.

I'm not sure I go along with him in all this, but you've heard Mal. He's hard to resist once he starts spouting ideas. Also, just about anything was better than moping around in that room of mine. Things were really bad for me at the end. I won't go into the reasons why (they're past history now), except to say I got myself into a mess and this move south with Mal was the best way out. Running away, I suppose you'd call it, and partly you'd be right.

So here I am trying to rescue the forests of the world! Only joking. Just one forest to be exact. There's an old-growth area back from the coast that a whole lot of us are out to protect from the logging companies. I expect that sounds pretty exciting. It did to me until I got here and found out how boring it could be. Most of the time we sit around in our humpies and wait for something to happen.

I can almost see you eyeing the word 'humpies' and starting to freak out, but like I said, there's no need. Mal and I built our humpy between us. It's more of a lean-to really, made of woven sticks and plastered with mud and leaves. It gives us plenty of cover most of the time. Except for when it rains of course. Then all you can do is sit the weather out.

Last week it rained for two days and everything was soaked – us, our clothes, our food and gear. There wasn't a dry spot in the entire camp. We had to huddle together just to stay warm. Bonny – a girl here, about your age I'd say – she was on a demo up round Lismore and she said it rained non-stop for three weeks, with leeches nearly as big as your thumb. God, it must have been awful. We've had nothing like that. Here, the clouds soon roll away, and after a couple of hours of sun our gear's dry and everything's back to normal.

The mud stays around for a while though. That's the problem. It gets into everything. You'd hate that part of living here. The dirt, I mean. Mal calls it clean dirt, and I guess it is, but it still gets to you if you're not careful. Bonny says you have to switch off about things like rain and dirt, otherwise they end up as more of a problem than the loggers. She says the secret is to do something about your hair, so it doesn't bother you, either cut it all off or do what she's done and rub the clay right in and go for a dreadlock look. I'm kind of in between at the moment. Decisions . . . decisions . . . (Just joking again!)

You might think that to stay clean all you have to do is dive into the nearest creek, but if you tried it on you'd get eaten alive by leeches. They give me the shudders. Long skinny things with technicolour stripes down the side. Yuck! You'd hate them too. Last week Mal and I hitched to the coast for a swim in the sea. It was great at the time, but the salt on our skin turned out to be more of a problem than all the mud and grime we'd washed off. I was scratching for days afterwards.

I can see I'm going on a lot about the conditions here in camp. They're not too bad really. You have to get used to them, that's all. The same goes for the food. Most people are vegetarians, so I haven't seen a piece of meat since I arrived. Bonny says a meat-free diet keeps you clean *inside*, and that's what matters. I don't know. It's something else I have to decide on yet. The jury's out, as Mal likes to say. There's quite a bit of talk about it around the campfire at night, argument mostly, and I just sit and listen.

The campfires are the best part, with everyone talking and laughing until quite late. There're a couple of guitars, and we sing a fair amount too. My favourite thing is to walk off into the forest for fifty metres or so and watch. Bonny came with me one night. She was a bit drunk and feeling sick. Everyone else was dancing around the fire by then, waving burning sticks over their heads. 'They look like fireflies,' she said, and it was true. They were hardly like people at all, and the fire could have been a lamp or even a bright star.

On dry nights Mal and I bed down beside the coals. Once everyone's asleep the silence of the forest really closes in. You can almost *hear* it – like a kind of low whisper somewhere behind the buzz of insect noise. And the stars seem to come right down to tree height. Not the few pin-pricks you see in Sydney. I mean S-T-A-R-S. When there's no moon, it's like gazing into some giant intergalactic video game, with the whole universe, the stars and planets, about to rush down on you.

Mal's been reading this over my shoulder, and he says that last part finally proves I've lost the plot. (His exact words: 'You're fifty cents short of the full dollar, Danny boy.') He and Bonny have gone off now, laughing, so I can say that he's been a good friend, never mind what you may think. I wasn't feeling too great when we first got here, and he saw me through. That's more than Dad ever did for us.

Mal sends his regards by the way. 'Not that she'd care.' (His words again.)

Which reminds me, I've often thought Mal had a soft spot for a certain person with the initial C. Don't wince. He's not so bad when you see past all that preachy stuff. Bonny can, and she's not nearly as bright as you. The fact is, it'd make life a whole lot easier if you and Mal could get on better. And you could do worse than Mal after all. (Hint, nudge, wink!) At least give the idea some airplay and see how it feels. You never know.

As you've probably guessed, I've run out of news. I can't tell you much about the loggers yet because we've hardly seen them. A few people in suits have come out from town to 'reason' with us, and that's about all. Mostly it's talk and no action. Their side says we're endangering the jobs of 'good Aussie battlers', and our side reckons that the battlers and the companies they work for are endangering the planet. And so it goes on.

Bonny, who's been through it all up in the northern forests, keeps warning us that the situation will hot up soon. Personally I have my doubts. For one thing there's no real blockade here yet, just a bunch of people like me and Mal camped out in the forest. For another, no one's in the mood for trouble, not as far as I can see. Singing peace songs around the campfire is about as radical as anyone seems to get.

I said as much to Mal and he laughed. Just watch them, he said. He's developed this theory that even the most ordinary people have hidden depths. Push them hard enough and they'll fight back. Well, right or wrong there won't be much fighting here, for the simple reason that nobody's pushing us around. As I mentioned before, it's all talk.

The first week I arrived, for instance, a bunch of us went into the local timber town for supplies. The way Mal's been carrying on, I was ready for all kinds of hassles. But apart from some loud talk in the local pub – about greenies and dole bludgers, the usual stuff – no one bothered us much. One old-timer even bought us a drink. 'You're not so bad,' he said. 'You may look bloody awful, but then who's perfect?'

I told Mal about it when we got back to camp. 'All that friendliness,' he said, 'it's just a smokescreen. They'll show their true colours later on.' Mal can get things drastically wrong sometimes.

Hey! I must be getting the hang of this. A page or so ago I said I was out of news, and here I am still going. My old English teacher would be proud of me!

So, what is there left to say? Not a lot, except I'm missing you heaps – you, the old house, and Mum of course. Even Dad! It's funny, but I can't seem to get those last years together out of my head. I try. I bear in mind all the things you told me, about the past being dead and gone, but it keeps coming back just the same. That's why it's good for me to be here. Mal calls this my 'compromise solution'. Typical Mal. 'Why fight a skirmish', he says, 'when you can take part in a war?'

Well, this is me signing off from the war zone. Some war! You should see it: the morning sun through the trees, the whipbirds calling, and a wisp of smoke from the fire to sting your eyes and remind you that you're not really in paradise. (A few snakes to remind you of that too!) Altogether, not bad. Better than I deserve maybe. Mum would have loved it if she'd . . .

But I've sworn off that subject. As Bonny said once, 'I'm training myself to dream about trees.' In my case it'll probably take a while, but I'll get there.

In the meantime, look after yourself. I think of you lots and wish you were here with us.

Best love,
Danny

PS If you write care of the local post office, it should reach me. I'd *love* a letter.

South Coast
Feb 5

Dear Cath,

It was great getting your news, about the new job and everything. I went off on my own and read the entire letter out loud amongst the trees. It felt exactly as if you were there next to me, chatting away. I didn't even mind the angry parts, because you're right, I shouldn't have left Sydney without a word. I'm sorry, and that's the God's truth. The only part where I disagreed was where you compared me to Dad. I can see why you said it, but honest, I wasn't running out on you. I'd never do anything like that. I was the one I was running away from, not you, because of how I'd messed up.

It's over and done with anyway, and although I'd act different second time around, I'm not sorry I let Mal drag me down here. For once I don't feel like the odd man out.

Quite a few people in camp talk about the bad trips they left back in Sydney or Melbourne. I never pry because there's this unspoken rule that you don't sticky-beak into other people's business. Still, it helps to know you're not the only weirdo around.

Mal, of course, hates it when I call us weirdos. We're the sane ones according to him. All the others, the people in suits or driving the logging trucks, they're the crazies.

We had a big argument about it the other day. 'How can you stand there and defend the bastards after what they did to her?' he shouted – meaning Mum. I warned him to keep Mum out of it, but Mal being Mal, he couldn't. He started chanting her name, to bug me. I nearly hit him, then picked him up and threw him into the creek instead. 'Party time for the leeches,' someone shouted, and everyone burst out laughing. Mal did too in the end, so there was no harm done.

I hope I'm not giving you the idea that we're at each other's throats, because we're not. Mostly we get on pretty well. It's just that there's been some trouble with the townspeople since I last wrote, and we're all a bit jumpy. Me as much as anyone.

What happened was this. One Saturday night a group of young blokes from a local sawmill got drunk and decided to pay us a visit. It wasn't the first time they've been out here. Usually they ride up and down the logging road beside the camp, yelling and chucking bottles, and that's about it. This time it was different. They sneaked up on us in the dark, when we were all asleep, and grabbed one of the girls.

The first thing she knew, someone had clamped a hand over her mouth to keep her quiet, and she was being dragged off into the bush. They weren't just out to give her a scare as they claimed later. They meant business because they stripped off her clothes and tried to force her into their ute.

Luckily she broke free long enough to wake the rest of us with her yelling, and after that there was a really bad fight.

Quite a few people got hurt, including Mal, and one of the sawmill blokes was knocked out cold. His mates had to carry him to the ute, and in the light of some flares we'd lit, you could see the side of his face was bloodied.

Mal was all for sending the others back in the same state, but most people had calmed down by then and we managed to keep Mal talking while the ute drove off. I've never seen him so fired up before. 'This is war!' he kept saying. 'War!' The words came out kind of muffled from where his lip was split and his mouth puffed up.

Some of the others agreed, but not Bonny. 'No, this isn't war,' she said. 'Not yet. This just spells trouble. *Police* trouble.'

Because she's been through this before, we all listened. And sure enough the cops arrived soon after dawn.

Polite but menacing is the way I'd describe them. Or to put it another way, there wasn't much doubt whose side they were on. That's understandable, I suppose, when you take into account how some of them are local people. Also, they do have to live down here. They're not just blowing through like us.

Mal wasn't in the mood for taking any of that into account though. 'You time-serving bastards!' he yelled, and charged straight in. You should have seen him. In the dawn light, and in his filthy gear, with his hair piled on top of his head and his jaw swollen, he looked like something out of the dark ages.

To be honest, the cops acted fairly restrained and got him into the wagon without too much rough stuff. Not that it quietened him down much. You could hear him crashing around inside the wagon, yelling out every insult he could think of.

'The greenie from hell,' one of the cops said, and they all laughed.

None of us found it too funny. Especially when the head cop explained about the sawmill bloke being in hospital. He reckoned he'd been hit with something heavy like a club, which was news to us. I think the cops must have seen that because they didn't press charges, or whatever they do at times like this. They just left us with a warning to clear out while we had the chance.

We discovered why they'd soft-pedalled a few days later. The hospital case had only been concussed. He'd been released that same morning, so he wasn't any worse off than some of the others. The cops also released Mal, by the way. He walked into camp in the late afternoon, as bouncy as ever.

'It's started,' he said, and rubbed his hands together as though warming them at a fire.

No one asked him *what* had started, because even Mal couldn't tell us that. But we were given some idea the following Tuesday when a group of us went into town for the weekly supplies.

There were only four in the group – Bonny, a girl called Cherry and her boyfriend Dave, and me. Not Mal. The whole camp voted for him to stay behind, to avoid trouble. The plan was to keep the trip low key.

That was the plan anyway, but it didn't work out. On the edge of town a ute swung in behind us, and another headed us off, forcing us into a dead-end street. Nothing was said, not at first. A lot of big blokes surrounded our car and without saying a word started rocking it from side to side, pushing harder and harder until I thought we'd roll right over.

Bonny was yelling blue murder. We all were, but Bonny the loudest, and not because she was scared. She sounded really wild. 'Creeps!' she kept shouting, which reminded me of you. It's what you say when you're mad.

The rocking stopped after a while and these hoons stepped back. All except for one who poked his head in through the window, his mouth only a few centimetres from Bonny's ear. 'You're not welcome in these parts,' he said, quiet but in an I-mean-business kind of voice. 'D'you hear me, darlin'?'

He'd begun kicking the car door with his boot, a regular click-click-click against the panel. Quite hard. And Bonny had the sense not to answer. She didn't look at him either. Like me and the others she went on staring straight ahead while he told us what a lot of layabouts we were, and how, if we didn't move on in the next few days, there was a whole townful of people keen to come and give us a helping hand. He didn't raise his voice once, but with his boot still clicking against the side of the car you didn't have to be a genius to get the message.

Then he and his mates piled back into the utes and escorted us out of town. We didn't collect any supplies of course, though that was the least of our worries.

We held a camp meeting in the evening, around the fire, to decide what to do. Whether to go or stay. Mal was in his element, carrying on about 'war' and urging us all to 'stand and fight'. I don't know about the 'fight' part, but except for a Queensland couple who cleared off at dawn, the rest of us opted to stick around.

That was the night before last, and since then the camp has been gearing up. If you'd been here before, you wouldn't recognise the place now. There's no more sitting in the sun and strumming on guitars. One group, headed by Mal, has finally set up the road-block we've been talking about ever since we arrived. Two others – Cherry and Dave – have started work on tree platforms. It makes me feel ill just looking at them, perched there thirty or forty metres up. They reckon they're not coming down till the logging companies back off from clear-felling this part of the forest. There are a few others who plan to chain themselves to some big trees they want to save. As for the rest of us, we've done what we can to get ready, and now we have to sit tight.

Mal keeps calling us 'the troops', but Bonny says that's bullshit. She says it's thinking like the other side. We're not soldiers or cops or company people. They're the 'troops', the ones we're up against. We have to think differently. But Mal and some of the others just laugh. 'Yeah, try singing peace songs to the bulldozers,' they tell her.

In fairness to Bonny, she's tough. Not physically strong, I don't mean that. She's actually small and skinny, with dreadlocks dyed a kind of orange colour. On the inside is where she's tough. She knows what she knows, and no one's going to push her around. That's the feeling she gives you. She's – and I can't help saying this, Cath – she's the opposite of Mum. And of me, too, I sometimes think. Because she decided long ago, when she was about fourteen and ran away to join the green movement, that she wasn't going to stand by and watch the planet being wrecked. Trees and rivers and animals and oceans can't fight back, she says, so we have to fight for them.

'What about helpless people?' I asked her once.

'Them too,' she said, which made me feel bad, because of Mum and how we never really stood up for her. Neither of us.

In a way that's why I've come here, to stand up for her, whether she'd want me to or not. I know you think it's unnecessary – 'going to extremes' you called it in your letter – but it's how things are. As Bonny would say, I know what I know. And this time I'll keep to my promise, one I made on the day of the funeral.

Sorry to sound so serious, Cath. Also, I hope this letter doesn't set you off worrying again. My personal opinion is that if there is any trouble between us and the loggers, the cops will soon get in between. 'I'd like to see them try,' Mal says, but as usual with Mal it's just talk. The cops have already released him without laying any charges, so he knows better than anyone that when push comes to shove they'll probably do their job. If you ask me, it's what both sides are relying on.

Not that there's any sign of trouble around here right now – just trees as far as you can see, and sunlight slanting down through the canopy, and the creek about the loudest thing for miles. This is the sort of peaceful place Mum must have dreamed of at the end, which is another reason for not letting anyone smash it up. Or for at least doing our best to stop them. *The Word for World is Forest* – that's the title of a book doing the rounds in camp. I haven't read it yet, but I reckon the title sums up most of what I'm trying to get across here.

You might be wondering, by the way, how this big confession of mine is going to reach you now that we're holed up in the forest. Well, if there's no sign of loggers tomorrow morning, someone will take the car and head off through the back roads for a town further down the coast. To load up with supplies mainly, but also to post out our mail. I'd ask you to write back, except maybe there's not much point for a while. Not until all this blows over. You'll probably learn when that is from the headlines in the papers. (Steady, Cath, just kidding!)

I needn't tell you that keeping a sense of humour in this place is important. D'you remember how Dad was always going on about laughter being the best medicine? A pity he forgot his own advice when he was drunk. It's different here in camp, in spite of everybody being tense. Drunk or sober, people stay pretty cheerful. And at night, round the fire, they still manage plenty of jokes. Most of them about greenies.

Like: 'What's the difference between a greenie and a dole bludger?' Answer: 'Wow, that's a hard one. Would you repeat the question please?'

Hey, I'm rambling again, like in the last letter, and this is already pages long. Not to mention that the light's fading fast. There's even a mopoke calling from somewhere. You must know that sound, from our camping days with Mum and Dad. Really lonely. It makes me wish I was home, whatever that means.

Miss you lots, Cath.

Take care,

Danny

South Coast
Feb 14

Dear Cath,

Believe it or not your last letter did reach me. The police, of all people, brought a bunch of letters from the post office, and yours was amongst them.

I did the same as before and read it aloud to the trees. I'm not sure if they appreciated it, but I certainly did. It's funny how someone's voice can get locked into what they write. Yours does, so loud and clear that I can almost hear what you're thinking. It made me realise that if I'm ever in Mum's position I'll write as many letters and stuff as I can, for after. That way I won't leave a hole in the world. I'll be gone, the real me, but the other me that everybody knows will still be around. Kind of.

I explained my idea to Bonny and Mal, and he called it talking across the void. I like that. It's what our letters are doing, yours and mine. If you think about it, the distance between us is more than just so many kilometres. It's also a great empty space where we don't exist, with our words sort of flying across it.

I expect that sounds dumb. I saw an American movie once, set in a prison, where everyone was reckoned to be 'stir crazy'. We're a bit that way too, which isn't really surprising. You can easily get things out of proportion when you're shut off from the rest of the world, like now. We've been trying to get the press and TV people to come in, but so far they're not interested. Disaster is what they're after, and the trouble here hasn't progressed as far as that. Not yet, though we've come fairly near.

Just so *someone* knows what's going on, I'll fill you in on the latest developments.

When I last wrote we were more or less waiting for the loggers to make the next move. Well, we didn't have to sit around for long. They arrived one morning at dawn, as Bonny said they would, and in thick mist. We had sentries posted as usual, but in those conditions, with no one able to see more than a few paces in any direction, they were useless. There was no alarm, just the scream of a chainsaw somewhere off in the mist, and a crash as a tree came down close to camp. A few other trees went down, all around us, the noise really deafening in the still of the morning. Then the bulldozers and trucks came trundling along the road.

We didn't hear them at first. There was too much other noise – and confusion, plenty of that. For a while we were running in all directions. Like chooks with our heads cut off, someone said, and that's not far wrong. Mal kept yelling for everyone to take up 'battle stations', and a few others, including Bonny, were kind of talking under him, trying to calm everyone down.

What steadied us off was the morning wind, the way it tore through the mist. We heard the bulldozers then, and *saw* them, and after that everything went according to plan. In the early stages anyway. By the time the mist had blown clear, we were all in position. Dave and Cherry had climbed up to their platforms, others were chained to big trees flanking the road, and the rest of us had positioned ourselves along the top of the barricade.

The barricade was where the real trouble started, because one of the bulldozers tried to crash through while we were all up there. It was really hairy for a while. We'd stretched a cable across the road, to hang onto, which was just as well. Without it some of us might have fallen under the blade. The driver couldn't have cared less. He was an old bloke with this dead-set look on his face and both hands working the levers like mad. Yelling and swearing at him had no effect. Nor did the fact that some of us, the girls especially, were in real strife. He just kept coming. He'd smash into the logs we'd heaped up, reverse far enough to give himself some room, and charge in again.

At one point I actually stepped onto the top of the blade. I had to. The log I'd been standing on had disappeared. Even the big logs were being knocked aside like matchsticks, and all I had to hang onto was the cable. I saw the driver reach for one of his levers, and I got ready to jump clear. Then something sailed across my shoulder, real close, and hit him in the side of the face. A rock I think it was, something heavy. He didn't clutch at his face or anything like that. He just gave this surprised look, and the bulldozer jerked forward and stalled as he slid down off his seat.

His logger mates swarmed around the bulldozer then. A *lot* of them. I remember thinking, oh no, here comes trouble. But luckily the cops must have thought so too. Before you could blink, there were blue uniforms everywhere, a solid line of them right across the road.

The cop in charge had a megaphone. 'Leave this to us!' he kept yelling. 'We'll handle it.'

And something else sailed out of nowhere. Another rock probably, which knocked the megaphone clean out of his hand.

The cop's mouth went on working, but what with all the other noise you couldn't hear the words any more. Mind you, you didn't have to. The way some of the younger cops began scrambling up onto the barricade made it pretty obvious what he was bawling at them.

A couple of them came straight at me, and I jumped for it. Other people were doing the same, down into the scrub on the side of the road mostly, where there were more cops waiting. A big burly type snatched at my hair, but I ducked under his arm and he grabbed someone else instead. A skinny kid called Lenny. The cop didn't care who he was, nor did any of his mates. Any protester would have done. They just wanted to arrest *someone*, and once they'd carted him off to the wagon they drew back and regrouped across the road.

'Victimisation!' Mal was screaming out, right behind me, but by then the head cop had picked up his megaphone and got it working again, so all most people could hear was him.

'Everything's under control!' he shouted. Not so much at us. More at the loggers, who were still looking pretty ugly. 'Stay out of it!'

Most of them did, but not all. Some tried to rush the police line and were pushed back. One oldish guy started swinging an iron bar around his head. It was us he was dead keen to get at, not the cops. They grabbed him just the same and carted him off too.

The second arrest was probably what settled things, evening them up the way it did. There was still a lot of yelling, from both sides, but not much more than that. Mal, as you can guess, was making more noise that most. You only had to look at him to realise he was still fired up, but a few of us managed to wrestle him back behind the barricade.

It wasn't easy. He was shaking all over, and he gave me a hard time when I wrapped my arms around him and pulled him down onto the road.

'What are you then?' he shouted. 'Some kind of cop in disguise?' And he spat in my face.

That's how bad things were, because you know Mal. He wouldn't normally turn on his friends. It wasn't really me he was turning on, of course. He'd lost it, that's all, and I know how that feels.

I didn't get mad. There was no point. I just held onto him. 'It's me,' I kept saying. 'It's Danny.' I went on saying it until he stopped struggling and sagged down in the dust. Even Bonny was worried about him because his face had crumpled up and he was letting out these small choking noises. If it had been anyone else, I'd have sworn he was crying.

I bet that sounds hard to believe. Mal crying! But if you'd been there you'd have understood. I can describe all the noise and violence, all the yelling and confusion, but not how any of it felt. Mal came closest to putting it into words, earlier, when he talked about going to war. That's about right. It was like being in the middle of a battle, scary and exhilarating and everything else you can think of.

While it lasted I didn't think about Mum or the Company or any of that old stuff, not once. I didn't have a chance. They were why I was there – I know that much – and yet at the time I felt free of them somehow, the way you want me to be. Does that make sense? It's true all the same.

Then in just a few minutes, not much more, the whole thing was over. Finished. The cops were barking out orders, the bulldozers had begun pulling back along the road, and there was this feeling of coming down to earth. Really crashing, I mean. I reckon that's why Mal got into such a state. I tell you, Cath, I was in quite a state myself, and most of the others didn't look too good.

'We showed them a bit of stick, eh, Danny?' Mal managed to get out, his voice sounding as though it was bubbling up through mud or something. All thick and strangled. And he looked the pits. Terrible. I never saw Gramps at the end, but whenever I picture him he's exactly how Mal looked then. His face pinched and skinny and pale.

'Yeah, we showed them, Mal,' I said.

On the other side of the barricade the cop with the megaphone had turned his attention to us.

'Who's in charge here?' he bawled out.

Strictly speaking, nobody is. We regard ourselves as a people's democracy, all for one and one for all, etc. We voted for it and everything. There's a general understanding, though, that when someone *has* to front for us, it's Mal.

The cop called again, and Bonny and I looked at each other, worried that Mal wasn't up to it. Our mistake, because he was already struggling to his feet.

'They're playing my song,' he said, his voice shaky but clear, and he limped around the barricade.

I couldn't hear what was going on between him and the cop. Most of the time Mal nodded his head while the cop talked and did a lot of finger wagging. Mal didn't have a go back as you might expect. Like everyone else he'd probably had enough for one day. The best he could manage, when the cop let him go, was a funny sort of victory grin.

'We've been officially warned,' he called out, and made a secret V-sign, his fingers pressed against his chest so the cops wouldn't see.

Once the cops had pushed off, I had this idea in my head that we'd have a big victory celebration. But no one was interested. We felt too flat. People didn't even get into the booze (or other things!) like normal. All that happened was, we had this serious firelit discussion about the pros and cons of violent demonstrations.

I can't remember anyone starting it. We didn't plan for it to happen. We were sitting around after supper, pretty gloomy if you must know, and it kind of crept up on us. The next thing, we were all arguing as hard as we could go. Well, not *all* of us. I didn't say too much. You know me, Cath, I'm not a great one for words. Except for when you put a pen in my hand. It's different then because no one can argue back.

Anyway, there I was listening to the discussion, trying to work out where I stood, when all of a sudden Mal says:

'We didn't start the violence. They did. A logger chucked that first rock, at one of his own men. Those are the kind of people we're up against.'

I knew that was a lie because the first rock had sailed past my ear, and it had come from behind, from our side. I looked at Mal, and even in the half light I could see he knew it too. I didn't contradict him. I thought everyone else would realise he was lying, it was so clear from his face. But they didn't. People were nodding and saying things like, 'Yeah, we have to fight fire with fire,' and 'A rock or two is the only language these bastards understand.'

Not everyone agreed. Bonny for one.

'If you play their games,' she said, 'you'll lose. They've got more fire power than us, and there're more of them. You can't take on the whole of Australia.'

'Who says so?' Mal answered. 'Numbers aren't everything. Whatever they do, we'll go one better. We'll stay a step ahead.'

'Always?' Bonny said, and gave him this disbelieving smile.

'Always.'

They didn't say any more. Bonny had stopped smiling, the two of them eyeing each other across the fire.

'So where does it all end?' someone else asked.

And out of all that was said around the fire that night, it's that last question I remember best. I keep thinking about it, and never seem to get any closer to an answer. Where *does* it all end?

But I'd better stop this. It's nearly midnight, which is really late here in the bush. The rest of them are asleep, and I'm having to write by the light of the fire, what's left of it.

We're planning another mail run tomorrow morning, so you should get this soon. Please write back if you can. We all hang out for letters, they make us feel less isolated. Though it's more than that with me. Sometimes, when I'm on my own like now, and I think back over the past, I get this weird feeling that you're my other half. My good half maybe. And that if you stopped writing, if you stopped talking to me through your letters, a big part of me would go missing and I'd be all in bits.

I told you it was a weird feeling, didn't I?

Anyway, sorry to end on a gloomy note. I'll do a whole lot better next time.

Love,
Danny

Dear Cath,

No letter from you, worse luck. We asked the cops yesterday if they'd brought any mail, and they laughed. 'In your dreams,' one of them said, which will give you an idea of how things stand with us right now. We're not exactly top of the hit parade with anyone around here.

But I'll try and bring you up to speed on what's been happening. On the surface it's mostly more of the same. You know, confrontations every couple of days. The loggers rock up with their bulldozers and trucks and chainsaws (*always* their chainsaws!), usually at dawn. A few big trees go down, to show they're serious. We mount the road-block, to show *we're* serious. And so it goes on, with the cops keeping score until things get rough, and then pitching in real heavy. There're a few arrests, of people they call 'ringleaders' (that's cop-code for the ones who can't run fast enough) and after a lot of shouting and arm-waving everyone backs off for a day or two, getting ready to do it all over again.

I swear, Cath, it'd be just like some comedy turn if it wasn't so nerve-racking. The worst part is always the start. You're fast asleep in your humpy, or curled up around the remains of the fire – the forest's as still as the grave – it's either dark or soon after dawn, with mist dangling from the trees like loops of grey cloth – and suddenly all hell breaks loose. You're barely awake, so you haven't a clue what's happening. Nothing seems real except the noise, and there's enough of that to wake the dead. All the rest has this phantom quality about it, because of the mist. There're vague figures appearing out of nowhere and vanishing again; these hollow-sounding voices, barely human most of them, calling through the trees; and when the chainsaws stop for a minute, there's the creak of big trees getting ready to fall.

Where're they going to fall, that's what you ask yourself as you struggle up out of sleep. Should you stay where you are or run? What's the safest? You're still trying to make up your mind when there's this swishing noise, followed by a godalmighty crash, and the mist kind of boils up around you as though the forest's one great big battle zone and you're in the middle of it. Pretty soon you're running around the same as everyone else, yelling blue murder like you don't know what it is to be scared, but really just looking for somewhere to hide.

Things settle down after a while. The mist clears, the bulldozers roll in, and the two sides line up. It's all happened before so there's nothing to get too worried about. But never mind how calm you may appear, you can't shake off that first scare – the feeling that the world's a dangerous place and the whole sky might come tumbling in if you're not careful.

Does that sound paranoid? Maybe. It's how you feel though, especially when the mist hasn't quite cleared and the bulldozers are crouched out there in the murk. 'Strange beasts,' Bonny calls them, with 'dragon breath' for exhausts, which is weird stuff, but typical Bonny.

The bulldozers are a bit like the Company, that's what I reckon. So big that even the people driving them can't see when anyone's in the way. The rest of us are just ants, and if we're trodden on, bad luck. Who cares? We don't count, any more than Mum did.

But whoa! I'm getting as bad as Bonny with all her talk of 'dragon dawns'. At this rate I'll spook myself, without any help from the loggers. Also, believe it or not, I didn't write so as to have a rave about all this, because like I said before, on the surface it's mostly more of the same.

What's going on *under* the surface, that's a different story. Since my last letter the whole feeling of the place has changed, and there've been bad rumours and gossip flying around. Here in camp, but in the town too – you can tell from the way the loggers carry on when they're out here. They used to yell things like 'bludgers' and 'greenie layabouts'. Now they accuse us of spiking trees and pouring sugar into the fuel tanks of their trucks. One old bloke, who managed to push through the police lines, yelled right into my face: 'I've seen you creeping round the timber yards at night. I know what you're up to. We all do!' He went on yelling even when the cops dragged him off. 'How much are they paying you? You and your commie mates? How much for your dirty work?' And you should have seen his face. Like I was a mortal enemy or something.

Plenty of the loggers feel the same. They've got this idea that we're not really here to save the trees. That's just a front. What we really want is to take their jobs away. Bonny says it was the same up in the northern forests. She says that there, the townspeople started talking about a world conspiracy, with somewhere like Libya behind it all. The word got around that the greenies were being paid by foreign interests to wreck the industry any way they could.

The word's got around here, too. When the loggers line up against us now, you can almost feel the waves of hate coming off them. 'What's the going price for a mercenary these days?' they shout. 'What do they pay you in? Joints?'

To be honest, the situation in camp's not much better. The talk around the fire is mostly about how the timber companies are bribing people to spread all these rumours, which may or may not be true, don't ask me. And a couple of nights ago a small group stole into town for a recce and came back with all sorts of stories. One is that the loggers have guns and are ready to use them if it comes to the crunch. Another is that they're planning a strike against us in the next few days, before we can get at them.

It's hard to know what to believe any more. I've tried talking to Mal, but he's up to his neck in the whole thing. When I pushed him he came right out and admitted it – some of the rumours *did* start with him. 'This is a war of nerves,' he told me. 'It's the war we have to win.'

Bonny agrees with him for once. The propaganda war she calls it, which is about right. It's always the hardest part of the campaign to get through, according to her. You have to grit your teeth and hold on.

But hold onto what? I don't know, Cath, it worries me, all these lies flying backwards and forwards. It makes me wonder what I'm really doing, whether maybe we've all started acting like company types ourselves. In which case what's the point?

I said as much to Mal, last night around the fire, but he wasn't having any of that. He kept urging me to get real.

'There's no such thing as a clean war,' he insisted. 'Means and ends, Danny boy, that's what it's all about. If you want to win, you have to get your hands dirty.'

I answered him with something Mum said once – how that's not the way we do things in our family.

He wasn't the only one who laughed.

'Good one, Danny,' he said, and wiped the tears away. 'Though correct me if I'm wrong, but wasn't one member of your wonderful family a hopeless drunk?'

I'd never stuck up for Dad before.

'So what?' I said. 'I'd rather be a drunk than someone who chucks rocks into people's faces and then lies about it.'

Nobody was laughing any more. You could hear the crackle of the fire and bits of burned twig settling in the ashes.

You can't put down Mal though. 'I don't remember

anyone electing *you* as Jesus Christ!' he said, real angry. 'And what the hell does it matter how you do something, as long as it gets done?'

'It matters,' I answered, which is something else Mum told us, though I disagreed with her at the time. 'It makes a difference to me.'

'Not to me,' Mal said. 'Oh, and by the way, old buddy, if you ever work out how to make an omelette without breaking eggs, give me a call. I'd love to see how it's done.'

There wasn't much I could say to that, so I shut up. A good thing too because it was a stupid argument. Mum was the one he was really arguing with, not me. I don't know even now whether I believe some of the things I said, and the bit about preferring to be a drunk was plain dumb.

It's often like that in arguments. The ones I seem to get into anyway. In the heat of the moment nothing comes out the way you want it to. What I should have said to Mal is what I'm admitting to you now, how I don't know where I stand any more. I thought I did when I arrived here, but now I'm not sure. Part of me thinks Mal's right. What does it matter how we go about things as long as we win? No one cared how Mum and Gramps were treated after all. On the other hand another part of me says the opposite – it says this is how everything went wrong before, in Sydney. Because I pretended I could act any-old-how there too, and I couldn't.

Mal of course says I'm underrating myself. He reckons I have hidden depths like everyone else, and when the world pushes me hard enough I'll sing a different tune. I suppose he means his tune. Perhaps. We'll have to wait and see. In the meantime I'm all in bits again, I'm afraid, with half of me wanting to stay here and tough it out, and the other half wanting to turn and run. Except I can't keep running, can I?

I know I shouldn't be heaping all my troubles onto

you, Cath. There's just no one else I can talk to openly like this. In fact there aren't all that many people to talk to, period. What with the arrests every couple of days, our ranks are looking pretty thin.

Which brings up another reason for this letter. There must be plenty of greenies out there, ready and willing to give us a hand. Letting them know they're needed is the problem. So could you get on the phone and try and raise some media interest? For the publicity, I mean. Radio, TV, the press, anything. Who knows, if there were some cameras in these parts, the war of lies might stop. With the spotlight on them, people might start worrying about the forest again, instead of how to win.

Fat chance, Mal would say, but what does he know? You and me, Cath, we're the ones for putting the world to rights. I wish!

Anyway, you must have had enough of me by now. Even I sometimes feel that way, so why shouldn't you?

My apologies if this letter's a mess. It probably takes after its writer! And talking of messes, you should see the mud here. It's been raining for a week and we're just about going under. Next time you take a nice hot shower, think of me.

Over and out for now.

Much love,

Danny

South Coast
March 4

Dear Cath,

Still no word from you. I can picture a whole heap of letters sitting in the post office, which makes me feel really frustrated, because going into town now would be like putting my head in the lion's mouth.

It's not too safe here in camp come to that. Most nights there are cars on the road, and since I last wrote there's been a two-way raid. Maybe 'raid' is a bit strong. 'Incidents', the police called them.

The other night, at about eleven, when the fires were low, a group from town came busting through camp on trail-bikes. They were onto us before the sentries could sound the alarm, yelling and swinging clubs. A couple of the bikes must have had ropes stretched between them because half the humpies were flattened, and so was anyone fool enough to put their heads up.

I was sound asleep at the time. There was this scream of bikes in the dark, and as I came awake I felt the humpy go. Whoosh! Just like that, and I was out in the open, with misty air damp on my face and dim clusters of stars showing through the gaps in the canopy. 'Keep down!' someone shouted, as if we needed any warnings. Like most of the others I was already burrowing into my sleeping-bag, lying doggo while the bikes circled camp a few times and finally pushed off.

Mal was mad as a snake that nobody had tried to make a fight of it. His answer was to organise a raiding party and hit straight back. Some of us objected, but it didn't do any good because they went anyway, and were gone the rest of the night. When they reached camp just before dawn, you'd have thought they were drunk the way they were laughing and carrying on.

I didn't stick around to listen to their stories. What they got up to is their affair. They can risk gaol if they want. Me, I'm here to blockade the logging trails, not take part in a running war with a bunch of country hoons.

I made that clear to Mal later in the morning, and Bonny backed me up. 'You're playing into their hands,' she told him. 'If you're caught messing up in the village, the logging companies will claim we're all vandals.'

'Who says we're going to get caught?' Mal said, and gave her a kind of smirk – you know how he looks when he's really sure of himself.

'Whether they catch you or not, who else is there to blame around here?' she said. 'It stands to reason. And while we're busy facing charges, the companies'll have a free hand.'

Mal didn't bother to argue. 'KFC,' was all he said, just like the kids at school, which made me as mad as he'd been the night before. I had to walk off on my own to cool down.

The cops were in camp when I got back, and there was a lot of talk going on. The second I appeared the head cop pointed straight at me and said, 'You! You've been warned, too.'

I didn't say a word, but of course Mal had to put in his two cents' worth.

'Is this an official warning or what?' he asked.

'Don't push it, son,' the cop said.

'You'll have to explain that to me, officer,' he answered, acting all innocent. 'What is it exactly that we're pushing?'

I tell you, if looks could kill, we'd all have dropped dead on the spot.

'Get this cheeky little bastard out of my sight,' the cop said, and some of his mates moved in.

So did a few of us. What else was there to do? We couldn't let them cart Mal off.

For a few seconds I thought we'd earned a ride in the wagon. Then the head cop waved his mates back and gave us a grim kind of nod.

'You'll keep,' he said, and strode off.

Since then there's been this uneasy silence, with no sign of the cops, the loggers, anyone. Sometimes at night we still hear cars further down the road, but they don't worry us any. I suppose we should feel grateful, being left alone like this. Except we all know it can't last. There's too much tension in the air, like before a storm when you sit waiting for the first flash of lightning and the first big heavy drops to start.

I was about to say I'll let you know how things turn out. Then I remembered that there's not much chance of getting this or any other letter off to you for a while, because we've decided against a mail run until the trouble's over. Everyone's needed around the camp right now.

I'll try and go on with this letter all the same. In fact I might as well keep it open and add to it day by day so at least you'll get the whole picture when it eventually reaches you.

For the time being, though, this is Danny signing off.

⊚　⊚　⊚

Another day of uneasy quiet. Eerie almost. Dave and Cherry – they're the ones up on the tree platforms – only had to whisper to be heard right across camp.

I couldn't stand the quiet in the end and I went off for a bit of a walk in the forest. Less than a hundred metres from camp I heard something. It could have been a roo, but I don't think so. There was none of that thumping noise you get when a roo runs off. This was just a steady rustle of leaves, as if someone was scuttling away between the trees.

I didn't try and follow. I didn't tell the others what I'd heard either. Whoever was out there can spy on us all they want for all I care. I don't have any secrets to keep. Only a promise. And no amount of spying can make me break that.

⊚　⊚　⊚

The TV people have finally arrived.

They turned up early this morning, and within minutes this white-haired guy was humping a bloody great camera all over camp, shoving it into people's faces. He's not as pushy as the sound man, though, who had this long furry mike that seemed to be just about everywhere.

'What are you supposed to be?' Cherry called down to him. 'A man or a phallic symbol?' And everyone laughed, even this cool, good-looking interviewer type.

I think I've seen her before, on one of those TV news programmes. She came on all pally at first – we're-all-in-this-together kind of style – which was about as believable as snow at Christmas.

Mal was in his element. With a smile as false-friendly as hers, he gave her a lot of stuff about how we'd declared this area of forest an independent republic and how any attempt to log it would be regarded as a foreign invasion. I think she must have believed him because she gave the producer guy a hard look and he shot off in the car, and within an hour or two half the town was out here in force – cars, utes, bulldozers, the works – everyone dead-set on becoming TV stars.

I'd hoped that having the TV people around would calm everyone down, but no chance. It was the biggest confrontation yet. And the ugliest. I won't go into details because you probably watched it on the box. If so, you'd have seen the bulldozers go right through our blockade, for the first time ever. Someone could have got killed. Me, for instance. Especially when the cable we'd stretched across the road snapped in two. One end damn near took my head off before I jumped clear, and the other end lashed back and broke some-one's arm. Then there was that cherry-picker thing and the way they let it smash into the tree platforms.

'Come on, see if you can pick *this* one!' Cherry was yelling at them – she's one of those people who doesn't have a scared bone in her body.

And Mal was screaming at the top of his voice: 'You see! They don't care! They don't bloody care!'

Which was true. It was just as Mal had said right at the start. People like us, like Mum, we're nothing else but casualties of war. We just happen to be in the way, and as long as the timber or the asbestos or whatever keeps rolling out, no one gives a damn.

I can hear myself raving again, Mal-style, but honest, Cath, I can't help it. You should see our camp, what's left of it – our humpies flattened, our gear wrecked, the whole area churned up.

I wouldn't have minded so much, but when it was all over – when the TV people had gone and the injured had been carted off to hospital – the cops came round and blamed us.

'This was always on the cards,' the head cop told us. 'You're trespassers.'

Mal went so spare he could hardly talk, which must be a first for him. 'Us! Trespassers!' was about all he could get out.

Bonny was the calm one. She also showed she's much cleverer than she looks.

'Since when is it legal in Australia to assault demonstrators?' she asked. 'Whether they're trespassing or not?'

'Don't come the bush lawyer with me,' the cop warned her.

'It's your job to enforce the law,' she came back at him, 'not remake it as you see fit.'

'Don't tell me my job, girlie,' he said, going red in the face.

But that was too much even for Bonny. 'Listen,' she told him, her voice real quiet, 'I'm not your girlie and I never will be. You got that?'

I don't know if that's what pushed him over the edge. Maybe he'd made up his mind beforehand. Whatever, he gave us a final warning then.

'Three days!' he shouted. 'Three bloody days! After that we're clearing the camp any way we have to.'

'I'd like to see you try,' Cherry yelled as he stomped off.

'You will, girlie,' he called back. 'You will.'

And that's about as far as we've got. It's dark now and people are sitting quietly around the fire, which is where most of us will spend the rest of the night. I'm not sure there'll be much sleeping done, though, not by some anyway. Mal's in a huddle with a small group in the shadows. They're whispering together, and I can smell more trouble brewing. I went over there a while back, to listen in, but Mal waved me away.

'This is not for your ears, Danny boy,' he said. 'You get back amongst the lambs.'

Writing it down like that makes it sound as though he was being sarcastic, but he wasn't. The very opposite in fact. There's a real caring side to Mal that not many people know about. It's probably why we've stayed such close friends. Unless I'm fooling myself again and there's maybe something hard in me that links us together. Who knows? Right now I'm too tired to think straight. If I don't sleep I'll drop. Whatever Mal's up to will have to keep. I'll take care of it in the morning.

Look after yourself, Cath. I'm really missing you. Tonight more than ever.

⊚　⊚　⊚

At least I'm sure now that you'll get this letter, because they've promised to post it, and I believe them. Even so, you're not going to like this part. All I can say is that you shouldn't worry.

Although things are in a mess again, I'm sure everything will sort itself out. Mal thinks so, too. He says that after the cops have had a good look at our statements, I'll walk.

'It's a matter of lambs and wolves, Danny boy,' was how he put it.

But I'd better fill you in on the latest. I'll keep it short so as to get this off to you.

I was asleep when the cops arrived in camp. It was still half dark and I woke with this torch shining straight in my face.

'Yeah, that's one of them,' a voice said.

And I was carted off through the mist and pushed into the back of a police wagon. Three others were already in there – Mal, Bonny, and Cherry, who'd been forced down from her platform during yesterday's fight.

I asked Mal what was going on, but he wouldn't tell.

'Don't ask, bro,' he said. 'What you don't know can't hurt you.'

That was about six hours ago now, and since then we've spent most of the time in a temporary lock-up in the town. As far as I can gather we're being held because of a fire that broke out in a local timber yard. Arson, the cop called it, so they must be pretty sure it was deliberately lit. By all accounts the whole yard, including the mill and the machinery, has been wiped out, and a couple of blokes asleep in an outbuilding got badly burned. They're not in any danger or anything, but from what I hear they're not in great shape either. One of them may lose an eye, the cops said.

It's a lousy business, Cath, I won't try and deny it. But it's not down to me, and that's the truth. So like I said earlier, I don't want you to worry. I've already written out my statement, explaining how I was asleep and never left camp all night, and once the cops have checked it out they'll let me go. With luck I may even beat this letter back to Sydney, depending on what lifts I can find. Because I've decided to come home for a while, providing of course you've still got a place for me. I won't bring any trouble, I promise. After what's gone on here I just need to rest up for a week or so and get my life straight.

I'll give you a call from along the way if I get the chance.

Be seeing you soon, Cath.
All my love,
Danny

South Coast
March 10

Dear Cath,

I didn't think I'd be writing again. I wish I didn't have to.

The truth is, the bastards are charging me. They've checked my statement, I've explained everything to them, and they don't believe a word. They say they have an eyewitness who saw me near the yard around midnight, which is a lie. They reckon I've been identified all the same, and that's that. Nobody listens. You talk and talk and it's like there was nobody in the room with you. I got so fed up in the end that I lost it and had a go at one of the cops. It was a dumb thing to do, I know, but I was so frustrated I couldn't help myself. Now they've charged me with that too, which is really unfair because nobody punches a cop and walks away, if you follow my meaning.

Never mind about that. I'm all right, more or less. A bit sore, but what can you expect? It's what's going on in my head I can't handle. I feel like Mum all over again, the way she must have felt at the end I mean. Kind of helpless, and cheated, having to pay for something she had nothing to do with.

Maybe that's why this has happened, because I didn't stand up for her when I should have. I let them walk all over her. I didn't lift a finger. I stood by and watched her end her life in that crummy public ward. God, Cath, I didn't even try and squeeze enough out of them to pay for a private room. She died like a pauper, for Christ's sake. Well, like I said, maybe this is payback time.

Today, for instance, someone came and talked to me about legal aid. I asked if that was for poor people, and he nodded, so I told him he could stuff it. I meant it, too. Accepting free help from them would be like walking back into the public ward again, and I couldn't stand it.

I realise things are probably a bit tight with you at the moment, having to pay rent for the flat on your own – and I know I don't have any right to put my hand out, not after walking off like I did – but please, Cath, try and raise some money if you can. Do your best at any rate. If I accepted their freebies I wouldn't be able to look at myself in the mirror. All I'd see was her staring back at me, and I couldn't stand that either.

Don't let me down on this one, Cath, I'm really counting on you. I wish I could add that I'm sorry and all the rest of it, but I'm not. It's them who should be sorry. *Them!*

That's all I've got to say for now.

Your loving brother,

Danny

4 Behind Closed Doors

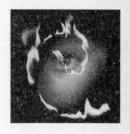

KARLIN DETENTION CENTRE
Summary of Preliminary Psychological Report

SUBJECT
Daniel Fenton

In all tests completed so far, subject showed signs of severe repression. This ties in with the Counsellor's earlier report, which referred to his being sullen and uncommunicative both prior to and throughout the Court proceedings. In a follow-up interview to our tests, the subject displayed these same behavioural patterns. Questions such as, 'Why are you feeling angry?' and 'Do you feel any remorse?' met with little response. Even the key question of whether he felt he had been justly or falsely accused, which usually produces a marked reaction, had no significant effect in this case.

All early indications point to an unstable personality. In such cases as this, it is not uncommon for bouts of severe repression to be followed by periods of hyperactivity, perhaps even of violence. We advise that his day-to-day demeanour, as well as his interaction with others, should be carefully monitored. In layman's language, this is a prisoner who needs to be watched.

There follows a brief extract from the actual interview, as a typical sample of his current attitudes (N/R stands for No Response).

Interviewer:	Do you know why you've been brought to a place like this?
Subject:	N/R
Int:	Do you *mind* being confined here?
Sub:	N/R

Int:	All right, let's talk about the length of your sentence. Do you think it's fair?
Sub:	What's fair mean?
Int:	It has an ordinary, everyday meaning, surely. One we all understand.
Sub:	*You* do maybe.
Int:	Don't you?
Sub:	N/R
Int:	We don't seem to be getting very far. Perhaps there's something you'd like to ask me.
Sub:	N/R
Int:	Something you'd like to tell me then. Anything at all.
Sub:	I want my amulet back.
Int:	Amulet? I don't understand.
Sub:	The one I was wearing around my neck. They took it.
Int:	I see. Was it made of metal?
Sub:	Yeah.
Int:	Then you know the rules. Inmates aren't allowed to retain any metal objects.
Sub:	They're *your* rules.
Int:	Yes, but they're for your benefit. For your protection. Can you see that?
Sub:	N/R
Int:	Aren't you scared of what might happen if there were no rules to protect you?
Sub:	I stopped being scared.
Int:	Of whom?
Sub:	N/R
Int:	Are you saying you aren't scared of anything? Of anyone?
Sub:	N/R

Int:	Okay, what about this amulet? Why is it important to you?
Sub:	N/R
Int:	Is it a lucky charm? Is that it?
Sub:	It's an *unlucky* charm.
Int:	Unlucky? I don't follow. You'll have to explain that to me.
Sub:	N/R
Int:	Do you think I'm incapable of understanding?
Sub:	You could say that.
Int:	Yes, but are *you* saying it?
Sub:	N/R
Int:	Is there anything at all you can tell me about this amulet? Think hard before you answer.
Sub:	(*After a lengthy pause*) Dust to dust, ashes to ashes.
Int:	What's that supposed to mean?
Sub:	N/R
Int:	Are you suggesting that this is all a waste of time?
Sub:	Isn't it?
Int:	You tell me.
Sub:	N/R

Final comment: I would point out that the subject sought at all times to retain a dominant position within the interview. Note, for example, that most of his responses take the form of demands or assertions; and even his occasional questions are intended to challenge rather than to elicit information. I need hardly add that as an inmate of this institution, the subject, in point of fact, is *not* in a dominant position. He is merely clinging to an illusion of dominance. Here, in part, lies the nature of his instability, for in my view any serious threat to that illusion may well give rise to violent, reactive episodes.

Signed: Dr M Stalt

⊚   ⊚   ⊚

Sydney
July 16

Dear Danny,

I hated seeing you so unhappy and angry during my visit yesterday. I'd really been looking forward to getting out there and spending some time with you. It's a long way, but I didn't mind. I'd been planning it all week. Then to find you like that, refusing even to talk!

I wondered at first if I was the one you were angry with. I thought, yes, that's why he hasn't written, because he's convinced I've let him down. In a sense that *is* what happened, I admit it, I *did* let you down. With Mum gone and no one else to look out for you, I should have made more of an effort to get you away from that awful demo on the south coast. I should have dropped everything and travelled down there. I could see the demo wasn't going anywhere (or not anywhere good) but I kept thinking, let him learn the hard way, which I realise now was a mistake.

I wanted to tell you so yesterday. I was going to. Then Dr Stalt asked to see me, and afterwards there didn't seem much point.

I might as well let you know what he had to say. He didn't swear me to silence or anything. According to him I shouldn't take your attitude personally. This is how you are with everyone, with the world in general, which is terrible if it's true and only makes me feel worse.

Have things really got as bad as this, Danny? Do you really hate everyone, me included? I know you feel you were treated badly at the trial, but you have to forget about that. You *have* to. I know too that you think your life is going the same way as Mum's. You told me so in your last letter from the south coast. Well, like I said yesterday, that simply isn't true. Mum was sick and dying; you're fit and strong, with your whole life before you. You have a chance to start all over again. Mum didn't.

There's one other thing I know about you. Down on the south coast, you were trying to put things right for her, you were out to make up for what happened to Mum all those years ago. And you can't. No one can, because she's gone. All you can do is put things right for yourself.

I don't like saying this, Danny, but I have to because it's important, and there shouldn't be any lies between us. You actually remind me more of Dad than of Mum. I don't mean the running away, I mean the drink thing. Before you went off with Mal, you were kind of drunk on grief, that's the only way I can describe it. Now, stuck there in that awful place, you seem to be drunk on anger, as if you're ready to fight the whole world.

Dad was a bit that way when he had a few bottles inside him. You can't have forgotten. How we had to lock our bedroom doors when he was rampaging through the house. 'They all hate me,' I remember him yelling out once. 'They all want to put me down.' It was so pathetic, because no one can take on the world and win. Not him, that's for sure. Not you either.

Here's something else I remember, from school. One time we had this stand-in teacher, just a student I think because she was really young, and she told us an old story about some Irish hero or other who was always fighting. It was the only thing he knew how to do, and it didn't get him anywhere. He finished up declaring war on the sea. Can you imagine it? How crazy he must have been? That's how he died, out amongst the breakers, trying to cut the heads off incoming waves. Some hero he turned out to be.

Okay, so it's just a story. Except that doesn't mean it can't be real, too. For instance, d'you know what Mum told me a few days before she died? She was lying in her hospital bed when suddenly she turned and said, 'So this is the story of my life.' You should have heard her. She sounded so calm, not angry at all. About as different from the mad old Irishman as you can imagine. If there were prizes for heroism, I know who'd win mine.

But here's what I'm getting to. How's the story of *your* life going to end, Danny? Out amongst the breakers or what? Ask yourself that while you're sitting there in Karlin, all quiet and full of anger. And while you're about it, remember this: Mum was the really brave one, out of all of us, the one we should both try and be like. She wasn't helpless either, the way you make out. I was with her in those final days, and she died with a lot of dignity, which is something the people who run the mining company couldn't take away from her. They took everything else, but not that. So you see, she doesn't need anybody to change the world for her. What she'd want is for you to forget about revenge and to start afresh once you get out of there.

She can't speak for herself any more, so you have to believe me in this, Danny, and trust me. You were always the one she worried most about. Her 'wild child' she called you when you were a little kid, because of the fights you used to get into. And I know she'd hate you to end up like Dad. So would I. You're too good for that.

I didn't mean for this letter to become preachy. I'm sorry if it has. It's just hard for me to picture your face as it was in the visitors' room and not feel frightened for you. If I'd been accused of a crime I didn't commit, I'd be angry too. I'd also want to fight back. That's only natural. What's unnatural is to let what they've done eat into you, to let it change you for ever. If that happens they've won, and the only person you'll be fighting against is yourself.

Judging from my reception yesterday, I'd say you won't be too thrilled to receive this letter. Don't tear it up even so. Keep it a week or two and read it over, that's all I ask. By then I hope to get out and see you again. Not this coming weekend when I'll be on at the restaurant, but the weekend after. I hope too that we'll be able to talk next time, talk properly I mean, the way we used to. Even before Mum I was mainly the one you confided in. You mustn't let anyone change that, whatever happens.

I'm going to end with an admission. Nothing's right for me while you're locked away. I can't seem to get on with my life. It's like you said in one of your letters from the south coast: we're all in bits, was how you put it, and I agree.

Don't drift too far away then, Danny. I'm hanging onto you with my thoughts as hard as I can, and that's how it'll always be, even when you're old and married and have kids of your own and all this is years behind you. Just watch me and see.

Always and ever.
Love,
Cath

⊚   ⊚   ⊚

KARLIN DETENTION CENTRE
Interim Psychological Report: Extracts from interview

SUBJECT
Daniel Fenton

(i)

Interviewer:	Can you perhaps give me a reason for your attack on the guard? He claims it was unprovoked. Is that true?
Subject:	N/R
Int:	You can speak without fear of any comeback here. You do understand that, don't you?
Sub:	N/R
Int:	Look, let's be sensible about this. We both know nobody attacks somebody else without reason. So what was yours? Give me a clue, that's all.
Sub:	He reminded me of someone.
Int:	Who?
Sub:	Someone I never met.
Int:	How is that possible? You'll need to tell me more. Who was this 'someone' for instance? This other person?
Sub:	He worked for a big company, years back.
Int:	Before you were born?
Sub:	Probably. And after.
Int:	But you never met him. Do you imagine him perhaps?
Sub:	Oh yeah, I can imagine him all right.
Int:	I see. And what precisely does he have in common with the guard?

Sub:	N/R
Int:	Is it the way they both look?
Sub:	N/R
Int:	Their attitudes then?
Sub:	Maybe.
Int:	What is it about their attitudes that you object to?
Sub:	They don't care who you are. They don't treat you as a human being.
Int:	You think that's reason enough to attack someone?
Sub:	N/R
Int:	Well, is it?
Sub:	I ended up in the infirmary, too.
Int:	Yes, but according to the guard's report you were the initial aggressor.
Sub:	So I hear.
Int:	Are you denying it?
Sub:	N/R
Int:	You're not?
Sub:	N/R
Int:	I take it then that you *did* start the trouble, and all because the guard reminded you of someone you don't really know. Have I got that right?
Sub:	There was another reason.
Int:	Go on.
Sub:	He was wearing a uniform.
Int:	So am I.
Sub:	Yeah, I've noticed.
Int:	Do I anger you, too?
Sub:	(*Laughs*)

Int:	I'll take that as a yes. What is it about people in uniform that angers you?
Sub:	N/R
Int:	Do we remind you of the police?
Sub:	Kind of.
Int:	I assume you dislike the police.
Sub:	So would you in my position.
Int:	Why? Because they took you into custody? It's what they're paid to do. It's their job.
Sub:	They were doing more than their job when they arrested me.
Int:	Ah, I see. You feel you were falsely accused. That's a common complaint in here.
Sub:	(*More animated*) When I hit the guard I wasn't making a complaint.
Int:	What were you doing?
Sub:	Making a statement.

(ii)

Int:	It's been brought to my attention that you only act aggressively towards the guards, not towards other prisoners. Why is that?
Sub:	N/R
Int:	Very well, let's keep it simple. Am I right in believing that you've been bullied by your fellow inmates?
Sub:	N/R
Int:	And that you've made no attempt to retaliate or defend yourself?
Sub:	N/R
Int:	Do you *want* to be a victim?
Sub:	It's not a question of wanting.

Int:	So that's how you see yourself.
Sub:	(*Sighs*) If you like.
Int:	Why exactly?
Sub:	It's pretty obvious, isn't it?
Int:	Not to me.
Sub:	(*Laughs*) Gee, I'd never have thought that.
Int:	Let's get back to this bullying business. Victim or not, you're quite ready to hit out at the guards. Why not at other prisoners?
Sub:	I have no quarrel with them.
Int:	Do you see them as fellow victims?
Sub:	Not necessarily.
Int:	Are you implying that you're the *only* victim in here? That you're unique?
Sub:	I'm more unique than you are, that's for sure.
Int:	Why do you say that?
Sub:	N/R
Int:	At least tell me what makes you so special.
Sub:	Special? That's your word.
Int:	But I am right, you do see yourself as someone set apart.
Sub:	I'm in a prison, for God's sake.
Int:	So are all the other inmates.
Sub:	(*Laughs*) Yeah, well maybe that's why I have no quarrel with them.

(iii)

Int:	Your sister was in here last week. She told me you wouldn't speak to her.
Sub:	Couldn't, you mean.
Int:	Pardon?
Sub:	I was correcting you is all.

Int:	Oh, I see. You *couldn't* speak to her. Why was that?
Sub:	Because I had nothing to say. Nothing she'd want to hear.
Int:	Do you feel very distant from her? Is that the trouble?
Sub:	N/R
Int:	Or have I got it wrong? Were you trying to protect her with your silence?
Sub:	N/R
Int:	What then?
Sub:	I've told you, there are things people want to hear and things they don't.
Int:	People? What people?
Sub:	You, for instance.
Int:	What is it I don't want to hear?
Sub:	Just about everything.
Int:	Am I like your sister in that respect?
Sub:	(*More animated*) Nothing like.
Int:	How are we different?
Sub:	N/R
Int:	How are we similar then?
Sub:	You're not.
Int:	But you said ...
Sub:	(*Animated again*) Look, didn't your mother teach you not to sticky-beak?
Int:	Did yours?
Sub:	N/R
Int:	As we're talking of mothers, perhaps you'd like to tell me why you're so unwilling to discuss your parents.
Sub:	N/R
Int:	Did they mistreat you?

Sub:	N/R
Int:	I see. So I can assume that you regard them in the same light as your sister.
Sub:	What light is that?
Int:	The light of rejection.
Sub:	Who says I reject her?
Int:	You wouldn't talk to her when she came. Isn't that rejection?
Sub:	No.
Int:	What then?
Sub:	Like I told you, I had nothing to say.
Int:	This conversation is going around in circles.
Sub:	I've noticed.
Int:	Before we stop, is there anything you'd like to add?
Sub:	I've said too much already.
Int:	Meaning what? That you can't trust me?
Sub:	(*Looks away, unconcerned*) N/R

⊚ ⊚ ⊚

Sydney
Aug 9

Dear Mal,

You'll probably think it's funny, me writing to you and all. We haven't exactly been friends, as I'd be the first to admit, and you've got troubles enough of your own, locked away there in Long Bay, without me adding to them. But I have to talk to someone about Danny, and you're the person who knows him best after me.

As you may have heard, he's being held upstate in the Karlin Detention Centre, which is kind of half prison, half farm. I expect that sounds pretty easy compared with what you're going through. I thought so too until I visited him there and learned different.

It's not the place that's all wrong, Mal, it's him. The way he feels inside himself. I've seen him angry before, with Dad, and again while Mum was sick, but never like this. The first time I walked into the visitors' section I hardly recognised him. It was like looking at a stranger, and you know how open he is usually. Well, I couldn't get a word out of him. Just a few yeses and noes if I was lucky, and this sullen silence I could have cut with a knife the rest of the time.

I spoke to the doctor at the Centre. He's some sort of psychologist I think. He reckons Danny's at war with the whole of society right now, me included, and we have to give him time. I found that hard to believe – I mean the bit about Danny hating me. I thought if I wrote to him he'd come round, but he won't reply. It's the same as when I visit him at the Centre. There's just this deep silence, and nothing I can say seems to get through.

About the longest speech he's made in the past few months was when he said, 'You shouldn't mix with crims, Sis. Anyone'll tell you that.' I told him he wasn't a crim, we all know what really happened down on the south coast. You especially, Mal, so don't deny it. But it didn't make any difference. He gave me this bitter smile that I've had to get used to, which was the end of the conversation as far as he was concerned.

That's roughly how all my visits have gone until recently. Then last weekend when I went, I got this message about how he'd refused to see me. I nearly came straight home, which is probably what he was banking on, but then I changed my mind. I made such a fuss that they brought him out anyway, and his face was all swollen and bruised from where he'd been bashed.

I tried to find out who'd done it to him, but it was no good. It was like getting blood from a stone. At the end of half an hour of pleading, the most he would say was 'Leave it alone, Sis'. I felt so mad I couldn't stop myself yelling at him, loud enough to bring the guards running, and I think that must have given him a jolt because he ducked his head the way he used to as a kid. 'I'm sorry, Cath,' he said, really soft like he meant it, and for a second or two he was his old self.

That's why I'm writing to you, Mal, because he's still in there somewhere, the old Danny we both love, underneath all the layers of resentment and anger. What I need is someone to help me reach him. Someone who knows him as well as I do and can maybe find a way of breaking down his silence, or at least of breaking through it.

This is a big ask, I know, with you locked up for even longer than Danny, and in another part of the State. In a worse place, too. As I said at the beginning, you've got plenty of problems without taking on Danny's as well. Just the same, I'd be really grateful if you could start writing to him. He's always looked up to you, he thinks of you as a close friend, and a letter or two might make all the difference.

We've never got on, you and I, and I won't pretend otherwise. But this is a special case. It's Danny we're talking about here, not us. If you can get through to him, I'll owe you, and that's all I can really say. It's over to you now. I have this feeling you'll do your best for him all the same.

Keep well,
Cath

⊚   ⊚   ⊚

Dear Cath,

They say in here any letter's worth getting, and in spite of the bad news about Danny that was certainly true of yours. It *was* great to hear from you, even though you sound pretty upset. I just wish you'd had better news for me.

Having said that, I have to start with some baddish news of my own. I wrote to Danny weeks ago, twice in fact, soon after the trial, and didn't hear a word back. I figured he was mad at me for what they did to him, the way they stitched him up over that arson charge, and the best thing I could do was let him cool down. My guess is that he wouldn't exactly jump for joy even now if a letter from me popped out of the slot. Think about it – someone like you can't get a response from him, so what chance do I have?

Don't despair, though, because that's not the end of the story. I have a friend of sorts who's also stuck away in Karlin. He's an Aboriginal bloke, young like Danny, but clued up. I've written and asked *him* to have a word. I've more or less filled him in on the situation so there's no chance of him saying the wrong thing and making matters worse. He's had a rough time himself, which means he stands a reasonable chance of getting through to Danny.

The story doesn't end there either. Do you remember a girl called Bonny, who was sent down with us? As luck would have it she also knows someone in Karlin. Like most of her friends, he sounds fairly weird. He has something to do with the animal rights movement, I gather, but Bonny thinks he's okay, and that's good enough for me. Anyway, she's promised to shoot off a letter and get him in on the act. That way we'll have two people coming at Danny, both of them on the inside, which is important, because if Danny's going to trust anyone, it'll be one of his own kind if you see what I mean.

I wouldn't fret too much in the meantime. Danny's a good kid, the best, and what all this has proved is that his heart's in the right place. He isn't like a lot of seventeen and eighteen-year-olds who don't have a thought in their heads outside of what's showing at the movies or what's number one on the charts.

There's some real feeling in him, too. Right now it's all coming out in anger. At least that's how it sounds from what you say – and if anyone should recognise anger, it's me. Sometimes I feel as if my head's going to split wide open with it. But it doesn't last for ever, Cath, no matter how bad it is. It runs its course, and afterwards it leaves you cool and clear and able to look at yourself. It *purges* you, that's the word, and then you know who you are. The real you, deep inside. From then on you can see where you're going and you don't get side-tracked by all the bullshit out there ever again.

That's how it's been with me, and my guess is that Danny's going through the same process. Don't get me wrong, I'm not saying Danny and I are alike. We're not, as you and I both know. I've dived in and out of anger time and again. That's how I am. I have a low flash-point and I can't do anything about it. With Danny it's different again. For him anger is a slow burn that he'll only go through once. It's been building up over a long time, and it'll probably last a while longer, but when it's finally over he'll be free of it. He'll be licked clean, like when you hold a knife in the flame and it changes colour. I don't know when that'll happen, but when it does he'll understand the road he has to take better than any of us. He's a deep one, Danny, and once he's

103

decided on a course he won't be deflected by the likes of you and me.

All that's down the road a way of course. Still, at least things are moving, and in the right direction I hope. By the time you get this there'll be two friendly voices inside Karlin with him, talking him through, and that's the best I can do for the present. If any other ideas occur to me I'll let you know.

You mention in your letter that it's a big ask, your wanting me to write to Danny. (As a matter of fact it's not, and when the time's ripe I'll drop him another line. That's the least I can do.) What *is* a big ask is me looking to you for another letter. I wouldn't presume, except letters are a kind of life-line in this lousy dump. They're proof that the real world goes chugging on and that someone out there still knows you exist. You get a letter and you realise you're alive and sane, which most of us need to be convinced of pretty often, especially at night after lights out.

There's a bloke working in the library who calls prison the great leveller. Some of the other cons have gone a step further and called it the great flattener, which is about right. But you know me, I never stay down for long. And if you want my opinion, the same holds true for Danny. He may be a bit slow about bouncing back, but he'll make it. He's not the type to cave in, not Dan. So bear up.

If nothing else, keep me posted on his progress.
Cheers,
Mal

⊚   ⊚   ⊚

Dear Miss Fenton,

My name is Jimmy Campbell. Mal Arden might have mentioned me. He wrote a week or two back and asked me to try and make contact with your brother. Mal also asked me to let you know how things stand. So here goes.

I've had a couple of chats with Danny so far, and I've got to say he's not too friendly. That could be because of me. I have a reputation in here, and white fellers like your brother are often a bit careful at first. I don't mind. I was adopted out and brought up white, so I'm used to it. I reckon once he gets to know me he'll come round. He's not dumb, I can see that. He can listen, which makes a change from most of the white fellers you bump into. What I plan to do is keep telling him stuff about this country he doesn't know and see if it makes any difference. I'm betting some of it'll get through.

There's another con called Pete Chartiss who's also getting friendly with him. He's a mate of Bonny's, that you know about. I know her too from a Daintree protest we were on together. I've looked Pete over and he seems okay. We get along fine. He agrees with me that Danny's a bit closed up, but not for long. Between us we should be able to put him right. A few weeks is all it'll take probably, and I should know. I've been there and back myself. So has Pete I shouldn't wonder.

I've noticed you a few times when you've come to visit Danny. You always brighten the place up, that's my opinion. So it's a pleasure for me to write to you like this.

There's this old uncle I met once who never tells you goodbye. And he knows a thing or two. Here's all he ever says –

Keep walking straight.

Jimmy

⊚   ⊚   ⊚

KARLIN DETENTION CENTRE
Second Interim Psychological Report
Extracts from interview

SUBJECT
Daniel Fenton

Interviewer:	I've been hearing good things about you recently.
Subject:	Such as?
Int:	Well, the situation between you and the guards sounds a lot better. There've been no reports of physical aggression for some weeks now.
Sub:	Yeah, it wasn't getting me anywhere.
Int:	Would you care to expand on that?
Sub:	Sure. My sister wrote me this letter about an old Irish crackpot who was so keen on fighting that he couldn't see straight any more. As he saw it there were enemies everywhere, and he finished up wading out through the surf and having a go at the sea.
Int:	Is that how you think of the power of the guards? As like the incoming waves?
Sub:	Kind of.
Int:	What made you pull back?
Sub:	You can't beat the sea, can you? No one can. Not even that other old crazy who lived years ago. That English king, whatever he was called. The one who ordered the waves back.
Int:	You mean King Canute?
Sub:	Yeah, Canute, not even him.

Int:	So you gave up because you couldn't win. Is that the idea?
Sub:	More or less.
Int:	And if you could have won? What then?
Sub:	I still don't *like* the guards, if that's what you mean. But win or lose, there was no point. Like I told you, I wasn't getting anywhere.
Int:	Good. That's good.
Sub:	(*Laughs*) Glad you approve.
Int:	I also hear you're on a better footing with your fellow inmates.
Sub:	You seem to hear an awful lot.
Int:	Yes, but is it true?
Sub:	I'd say so.
Int:	Can you explain why?
Sub:	Maybe they've got used to me.
Int:	Is that all that's happened?
Sub:	Probably not. You need mates in a place like this. After I got to know a couple of the guys, things started to turn around.
Int:	Would you call these two people friends?
Sub:	(*Nods*)
Int:	And how have they changed your life?
Sub:	They've taught me stuff.
Int:	Go on.
Sub:	Like now, when I get pissed off, I don't do my block. I think about something else instead.
Int:	What kind of something?
Sub:	N/R
Int:	Your parents, do you think about them?
Sub:	(*Pauses*) No, not them.
Int:	What then? Memories of your childhood?

Sub:	(*Pauses again*) Not memories either.
Int:	Why? Do you find those painful?
Sub:	Some.
Int:	Tell me about them.
Sub:	Look, can we change the subject?
Int:	Of course. Let's get back to what it is that stops you feeling angry.
Sub:	Forests for instance. I imagine big empty forests. They have to be empty.
Int:	Why's that?
Sub:	(*Waves question aside*) There's nothing in them but birds, and a few wallabies maybe. And the wind. If I listen hard, it seems to whisper things.
Int:	Like what?
Sub:	N/R
Int:	Does it tell you to keep calm? Is that its message?
Sub:	(*Shakes his head*) It doesn't matter. Can we change the subject again?
Int:	No problem. These new friends of yours, what are they like?
Sub:	For a start, they don't ask a lot of questions. (*Laughs*)
Int:	I take your point, but that's how these sessions are. There's nothing I can do about it.
Sub:	You could resign.
Int:	Now it's *my* turn to change the subject. What else do you like about these friends of yours? How are they different from the guards, for instance?
Sub:	You must be kidding.
Int:	No, I'd really like to know.

Sub:	The list'd go on for ever.
Int:	Just one difference then, the main one.
Sub:	Okay, they accept me for who I am.
Int:	And who *are* you?
Sub:	Not the person I thought I was.
Int:	Can you describe this new self to me?
Sub:	Not really.
Int:	But it's a calmer self, less angry.
Sub:	Calmer. I like that better.
Int:	So how is this new you getting on with his sister?
Sub:	Just fine.
Int:	You're talking to her again?
Sub:	(*Nods*)
Int:	You told me once that she wouldn't want to hear anything you had to say.
Sub:	(*Laughs*) Yeah, but that was then, this is now.
Int:	And now's different?
Sub:	Heaps.
Int:	Is it also better?
Sub:	Some people would think so.
Int:	Would you?
Sub:	(*Sighs*) Listen, can we close this off? I'm getting tired.
Int:	All right, one last question. What have you and your sister talked about recently?
Sub:	You know, family stuff.
Int:	Can't you be clearer than that?
Sub:	You said *one* question.
Int:	Humour me.
Sub:	Okay, you're the boss. I told her about those forests I imagine when I'm feeling uptight.
Int:	The empty ones?

Sub:	Yeah, and how the wind whispers through the trees.
Int:	Was she as curious about those whispers as I am? Did she ask you what the wind was saying?
Sub:	No, she just listened, and I think maybe she heard it too. The wind I mean. (*Holds up both hands and laughs*) A joke. Just a joke.

Interviewer's comments

As the whole extract should make clear, the subject's overall attitude has improved significantly in recent weeks. He is far less overtly angry, disinclined to shows of physical aggression, and more amenable in his dealings with all levels of authority. Any optimistic prognosis, however, needs to be tempered by the following considerations:

(a) On occasion the subject still resorts to verbal abuse in his relationship with the guards.

(b) The case files of the two friends he refers to reveal that they are both committed arsonists, like himself. Furthermore, they are both classified by the guards as 'difficult'.

For these reasons I would recommend that, despite recent gains, the subject's progress should continue to be monitored.

⊚ ⊚ ⊚

Dear Mal,

I won't make this a long letter. It's mainly to give you the up-to-date on Danny that you asked for.

I didn't write earlier because there wasn't an awful lot to say, and it's no use pretending we're friends who exchange letters for the fun of it, because we're not. We're not enemies either. Just different.

All that aside, I do have something worth passing on at last. It's beginning to look as though Danny's coming out of the depression or whatever it was he'd fallen into. I don't want to sound too hopeful, just in case, but he *is* talking to me again. And although he's not his old self yet, he's far more open.

I noticed the difference a couple of weeks ago. I arrived there for my usual visit and right out of the blue he greeted me with a kiss on the cheek. It came as such a surprise that I burst into tears. I felt a real fool, blubbing away in front of everybody, but at the same time I didn't care. I kept telling myself, he's back, I've got Danny back. He didn't talk much after that. On the other hand he wasn't all sullen either. He was kind of there for me if you know what I mean. I don't have a word to describe it.

Then last Sunday when I went out there, he was better still. We actually joked and laughed quite a bit, can you believe that? It was almost like old times, before Mum got sick, which is really going back a while. I didn't push him for explanations or anything. I know Danny, he'll tell me what's been going on all in his own good time. About the closest we came to being serious was at the end, when I asked if he'd stopped feeling bitter about the trial. 'What trial?' he said, and laughed.

That may sound as if he was dodging the question, but he wasn't. Like I said, I know Danny, and it was his way of saying he wasn't fazed by the trial any more, and nor should I be.

I can't tell you how much better *I've* felt since then, and that brings me to the second reason for this letter. I have no idea whether or not you actually had a hand in helping him, but I do know you tried because I heard from that friend of yours in Karlin. I also know you went on believing in him. I have your letter open in front of me now, the part where you talk about his anger eventually burning itself out. Well, it looks as though you were right, and I want to thank you for everything.

I said I'd owe you if Danny came good, and I do. I'm not sure how I'll get to repay you, but somehow I will. I won't forget anyway. For the time being I'll just say this – when they let you out of that place, you're welcome here until you find your feet. That's if Danny wants to see you again. It's up to him.

You'll still have a way to go, of course, after they release Danny. It must be hard, especially in Long Bay. Karlin's bad enough, and that's supposed to be one of the best places. If I can, I'll try and get Danny to drop you a line, but I can't promise. It's early days yet and I don't want to push him too much. I'm sure you understand.

Thanks again for all your help.

Yours,
Cath

⑥   ⑥   ⑥

Dear Cath,

This letter's way overdue, I know. Every weekend while you're here, I see all those questions in your eyes and I mean to answer them, but I never seem to get round to it, not properly. It's too difficult I suppose. Also, in a place like this you kind of get used to keeping your thoughts to yourself. So, I decided this morning that it's time I *wrote* instead and cleared the air between us this way.

I won't make out I wasn't mad about what happened at the trial, and before. I was. I felt done over, because like I've explained a million times already, I wasn't anywhere near that timber yard and didn't even know there'd been a fire. But mad as I was, I never turned against you. I felt trapped was all, and didn't want to talk to anyone. I'm not a kid any more, I couldn't just lean on my big sister. I had to work it out as best I could.

In the end I got quite a bit of help from a couple of guys I met in here. Talking to them, I learned I wasn't the only angry person in the world. Nor the only one who's been hard done by. Jimmy, he's this black guy, he told me about the history of Aboriginal people since white settlement. And God, Cath, compared with them my life's been a picnic. You wouldn't credit the way they've been treated. It turned my stomach, I can tell you.

Then there's Pete. He's into animal rights and he's big on what he calls anti-vivisection, which I'd never heard of before, but which is all about stopping these scientist-types from experimenting with animals and treating them as though they don't have feelings or anything. What Pete taught me is that animals are at the very bottom of the heap. They have hardly any rights at all. They don't even have a way of complaining unless we speak up for them.

I said just now that I talked to Jimmy and Pete, but mostly I listened. And it's hard to describe, Cath, but sitting there listening to what they had to say, I felt like I was gradually coming out of the dark. It was as if I'd been locked away in this pitch-black room for a long time, and then these voices started getting through to me, and pretty soon a crack of light showed at one of the windows. Next thing the light was real bright and the door started to open. That's more or less how it was.

I can't say I'm ready to walk out of the room yet, or that when I do I'll be the same person who walked in. Before, I was all over the place. I didn't really know where I was going or anything. Now it's different. Jimmy talks a lot about 'focus', which is the closest I can come to what I mean. For the first time in my life I'm beginning to see how things are, and not how I'd like them to be. I haven't forgotten Mum, don't ever think that. What I'm getting at is that I can see now how she fits in. There's a kind of pattern, and she's a part of it. It's a lousy pattern, though, and somebody, some time, has got to do something about it.

Just as long as it isn't Danny! That's what you're thinking, isn't it? Well, I won't make any promises. Jimmy reckons it's crazy to decide what you'll do on the outside until you get there, and I agree. I have some ideas, but I'll have to wait and see. Right now I just sit and listen to those whispers from the forest I told you about. They're what keep me going, day by day, and I have no idea what they'll be telling me by the time I walk free.

Walking free! It sounds so great. I have this calendar on the wall over my bed, one I drew up for myself, and I'm marking off the days. Most of it's crossed out squares by now, which is the best news around. Only one more block of squares to go and I'll be home. Or four more visits from my ol' sis, which is a better way of thinking about it.

See you on Sunday, Cath. Don't let's talk about any of this then. It's the best day of the week for me, by a long mile, and I don't want to spoil it.

Lots of love,
Danny

Long Bay
Feb 2

Dear Danny,

I'll keep this real short because your long silence has made it clear how you see me these days. A pity, but there you are.

I see from the calendar that you'll be getting out in a week's time. Way to go, bro. Just don't let the big wide world grind you down when you get out there. Remember what you know and keep the faith. Hold a little bit of that anger in reserve, because if you don't the bastards will clobber you again. And again and again.

I'll think of you on the big day.

Good luck, break a leg, and all the rest of it.

Your one-time friend,
Mal

KARLIN DETENTION CENTRE
Final Psychological Report: A summary

SUBJECT
Daniel Fenton

The subject has continued to make excellent progress. His relationship with the guards appears to have plateaued at the level of mutual respect; and during our last interview he portrayed no signs of either anger or resentment. In sharp contrast to his sullen, untrusting behaviour at the time of entry, his overall manner has become for the most part open and candid, even humorous. He is still somewhat reticent about his parents, which suggests some unhealed wounds, but against this must be set his undeniably good relationship with his sister, who is the only traceable/surviving member of his immediate family. On balance, therefore, his prospects are excellent, and there is every reason for including him amongst those least likely to re-offend.

Signed: Dr M Stalt

5 Caged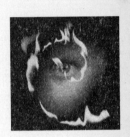

It's dark here now, the forest quiet except for a whisper of wind high in the canopy. There're no signs of movement from below, thank God. Not yet. They'll probably leave us a while longer. A day or so with any luck. Bonny keeps hissing for me to blow out the candle, but the leaf shelter should be enough to hide it from the outside. And I need the light if I'm to get everything in order, everything clear. Especially those parts I've left out. Like the time before I teamed up with Mal again. I need a record of that if I'm to keep it all straight in my head.

Well, this is as good a time as any for filling in the blanks. The only chance I'll ever have, maybe.

⊚　　⊚　　⊚

I won't bother about those first weeks on the outside. Cath was great, as always. We've never had any serious quarrel, Cath and I. At the same time I couldn't really talk to her, not about how it felt to be free, because no one can understand that unless they've been locked up. I couldn't tell her what I had in mind either. She'd have freaked.

'Get a job,' she told me, but I was marking off the days again. Only a month or so this time, till they let Jimmy and Pete out more or less together.

At first Jimmy was for heading off. He reckoned he'd had enough of white feller's business and had business of his own to see to. Pete and I kind of wore him down. Pete more than me. He can talk, I'll give him that much.

'This goes deeper than race,' he kept saying. 'This has to do with the Dreaming.'

'You should shut up about things you don't understand,' Jimmy said, but all the same you could tell he was interested.

What finally got through to him was the bit about animals

being related to us, how they're our brothers and sisters, as much a part of the life-blood of the land as we are.

'I see what you mean,' Jimmy admitted, a different look in his eyes. 'The bastards're trying to kill off the Dreaming. They want to choke the life out of it.'

That wasn't how I saw the situation. Not then. For me animals were plain helpless, something else for the wrong kind of people to trample on. But as Pete said, it all came down to the same thing in the end, so the three of us stuck together.

We chose as our target a building in one of the universities, the sort of place where they keep a whole collection of exper-imental animals. The plan was to break in, let the animals loose, and then fire the place. According to Pete we'd need extra pairs of hands to get the job done quickly, and he brought in two other people, Fay and Kris.

They were just up from Melbourne then, sisters, though they didn't look alike. Kris in her mid-twenties, big and slow and nearly white-blonde, with skin so pale you wondered if she was albino. Fay the very opposite, maybe two or three years younger, small, dark, and with a quick, jumpy way of doing things. What they had in common was a belief in the Gaia theory, which is this idea that the whole world is a single giant organism, and we're all a part of it. That's how Fay and Kris described it, anyway.

Gaia freaks, Pete called them, but if you ask me they know a thing or two the rest of us don't. Fay, for instance, who always has this faraway expression, as though she's off in some world of her own where things make more sense than they do here. Looking at her, you'd think she was dead vague, and you'd be wrong. Underneath it all she's a hard case. Even big quiet Kris isn't someone to mess with in a tight spot.

Well, once we'd put our plan to them they were on side straight away. Kris, she gave us this slow smile, as much as to say, 'I'm in'. So was Fay, though she was worried that five people weren't enough to carry the plan through, not if we wanted to get in and out fast.

That's how we came to include Mick. I didn't trust him at first, and I'm sorry about that. I'm extra sorry for all the lousy thoughts I had about him afterwards. It wasn't his rough, shaggy look that put me off. I didn't look so different myself when I was down in the southern forests. What really got to me was the way he carted that kid of his around everywhere – Zizi, his four-year-old daughter, who'd been dragged from one demo to another from the day she was born. Somehow it didn't seem right to involve a kid in his kind of life. What I didn't realise is that everything Mick does is for Zizi, no one else. 'It's her future I'm looking out for,' he likes to say, and he means it.

She's a great kid, too. On the night of the raid, when Mick put her to bed in Pete's Newtown terrace, she didn't complain about being left on her own.

'When you wake up tomorrow,' Mick told her, 'there'll be monkeys in the tree outside.'

'Monkeys?' she said. 'Really?'

'Sydney'll be swarming with them,' he promised.

I remembered that later, when everything had gone wrong. But there and then it was just a promise to a kid, and I didn't give it a second thought. I was too busy getting ready like everyone else.

For obvious reasons we'd decided to dress in black, with balaclavas to hide our faces in case we ran into trouble.

'Not that there'll be anyone around,' Pete said as we set off. 'You know what these university outfits are like. Bloody hopeless.'

In fact we were the only hopeless ones – all six of us dressed like burglars and packed into his old bomb of a car, with the crowbars and heavy-duty jack rattling around in the boot every time we turned a corner. If the cops had stopped us, they'd have had a field day.

We made it as far as the campus all the same, and parked outside on one of the side roads. Pete was all for marching in at the main gate, but Jimmy wasn't having any of that, and we chose a spot between two street lamps, where it was darkest, and bunked over the fence.

Getting into the building itself was almost as easy. Thick bushes grew right up against the windows on one side, and they supplied all the cover we needed while we slotted the jack between the burglar bars and cranked them apart. There was a crunching noise as the bricks holding the bars gave way, and the sound of splintering wood when we levered up the window, none of it loud enough to bring anyone running.

Then we were in. Not amongst the animals as we'd expected, but in a long corridor with doors leading off down one side. We tried most of the doors, and they opened into these empty rooms that looked like the labs at school. In any case the smell of the place was wrong. That musty animal scent was missing.

We caught a tang of it as soon as we reached the stairs, and it got stronger as we went up. That's maybe when we should have called the whole raid off, but instead Pete started making excuses – explaining how all he'd had a chance to see was the layout of the animal section and how no one had told him it was up on the first floor. He carried on as if none of this was his fault and someone else had let us down.

'We've still got a problem,' Fay whispered. 'How are we supposed to get the animals out from up here?'

'They'll find their own way out,' Pete said, which was crazy.

'Yeah? How?' Jimmy asked him, and straight away Pete started acting all high and mighty.

'Just do it, okay,' he said, which got everybody's backs up.

For a while after that there was a free-for-all, with the six of us huddled together in the dark on the upper landing, whispering away like mad. You couldn't see anyone's face, just the shadowy blobs of the balaclavas, and half the time you couldn't tell who was saying what.

Mick was the one who finally sorted things out.

'Look, this isn't getting us anywhere,' he said, his voice so loud in the empty stairwell no one else dared say a word. 'We're here now and it's too late to back out. So the rest of you get started while me and Pete have a go at opening the main door downstairs.'

'What if it won't open?' Fay said. 'What'll we do then?'

'God knows,' Mick said, which about summed up how the rest of us were feeling.

We'd decided beforehand that I'd team up with Jimmy, and I could hear him swearing to himself as we groped our way into the nearest holding area. It was lined with perspex cages or boxes, and there were these long scurrying shapes inside. The smell alone should have told us what they were, but the penny didn't drop until Jimmy switched on his torch.

'Christ, rats!' he muttered, and backed into me.

It turned out he had an absolute thing about rats. I could feel him shaking. He began yanking open the boxes all the same, moaning to himself as the rats scampered out.

I wasn't feeling too great myself, not with these mushy shapes underfoot. Every time I took a step I could feel them milling about my ankles. The worst, though, was when a couple started climbing up my jeans, their little feet sort of plucking at the cloth, and I had to knock them away with the torch.

'I'm out of here,' I told Jimmy, and pushed through to the next room.

The smell was different in there. Less musty. More of an earth

125

or dry grass smell. I swung the torch and saw why. Rabbits. Pink-eyed and dead still, as though stunned by the light.

Jimmy was right behind me, the beam of his torch still shaking like crazy.

'What are you waiting for?' he said in this strangled sort of voice, and shoved past. 'Doomsday?'

I followed him into the room. He'd stopped caring about how much noise he was making. Most of the time he wrenched at the cages, and when they wouldn't come open at the first try he kicked at them until the metal bases broke loose.

'You're going to bring the guards at this rate,' I warned him.

'What guards?' he said, but he stopped all the same.

He'd turned off his torch for a minute and I could hear him breathing hard. Underneath the sound of his breaths there was this soft rustling noise made by the rabbits. You couldn't see much, only these vague white blobs hopping around in the dark.

I waited for him to calm down, then I said, 'Come on, let's get this over with.' And we moved on, quieter now, our feet pushing through the warm bodies.

We'd just about finished when there was a shout from somewhere back in the building. At least I thought it was a shout, but it was so muffled I couldn't be sure.

'What was that?' I said.

Jimmy had steadied off by then. He was more like his old self, the cool guy I'd known in Karlin.

'Never mind about that,' he said. 'We're here to clear this end of the building. Let's do it.'

The end room was stacked with monkey cages. I don't know what kind of monkeys – quite big, with whitish stripes on their faces, and bright intelligent eyes that followed your every move. Some of them were fierce too, lunging at you when you tried to unfasten the cage doors.

'Watch these buggers,' Jimmy said as we began moving along the first line of cages.

It was slow work, and we hadn't gone far before there were more shouts, closer this time and clearer. Then something else, a kind of feeling in the air that I couldn't put a name to. The monkeys knew what it was though. They were jabbering and jumping around in their cages, getting more worked up by the minute.

'Christ!' Jimmy said, and swung his torch back over the way we'd come.

I realised what it was then, the faint tang of smoke. I could even see it, the first thin haze drifting in through the door behind us.

There was a sound of footsteps and Mick appeared in the doorway, looking really wild.

'They're onto us!' he shouted. 'Get the hell out while you can!'

The smoke was a lot thicker already, the monkeys going crazy, and I'll admit it, I was feeling pretty scared. But mad too. So was Jimmy. Grabbing Mick by the collar, he shoved him up against the nearest cage.

'This wasn't supposed to happen till the place was cleared!' he said. 'That was the plan. What stupid bastard decided to start splashing kero around?'

Mick tried to pull free, but I grabbed him too.

'It was you, wasn't it?' I said.

In the torchlight Mick looked wilder than ever.

'You're going to get us killed!' he shouted.

'I'll bloody kill you myself if I have to!' Jimmy told him, and started to cough as the smoke got thicker still. It had that kero smell that catches in the back of your throat.

Mick wasn't thinking too straight any more. Maybe none of us were.

'These guards arrived!' he said, the words kind of tumbling out. 'They damn near got me! They were chasing us and then ... and then there was this line of flames ... from one room to the next!'

'A bloody kero-trail!' Jimmy said, and shoved Mick away.

I didn't see what happened to him after that. He seemed to disappear into the smoke, and Jimmy was hauling me past the screaming monkeys towards the nearest window. The dozen or so monkeys we'd freed were scrambling over us, as though they'd guessed what he was up to even before he yanked the window open. I could feel their hands and feet on my neck, and then the cool clean air from outside that I could breathe without coughing.

Jimmy pulled his sleeve away from his mouth and nose. 'We'll have to jump,' he said, and tried to push me through the opening first.

I nearly went. There were no window bars on the first floor, and I nearly followed the monkeys, the way they crouched on the sill for a second and then launched themselves out into space. It's too long ago to remember what stopped me. It may have been Jimmy's face, completely black except for the eyes that showed as silvery points of light. Mirrors really. I know they were what made me turn around, which was how I came to see it. The ball of flame that had once been a rabbit, still moving, still alive, blundering into the cages it couldn't see any more. Bouncing off them and struggling on. With more burning shapes close behind, lured on like the rest of us maybe by the fresh air from the open window.

I could hear Jimmy shouting at me not to be a bloody fool, but the thing is, I didn't actually decide to turn back. It happened all on its own. My mind seemed to slip out of gear, or into a different kind of gear or something, and I was in amongst the cages again.

By this time there was smoke everywhere, and the noise from the monkeys was awful, like the screams of trapped children. They were crashing around inside their cages, their eyes real wide, blind with panic. I tried to make soothing noises, but I could hardly breathe, and they couldn't hear me anyway. They were on their own. As far as they were concerned the whole world had turned against them. Even when I pulled open the cage doors, it wasn't me they saw. My arm was just a branch or tree, something to run along on their way to the window. Maybe a couple of them registered who I really was because I felt this pain in my ear, and another sharp jab in my cheek, from where they bit me, but I didn't mind about that. How could I?

Mick! I thought. Bloody Mick! Because by then I'd forgotten where the window was located. There was only the smoke-filled dark, nothing else, and I had to blame someone for it.

I don't know if I blacked out or what. I was down on my knees, my eyes stinging so bad I couldn't open them. The coughing was even worse. It was all I could hear now. I remember thinking, So this is it, this is how Mum must have felt on the last day. But I didn't feel close to her or anything. I was on my own, the same as the monkeys.

And then the rain came down.

I was so confused I honestly thought it *was* rain, one of those sudden spring showers you get in Sydney, that seem to arrive out of nowhere and drench you in two seconds flat. Except this was a lot fiercer than any shower I'd ever known, more like some weird tropical storm crashing down from the dark.

Jimmy had dragged me as far as the window before I realised what was going on. The automatic sprinkler system had cut in, triggered by the smoke.

The last of the freed monkeys squirmed past us. In the light of Jimmy's torch they looked like half-drowned rats, their fur all spiky as they sailed out into space. I don't know where my torch had got to. I remembered it and tried to turn back for the second time, into the steady downpour that had once been a room. All I could see was a single cage, the one closest to us, with a huddled shape inside and these eyes watching me. It wasn't good being watched like that. Then Jimmy was pushing me out and calling me a silly bugger when I made a last-minute grab for the wooden frame of the window.

It's funny how quick you think when you have to. The fall couldn't have lasted more than a second or so, but it felt like an age. Long enough for me to believe all over again that I'd had it, that I was going to crash down onto the road outside. I can't say my whole life flashed before me the way it's supposed to. I only remembered one thing, but I knew it was important. It was what Mum told me once, when I'd chucked some flowers down in the hospital. 'You'll regret that my boy,' she'd said. And already I did, even before I landed in the bushes alongside the building.

I rolled clear and Jimmy landed with an 'ouf' behind me.

'You all right, brud?' he said. That was his first thought. A good feller, Jimmy.

The others were waiting for us beyond the bushes, grouped together in the dark, but it was only Mick I was interested in. I was still so worked up I'd have had a go at him there and then if Jimmy hadn't got between us.

'This isn't the place for it!' he said. And when I went on struggling, he kind of hugged me and pressed his lips to my ear. 'Listen!'

We all heard it then. The police siren, or the fire engine maybe. I'm not sure which.

'Scatter!' Pete said, and we took off in different directions, according to plan.

My route took me round behind the building into the real dark. After that everything was a jumble. Trees and more buildings and finally a metal fence with a busy road on the other side. I stayed inside the fence until the road was clear, then climbed over and ran off into the quiet streets beyond.

I kept running even after the sirens had faded. I had to, because of the way I felt about Mick. But it's dumb running through the suburbs. You only draw attention to yourself. After I'd set a whole lot of dogs off barking I made myself stop and crouch in the shadows between two street lamps.

That was when it really hit me, the lousiness of what we'd done. Not just Mick. All of us. And I didn't need to be some creative genius to imagine what Cath would have said, which only made me feel worse.

I walked after that. I took the long way home so I could cool off. It must have been about one when I reached Pete's terrace. 'Home base' we'd called it while we'd been planning the raid, but it didn't look much like home any more.

Kris answered the door, her face and hair all shiny and clean. 'God, look at you!' she said.

The others were having a drink in the front room. They called out as I passed, but I wasn't ready to talk to anyone yet, and I went straight up to the bathroom.

Kris was right, I did look a mess. I had big splotches of dried blood on my cheek and neck, and my face and clothes were streaked from the water and the smoke. Most of it soon washed off under the shower, but not the smell of where I'd been. That seemed to stay with me even after I'd dried myself and put on fresh clothes.

My old clothes I stuffed into a garbage bag with everyone else's, and then I carried the bag downstairs.

'I'd better go out and dump this lot,' I told them, because I still wasn't ready to talk.

'Have a drink first,' Pete said, and tossed me a can, though he knew I didn't drink, and why. I'd have thrown it back at him if he hadn't been a bit smashed.

'Steady, brud,' Jimmy whispered, and took the can from me. I had to be careful not to look at Mick.

'That wasn't what we planned,' I said, talking only to Pete.

He gave me a hard look back, and I realised he wasn't as drunk as I'd thought.

'It wasn't all loss,' he said.

'Wasn't it?' I couldn't bring myself to say anything else.

'Property, Dan,' he said, and wagged a finger at me, as if he thought he was Mal or someone, which he wasn't. 'Property, that's what it's all about. Money. Hit them in the hip pocket and they'll stop funding their so-called research units. It'll be too expensive. Well, we hit them hard tonight. Did you see that place go up? Like a bloody torch. We really made them sit up and listen, never mind what you think.'

'Why should anyone mind what I think?' I said, and I picked up the bag of clothes and headed off along the passage.

Kris walked me to the door.

'D'you want some company?' she said.

When I didn't answer, she did something surprising. She wrapped her big pale arms around me and eased me towards her. I could feel her nose and lip rings against my cheek, and her hair smelled of shampoo.

'I hated what happened tonight,' she whispered. 'It was horrible.'

'Then why're you sticking around here?' I said, and pulled free.

She wouldn't look at me.

'What else is there to do?' she said. 'This is the only way if we want to make them listen.'

I couldn't really argue with that last part.

'Yeah, someone has to make them listen,' I agreed, and left.

◎   ◎   ◎

I dumped the bag of clothes in one of those Vincent de Paul bins. Afterwards I went round to Cath's. She was forever saying it was *our* flat, not hers, even though she paid the rent. Sometimes I half believed her, but not that night. There was just nowhere else to go.

She's always been a light sleeper and she woke the second I let myself in.

'Is that you, Danny?'

Then she was standing in the darkened passage in her nightie, her hair all over the place.

I said, 'Okay if I crash here?'

She pulled her hair away from her face as though trying to get a good look at me.

'Since when d'you have to ask?' she said. 'Or have I got it wrong? D'you only look like Danny?'

She's never too pleased about being disturbed in the middle of the night. Who is? But she must have sensed something was up because she didn't say anything else. She just stepped aside and nodded towards the door of my room.

Five minutes later she followed me in, carrying two cups of hot chocolate. I saw her take in the bloody mark on my face and glance away.

'I walked into a door,' I told her, and laughed, except it didn't come out right.

She settled cross-legged at the other end of the bed, her nightie pulled tight across her knees, the cup cradled in both hands. She didn't speak until I'd finished my drink.

'Feel better?' she said then, as though a hot drink can cure anything – she's a lot like Mum that way.

I stretched out on the bed without answering, and she crawled up to my end and lay down beside me, our shoulders touching.

'I need you to explain something,' I said.

She waited for me to go on.

'Why is it that when we try and put things right, they only seem to get worse?'

She thought about her answer for a while.

'Because we're not God I suppose,' she said at last.

I couldn't keep the bitterness out of my voice. 'You could be right,' I said. 'Maybe God's the one who messed up.'

I felt her turn her head and look at me.

'You don't believe that,' she said.

But I wasn't so sure.

'If God's so brimming over with love and kindness,' I said, 'why is it always the innocent who get trampled on?'

'It's people who do the trampling, not God,' she pointed out, which was so close to the bone it really hurt.

'Yeah, people like me,' I said.

She reached over and touched the bite mark on my cheek with the tips of her fingers.

'What went on out there tonight?' she said.

And I almost told her. Maybe if I had, I wouldn't be here now, crouched in this leaf shelter in the middle of the night, with the forest all around. Don't get me wrong, I'm not complaining, just wondering whether everything could have been different, that's all. Probably not. And in a way I'm glad, because this is who I am now. Someone who'll never wake up on a closed-in veranda and watch the white dust flying around. Never. I won't live and die in a cage either, like those animals at the research centre. I'm certain of that, too.

So back to that night in Sydney where I was just about to blurt everything out to Cath. What stopped me was this pounding on the front door.

If it had been the cops, I'd have been stuck. The flat's two floors up, and I'd had enough of jumping out of windows for one night. I was shit-scared, I'll say that much, but when Cath answered the door it was only Pete. And with quite a few beers in him.

'Where is he?' I heard him say, and the next minute he was standing in the bedroom doorway, looking surprised to find me there.

'What's up?' I said, and this guilty look came over his face.

'Just making sure you're all right, mate,' he said, but not easy like that. He kind of stammered it out as if he was making it up on the spot, and I realised why he'd come. To check up on me, no other reason.

'You thought I might have gone to the cops, didn't you?' I said.

'Cops? Not a chance, mate.' He was putting on a big act now. 'Why should I think something like that?'

'Because of Mick and what he did.'

He blinked a few times before he worked that one out, and I should have guessed then.

'Oh yeah, Mick.' He shook his head. 'I see what you mean. The rotten bugger doesn't care, does he? A few monkeys and rabbits go up in flames, and it's all in a day's work as far as he's concerned.'

'What about where *you're* concerned?' I said. 'You told me earlier tonight how the raid was a big success. You said we'd really been out to damage property, and it was bad luck if animals got in the way.'

He leaned against the wall, dead casual. 'Me? I said that?'

'In so many words.'

'Yeah, well that was for the sake of group solidarity, wasn't it?' he said, and I could almost see him fishing the words out of nowhere. 'I didn't want to scare the others off.'

'So you wish the fire hadn't happened?'

'Too right, mate. It's the animals that count, first and last.'

It was such a feeble lie that I wondered then how I'd ever believed him, and I wonder now why I didn't just kick him out and end it all. That's the mystery. Why did I go on pushing him the way I did, and myself too? Unless maybe I needed to make someone pay for what had happened, and we were the only ones around. For whatever reason, I got up from the bed.

'You ready to prove your credentials?' I said.

'Credentials?' He was a bit too drunk to understand.

'You said it's the animals that count. Their rights. You want to prove that to me?'

'Any time, mate.'

Cath was standing behind him in the doorway, waving her arms for me to shut up, as if she'd guessed already what I was on about.

'Well, there's no time like the present,' I said.

⊚　　⊚　　⊚

Here's the other part of the mystery. Why did I have to go and choose Taronga Zoo? There of all places? I've thought about it a lot since, and it could have something to do with a book I read once, at school, and set in the future, about these teenagers who decide to free all the animals in Taronga.

That's one explanation. The other's much simpler. In a big city like Sydney there aren't many collections of caged animals, and with the research centre already swarming with cops and firefighters, the zoo was about the only option left. For what I had in mind anyway.

Cath, as usual, didn't want to let me go.

'This is about revenge, isn't it?' she said. 'It always is with you.' And when I wouldn't listen: 'Didn't you learn *anything* in Karlin?'

But she saved her big guns for when I was actually climbing into Pete's car.

'How many times do I have to remind you she's dead and gone?' she said, standing there on the darkened street, still in her nightie. 'Nothing you can ever do will bring her back. D'you hear me, Danny? Nothing!'

I slammed the car door.

'I can help her rest though,' I said, and we drove off.

Cath was mainly right of course. Most things go back to Mum and to what they did to her. All the same, Mum wasn't behind what happened during the last part of that night. If it was anyone, it was Dad. As Mum once said, in the hospital when she was dying, 'There are more ways of getting drunk than from a bottle.' And that's how it was with me as we drove across Sydney. I was like the old man on one of his mad binges, how he'd push himself to the limit as though all he wanted was to see when he'd break.

Anyway, there we were in Mosman at about three in the morning, in the parking area outside the zoo's main gates.

'We're not going in there!' Pete said, staring at me like I was crazy.

'Where else?' I said. 'It's a kind of prison, isn't it? Like Karlin, only worse. If you want to help animals, this is the place.'

'Yeah, well ...' he began, and ground to a halt because he knew I had him.

'Let's give it a go then,' I said, but he just sat there, glued to the seat.

'Look, any other time and I'm with you,' he said, sounding shaky as hell. 'It's been a long night, that's all.'

I climbed out of the car and went around to the boot. 'You're not turning chicken on me, are you?' I called back.

That got him going. His door clicked open and he was standing right next to me.

'Just lead the way, mate,' he said, sounding more sober than he had for hours.

I found a bolt-cutter in amongst the other gear in the boot, perfect for cutting through the fence wire. Though as things turned out we didn't have to bother with the fence. When we crept off down the side of the zoo grounds, we came to a building set right on the boundary. We only had to climb up over the roof and we were in.

I remember best the smell of the place, from so many animals lurking in the dark. You could hear them, their weird hoots and yowls that didn't seem to belong in Australia. The noise was loudest when we passed close to any of the cages or buildings, then they'd really start up. The big cats most of all. Their snarls were the creepiest of the lot. They made you feel as if a tiger or something was actually stalking you across the open hillside.

'We can't let *them* go!' Pete said, meaning the cats.

We'd stopped on this broad path, and in the faint moonlight I could see the sweat on his forehead.

'What about these then?' I said, and pointed to a big cage next to the path.

There were small, bunched-up shapes inside. I didn't realise they were monkeys until we tried hacking our way through the bars. Pete was struggling with the bolt-cutters and not getting anywhere, when suddenly there was this piercing scream and all these tiny bodies started hurtling around inside. The din was awful. And Pete, he just dropped the cutters and took off.

I nearly let him go, but like I said, it can get pretty creepy in there and I didn't fancy being left on my own, so I snatched up the cutters and took off after him.

It was just as well, because when we stopped for breath we could see these lights moving up behind us, three or four of them bobbing around in the dark like fireflies.

'The bastards know someone's here!' Pete whispered, and would have headed off again, except this time I grabbed hold of him.

I wasn't feeling super-calm or anything. I just realised that running blind wouldn't do any good. It's a big place, Taronga, and easy to get lost in during the day, let alone at night when you're surrounded by shadows and shapes you can't recognise. While we still had some sense of direction, my idea was to double back to where we'd climbed in.

But what with those moving lights and all the animal noises coming at us out of the dark, Pete was in too much of a state to listen. And when I held onto him he panicked and started to struggle.

'This is all your doing!' he hissed at me. 'All for a few lousy animals!'

Okay, so I knew he was scared. Even so, there was something about the way he said it – the part about the animals I mean – that gave him away.

'Mick didn't lay that kero-trail, did he?' I said. 'It was you.'

'Kero-trail? What are you talking about?'

I shoved him hard against the nearest tree. I was glad I couldn't see his face because I might have done something worse.

'You know,' I said.

The lights were a bit closer now, an arc of them over to our right, and someone called out for us to stay put.

Pete's voice had gone high and scared. 'All right, I set fire to the place! So what? Someone had to!'

'And the animals? What about them?'

'What *about* them?' he said, as if he didn't care a damn, and I think that was what did it, what pushed me over the top.

'You're just like the others!' I said, my throat so tight I could hardly get the words out, and I hauled him off into the dark, away from the lights.

I wasn't out to save him. Not any more. And I wasn't running blind either. Mad as I was, there was still a part of me that was thinking, planning what to do next.

'Get your bloody hands off me!' Pete said, sort of pleading and threatening. Then a bit later, when I kept shoving him along: 'Have a heart, Dan.'

But I was too strung out to start feeling sorry for him. For him especially. Apart from all the anger, the one clear thought in my head was that this time things would be different. I wasn't going to mess up again, I was a hundred per cent on that. So when Pete got desperate and took a swing at me, I didn't hesitate. I clipped him on the side of the jaw with the bolt-cutters, hard enough to give him a real jolt.

He sagged at the knees and would have fallen flat if I hadn't grabbed him by the hair. With a bit of urging he climbed back to his feet. He was still groggy though, staggering all over the place when I pushed him on ahead.

'Where ...?' he said in this croaky voice, like he'd been asleep for a while, and waved his arms around in the dark.

'You'll find out,' I told him.

'Christ!' he said, and spat some blood maybe, from where I'd hit him. 'Christ!'

'Shut it!' I whispered, because the people with the lights weren't far behind, and also because I was listening, for one sound in particular, out of all the night noises in Taronga.

I didn't locate it till we'd circled round to roughly where we'd been before. We crashed through a line of trees and bushes, onto another path, and it floated up from directly below us – the rumble of big cats. They broke into these deep roars as we got closer, and by the time we reached the main door to their building they were going pretty wild.

So was Pete, who'd begun struggling like crazy. He'd guessed what I had in mind.

'You off your head or what?' he said in this horrified whisper, and I didn't even have to stop and think, not with all that roaring in the background. As he tore himself free, I clipped him again and down he went.

'Payback time,' I said, and left him groaning on the ground while I groped in the dark for the padlock.

Except there wasn't one. The door had an ordinary lock I couldn't get at. The best I could do was push the metal handle of the bolt-cutters in beside the door and try and prise it open. I made plenty of noise, and a few scraps of wood splintered off, but that was about all.

Then I had to stop and see to Pete again. He was up on his hands and knees, sobbing to himself as he crawled off.

'Where're you off to?' I said, and dragged him back.

He didn't resist. By then he was as helpless as those freed rabbits in the research centre. Not that it made me feel any better. I tell you, I really wanted to get him in there and make him face those cats. I wanted him to know how it felt to be treated like nothing. Like some worthless piece of meat.

But never mind how much I smashed at the door, it refused to give. Meanwhile the moving lights had reappeared on the open hillside above us.

I had just enough time for one more go at the door, with the same result. And that was that. So near and yet so far, as they say. There was nothing for it but to give up on the whole idea. It wasn't easy, but the moment I let it go, all the anger seemed to flow out of me and I saw how dumb I'd been. Because even if I'd managed to break into the building, I'd still have had to deal with the cages. And if I'd somehow got Pete into one of *those* ... what then?

Judging by the mood of the cats, I probably wouldn't have walked out alive either. They'd have had us both. End of story. Not just my story and Pete's, but a much bigger story that began years ago in a small mining town. One bit of cheap revenge and it would all have been over, with Mum and Gramps lost for ever if you see what I mean.

I can't say all this came clear as I stood there in the shadows, but I did understand enough to realise that Pete himself wasn't worth the risk, any more than my Company man had been.

'This is your lucky night, d'you know that?' I told him, and chucked the bolt-cutters into the dark, up towards the advancing guards.

They landed on the hard path with a clatter you could hear even past all the cat noise. Straight away the lights picked them out, held steady for a while, and then swung in our direction.

It's funny how, when really important things happen, everything seems to slow down. I could only have had a second or two to decide my next move, but that was enough. Grabbing hold of Pete, I heaved him up in front of me, as a kind of shield, so when the lights hit us he was the one caught in the glare.

'Get away from that door, son!' someone called, having to shout above the roars and growls.

My head was directly behind Pete's, my mouth only a few centimetres from his ear. 'You heard the man,' I whispered, and shoved him forward.

For once he didn't let me down. He staggered, nearly fell, and veered off to one side, with the lights following him all the way. The dark only held for a second or so, like before, but again it was enough, and I was nearly to the corner by the time the lights caught up with me.

'There he goes!' someone yelled. 'The other one!'

I could hear footsteps on the path, but I had a good lead. I reckoned that if I headed across the slope I'd reach the fence sooner or later and be able to climb out.

That was the idea, but when I ran past this bunch of trees and blundered straight into the fence, I changed my mind. It was so damned high! With barbed wire all along the top! I knew if I got tangled up in *that* I'd be in trouble, because there was still someone after me. I could see this light bobbing around beyond the trees, and I didn't fancy joining Pete in a trip back to Karlin. Or maybe somewhere worse.

So I did what I thought they'd least expect. I crept away from the fence and off down the slope until I reached a thick patch of bush. Then I crawled in through a tangle of leaves and branches, to where it was too dark even to see the sky, and settled myself in a soft mess of leaf litter that smelled of eucalypt. Through the leaves I could just see lights moving along the line of the fence, but no one came near my hiding place. They were looking for someone who was trying to break out, whereas I'd decided to stay right where I was, well inside the fence, at least until the day came and the zoo filled up with people. After that I planned to use the normal exits like everyone else.

It was a long wait. I had plenty of time to think back over the rest of the night. Most of it was plain depressing. Another failure. I remember thinking at one point how Taronga was about all I deserved, and how that was where I really belonged, in a prison for animals. What else was there after all? And from there I got to thinking just like Cath, that maybe I'd gone wrong somewhere along the line. I'd made a mistake and taken a false turn.

Sitting in the dark, surrounded by weird shadows and weirder animal noises, I went back over the years, searching for a split in the path, a time and place where I'd lost direction. But the road back looked dead straight to me, I couldn't imagine it any other way, and it always led to the same kind of place. To an empty corridor in our local hospital, or to the old veranda Gramps had closed in for an extra bedroom. If they were the crossroads I was after, then they had only one signpost I could see, and it pointed forward, right to where I was at that moment. Trapped in the dark with no quick way out.

Things didn't seem quite so bad once dawn arrived. I don't mean that first grey light when everything's drab and still, that's the worst time of all. I mean after, when the sun's about to come up and the sky's a pinky-white and the grass and trees are turning from black to green again. I was cold by then, and cramped from sitting too long in one position. Tired too after all that had gone on. It had been a hell of a night. Still, it was a relief to be able to look around and see more than shadows.

And it's funny, but with the night behind me I felt as if I could see other things as well. Like the simple fact that I'd only messed up so badly, at the research centre and there in Taronga, because I hadn't been organised. I'd rushed in without a real plan of action. Or what amounted to the same mistake, I'd relied on a dead loss like Pete. That was the only way I'd gone wrong that I could see. Looking at the green slopes of Taronga, dotted with cages and stuff, I was convinced I hadn't been 'wrong' in any deeper sense, because carving up animals or sticking them in cages can't be right, I don't care what anybody says. It's as cruel as letting a little girl lie in a room full of asbestos dust, thinking all the time that it's snow. In my book that's wrong.

Well, she'd ended up in a different kind of dust altogether. Her own, which was all they'd left her. It was something I could hardly forget, what with the amulet round my neck and all.

I touched it for luck, like always, and round about then I found out something else. How I'd been an idiot to break with Mal. He wouldn't have let me down the way Pete had. If he'd come up with a plan, it would have been watertight. That's how he is. Cunning. And like it or not, I needed him. We were a team. Not two sides of a coin like me and Cath, but a team all the same.

Pretty soon the zoo started to fill up. I waited till there were quite a few people around before I crawled out of the bushes. No one so much as glanced at me. Why would they? And as I walked past all the kids and their mums and dads on my way to the lower exit, I imagined Mal right there at my side. The two of us matching each other step for step.

I grinned at an old bloke on a day out with his grandkid, and he grinned back. It was the same with a couple of girls I passed a few minutes later. Nobody guessed. Nobody saw me as different. As far as they were concerned I was all alone, just another visitor to the zoo.

Here we go, I thought.

6 The Journal

Bonny was already waiting outside Long Bay when I arrived. She looks older, but I probably do, too. Her hair's short-short now and dyed blonde, and she has a tat on one shoulder, in the shape of a leaf, with the word 'green' printed inside it. I asked when they'd let her out. She laughed and said, I didn't know you cared. Then she kissed me on the cheek.

When Mal appeared a few minutes later, he walked over and kissed us both.

Welcome back, Danny boy, he said, as though I'd been the one locked away.

He's thinner and more nervy than ever. His face is so gaunt you can almost see the shape of the bones under the skin. His hands and elbows are the same. He looks like he's been on a hunger strike or something.

We drove back in Bonny's bomb of a car, an old VW. I kept turning to look at him and he leaned over and hugged me round the neck with one bony arm.

Yeah, this is the new me all right, he said. Now, how're you faring in this wicked world?

Don't bother to ask, Bonny said. Just check out the eyes.

Meaning, I think, for him to take a good look at me.

I'm checking, Mal said, but it's still a bit murky down there in the depths. The secret soul's a hard book to read.

I didn't have much of a clue what he was talking about, and said so.

You see, Dan, that's our problem, he said, which also didn't mean much.

Later on in the trip he relaxed more and stretched out on the back seat.

D'you know what? he said, talking to Bonny's neck. I feel

like one of those animals they hand-rear in a cage and then release into the wild.

Tell me about it, Bonny said, sounding real bitter.

Mal grinned and rolled his eyes, more like the way he used to be.

So what do you say to a spot of action?

Bonny didn't miss a beat. I'm ready when you are, she said, as if all along she'd only been waiting for him to ask.

In that case, he said, and his breath came out in this long sigh, I say let the conflicts begin.

Again, I wasn't too sure what they were on about, but he still wouldn't tell.

It'll keep, he said, and hardly spoke another word for the rest of the trip, which is unusual for Mal.

Kind of ominous.

Oct 19

Mal came round today and quizzed me on how I'd got on inside, so I talked about meeting Jimmy.

Oh yeah, Jimmy, he agreed, a terrific bloke. The best. But Jimmy aside, what did you *learn* in there?

I was too angry to learn, I said. At first anyway.

He liked hearing that.

Hey, that's good, he said. Angry's good. Except it didn't last, right?

It lasted, I said.

He didn't seem all that convinced.

So how come this anger of yours doesn't show? How come you hide it so well?

Maybe that's what I learned inside, I told him, and he swung around and stared hard at me.

Mal told me once I wasn't the wolfish type. He can be

wolfish enough for both of us sometimes. Like then.

Tell you what, bro, he said. You're a surprise package these days. It's like Bonny keeps telling me, you're well worth watching.

I asked him why, but he wasn't letting on, the same as when we drove back from Long Bay.

All good things come to those who wait, he said, and walked off.

Went down to Bronte with Mal. He doesn't talk as much as he used to. All the way there, in the bus, he stared moodily out of the window.

On the beach, with the wind blowing hard against us, you could see how thin he really is. Sort of whittled down.

I said to him: You're like a walking skeleton, and he laughed.

Yeah, Doctor Death in person, he said. The ol' Grim Reaper enjoying his day off.

The trouble was, he didn't look as though he was enjoying anything. He never does any more.

Later, drinking Cokes and watching the miniature train go round and round, I tried having a serious talk about things we could do, start some kind of group action maybe, but he still wouldn't open up.

Don't know what you're talking about, he said, and winked at these little kids who were whirling past us on the train. I tell you, Danny boy, these plans of yours, they all sound a bit *risky* to me. I mean, like off the planet.

Since when did you worry about things being risky? I said.

He kept turning away, not looking in my direction.

You've got me wrong, bro, he said. What you have here is

a reformed character. Sadder and wiser and all that stuff. I've given up rocking the boat, or haven't you heard?

I told him: All I keep hearing from you is bullshit.

The train had stopped and the kids were piling off. One of them, with his half-melted ice-cream, tipped the cone over, and what was left of the ice-cream plopped at his feet. He looked at it for a minute as if he couldn't believe his eyes, then started to cry, with bits of chewed cone running down his chin.

Now *there's* something worth getting upset about, Mal said. You see, Dan, you've gotta keep things in perspective. Horses for courses and all that.

I was so fed up with him, I just headed off through the park that backs onto the beach. I could hear him running after me, and when he grabbed me by the arm I nearly flattened him.

Hey, steady, bro, he said. Steady.

I chucked my empty Coke can down on the grass, and for once I didn't care.

So talk to me, I said.

He did in a way, afterwards, when we were sitting with our bare feet dug into the damp sand at the edge of the surf.

I have to tell you the sad truth, Dan, he said. You're a Little Leaguer. You always will be. You know, the odd demo, a bit of placard waving, that's what you're really on about, and I'm not knocking it. Someone has to do the up-front stuff. All I'm saying is that you should stay where you belong. You'll be a lot happier there.

I looked straight at him.

Is that what Bonny thinks, too? I said, and I saw him hesitate.

Yeah, she agrees with me, he said.

But we both knew he was lying, and when you reach that

stage there's not much point in going on. In fact I thought all the talk was over for the day.

Then, on the way back in the bus, he suddenly turned to me and said: I wouldn't set too much store by what Bonny thinks, not if I were you, Dan. She's not exactly objective where you're concerned. Know what I mean?

This time I wasn't sure whether he was lying or not.

You're having me on, I said.

Aha! Gotcha! he said, and gave me a sly grin which could have meant anything.

Oct 29

Mal and Bonny have decided to take a place together in Chippendale, a beaten-up terrace in one of the back streets, away from the traffic.

I went round to help them move in, and Jimmy was there, with an old Holden ute he's bought, piled high with gear. It's the first I've seen of him since the break-in at the uni, and he gave me a big hug.

Good to see you, brud.

What I like about Jimmy is how, when he says something like that, you feel he means it.

I thought he'd come just to help, same as me, but when I asked who was taking the room at the back – thinking maybe I could rent it myself – he did this funny little dance and sort of bowed.

Hey, boy, haven't you heard? he said in this put-on accent. Jackie-Jackie's movin' in with the big boss.

Mal, who was out on the landing, came storming into the back room.

We're not having any of that racist crap in this house! he said, really mad.

What's the matter with you? Bonny called from the stairs. Can't you tell when someone's joking?

There're some things we don't joke about, he said. Not even amongst ourselves.

And when I heard him say that, I guessed straight off how Jimmy had done more than take the third room. The three of them had teamed up together. I sensed it again when Bonny came to the door, from the way they looked at one another, kind of shutting me out, as if I was the hired help or something.

Yeah, well you don't need me here, do you? I said, and I'd reached the bottom of the stairs before Bonny caught me up.

Let him go, Mal called after us. He'll be better off out of here.

But she didn't take any notice.

Where're you going in such a hurry? she hissed, and pushed me into the corner behind the front door.

I can tell when I'm not wanted, I said.

You're wanted, she said, and pushed her face up under my chin.

I could feel her whole body warm against me and sort of trembling. It was hard not to move, just to stand there, but I made myself do it.

Then why doesn't Mal trust me? I said.

He's trying to protect you, that's all.

And you?

She grabbed the front of my shirt and bunched it up in both fists.

Shut up, Danny, she said. For once in your life stop asking questions.

Oh yeah, you don't have to tell me, I laughed, and I could hear myself sounding like some spoiled little kid. It's for my own good, right?

Right, she said.

Cath reckons I've changed since Mal's been back on the scene. She says I've got moody again, which I can't deny. This morning we had a bit of a run-in over the whole thing, with Cath yelling at me to ditch him and make a life of my own.

If you stick with Mal, she said, you'll only end up back inside.

No, you're wrong, I said. He's my only chance of staying free. Without him I'll really be in trouble.

Cath's sharp. She understood what I was getting at.

So you're keeping on anyway?

I nodded.

And I can't talk you out of it?

You know you can't.

Then God help you, she said, and grabbed hold of me like Bonny the other day. The same but different.

There's definitely something going on. I went round to the house earlier and the three of them were sitting in a huddle in the yard. They looked as guilty as hell when I let myself in through the back gate.

Guilty as charged, I said, trying to make a joke out of it, but Mal wasn't amused.

You can be a nosy little bastard, he said.

I tipped him off his chair, down onto the grass, just to straighten him out on the 'little' part.

Wow! he said, sarcastic. You're a real tough guy. You'll be pushing old ladies off pavements next.

I'll even do that if I have to, I told him.

He let out this tired kind of sigh and climbed back onto his chair.

Go home, Danny boy, he said. We love you and all the rest of it, but there's still no room for you here.

He's right, Jimmy added. It's for your own good.

When Bonny didn't say anything, I squatted down in front of Jimmy.

Is it 'good' for you to be here? I asked him.

He turned his head away, embarrassed.

Seems that way, brud.

That's really weird, I told him. Because as I recall, you were the one who was freaked out by the rats, the night we broke into the animal house, not me.

Jimmy glanced at Mal.

He's right, he said.

And there's another thing, I went on. I've heard tell that Pete's a bit of a hero since he climbed into Taronga.

So what? Mal said.

So this is what really happened, I said, and I told them the whole story, right up to where I'd decided I couldn't make it on my own.

No one interrupted, Mal scuffing at the ground all the time I was talking, till he'd worn a bare patch in the grass.

I didn't stay around once I'd finished, like I was hoping they'd change their minds or anything. I just had my say and headed for the gate.

We'll take it on board, Dan, Mal called softly.

Suit yourself, I said, and left.

Nov 12

I thought they'd given up on me. Then early this afternoon I got a call from Bonny, asking me to meet her in Victoria Park.

I've only ever gone past in a bus or car. I've never actually been in the park itself. It's a crazy kind of place. An oasis,

Bonny called it, full of grass and trees, with madhouse traffic all around. It's a wonder the birds don't choke on all those petrol fumes, and the leaves shrivel up. That's maybe the trouble with the natural world, it's too forgiving, it just goes on absorbing the punishment we dish out.

Bonny sat facing me in amongst the big bulging roots of a Port Jackson fig.

Jesus! she said, looking up. What a tree!

It was pretty impressive, and worth a hell of a lot more than all the traffic roaring past. In my opinion anyway.

So what's the verdict? I said, bringing her back to why we were really there.

She didn't say yes or no straight out. Like Jimmy that day in the garden, she looked sort of embarrassed.

I don't want you to regret it in the end, she said. That's my big worry. Mal's too. Because there's no backing out once you're in. Not this time.

I took both her hands.

Listen, I said. I've had one lot of parents, and one was enough. I don't need any more. I can do up my own shoes and wipe my own nose from here on.

Is that how you think of me? she asked, disappointed. As a parent?

No, but it's how you're acting.

Jesus! she said again, but looking at me now, not up at the tree. Do I really sound that bad?

Only lately, I said.

She wiped at her mouth, which is wider and more full-lipped than I'd realised. Her close-cropped hair, in the sunlight through the tree, was practically white, with these dark roots that matched her eyebrows. The rest of her face looked nearly as pale as her hair.

It's not like being in the forest, is it? she said. You can't protect people the way you protect trees. You have to let them be whoever they are, even when you care a lot about them, and that's hard.

I don't know why, but that made me think about Mum. Maybe it was because of how she'd expected us to stop being angry and just forgive and forget. Then again, maybe I'm not so different, the way I go on trying to change the meaning of Mum's life and won't let her go – or so Cath claims. Either way, Bonny's confession made me feel a bit uncomfortable, I admit it, especially with her gripping onto my hands like she expected me to disappear in a puff of smoke.

Yeah, it's not easy caring about someone, I agreed.

She relaxed then, and I reached up to her shoulder, the one with the 'green' tat, and pulled her nearer.

What's been decided? I said.

For an answer, she leaned forward and kissed me on the lips, soft but unpassionate, not what I was expecting.

What's that mean? I said.

Think of it as a Judas kiss, she whispered, as though she didn't want to use those words but had to.

Why'd you call it that?

She tilted her head, and this tiny jewel in her nose caught the light.

You must know the old story, she said. How everything started with a kiss in the garden. It was the same then, too.

No, this is different, this is all of us together, I said, and kissed her back.

Nov 14

A long meeting with the others. Mal was in high spirits. He started everything off by cracking open a beer and pouring some on my head.

There, he said, laughing. You've been annointed.

The smell of the beer reminded me of Dad, but I made out I was enjoying myself. It was easier.

After that we kicked around a few ideas without coming to any conclusions. Without any real arguments either, which is good. That's mainly down to Mal, who kept stressing that we have to be 'objective' about all this. (It's his favourite word right now.) We have to put aside our personal wish-list and do what's really practical.

I did get the feeling, though, that he's not quite as open-minded as he looks. Whatever we do has got to be fireproof, he said at one point, which made me wonder. Anyway, we'll see.

Officially we all have a couple of days to mull things over.

Nov 17

Meeting in a pub wasn't as dumb as I thought it'd be. Like Mal says, the most public places are often the safest. The noisiest too, with this rock band nearly blasting us off our feet. We were screaming at each other most of the time, and even then I doubt if anyone else could have heard more than a word or two.

Mal didn't talk much to begin with. He listened mostly – to the music as much as to us, because when we finished going on about who we thought we should target first, he just shook his head as if he found us all hopeless.

There was a pause between songs, and he said: You've got it wrong, fellers. You're putting the cart before the horse. What we have to decide on first up is a method, a *way* of doing things. Call it our signature if you like, that people'll learn to recognise, never mind who we're trying to hit.

Somehow I wasn't ready for that last part, which gave me a jolt. Talking about a 'hit' sounded so cold and calculating, as if we were in a film or something. And I knew then it was really happening, what I'd wanted ever since the night in Taronga, for us to sit down and plan everything in cold blood, I mean. Well, there we were doing it, and I can't say it made me feel particularly great.

But this signature stuff, Jimmy was saying, I don't get it. If we sign our names to things, everyone'll know who we are.

Not a real signature, Mal explained. More of a . . . a hand-print, like in those old Koori rock paintings. No faces, no names, but instant recognition all the same.

What kind of hand-print d'you have in mind? Bonny asked.

Before Mal could answer, the band started up again, louder than before, and he dipped a finger in his drink and wrote a single word on the shiny black table-top:

Buddha

D'you know who that is? he yelled at us.

When we all nodded, he explained about some famous talk or other that Buddha had given once, called the Fire Sermon, which began with the words, 'All things are on fire'.

It was more or less what I'd been wondering about days earlier, but Bonny got in ahead of me.

Which things in particular? she asked him.

And he took us across to the far side of the pub – through all these boozy old drinkers and some girls boogying away in front of the band – to where a line of windows looks out onto the busy street. Rush hour wasn't quite over, and there were more cars streaming past than on that day in the park.

Everyone owns one, he screamed at us. Or at least *wants* to own one. So everyone's involved, everyone feels the heat. Got the idea?

Yeah, got it, Bonny and Jimmy said together.

When I went round last night Cherry was there, sitting with the others in the back room, the lights off and a couple of candles flickering away on the mantelpiece. It was the first time I'd seen her since the trial, and like the rest of us she looked older, though that could be because of the candlelight. Harder too.

She's in, Mal said, just like that, the moment I sat down. No 'what do you think', no 'how do you feel about it', nothing. As if we're all a part of his personal army and don't have any say.

I could see none of the others were impressed either, and I reckon if it had been any one but Cherry, Mal would have had a revolt on his hands. As it was, we all gave each other looks, and Bonny, she said:

So when did you get elected supreme ruler, Mal? I must have blinked 'cause I missed it.

Yeah, very funny, he said, not backing down. Hilarious in fact.

Cherry, to give her credit, looked dead uncomfortable.

I can walk if you want me to, she said.

Except that wasn't the point. It was the way it was done, not Cherry herself we objected to. I'd seen her in action down south, during the worst of it, and I knew she was the kind of person we wanted on side.

So did Jimmy, though that didn't stop him putting in his two cents' worth.

Okay, she's in, he agreed. But I want to get one thing straight from here on. I didn't leave my own mob to get pushed around by some old-style whitey.

Who you calling an old-style whitey? Mal said, bristling.

If the shoe bloody fits . . . ! Jimmy began, and Bonny slid in between them, the sudden movement making the candle flames shudder.

Is this what it's supposed to be about? she said. In-fighting? Even Mal can recognise when he's gone too far.

Tell you what, he said. Why don't I let the rest of you decide on the next move? I'll stay out of it.

Fair enough, Jimmy said, and then there was this deathly hush that went on and on as we all waited for someone else to lead off.

I don't think I'd have filled the gap if it hadn't been for this I-told-you-so-smile creeping across Mal's face. On top of everything else, that was too much, so I said:

All right, let's start with a mining company. They've got a lot to answer for. More than most.

If you're talking about *the* company, Mal said, the one that finished off your old lady, then forget it.

You're supposed to be staying out of this part of the debate, I reminded him.

Yeah, so think of me as your wicked conscience, he said, and laughed. You know, the little guy with the horns and the pitchfork, floating above your left shoulder. And what he's telling you is that it's dumb to let personal vendettas take us over. That way the bastards'll be able to track us down. They'll have a handle on us. Like I've said all along, play it cool. Be objective.

He's right, Dan, Bonny said, and the others nodded in agreement.

Well, there's no shortage of mining companies, I countered. All we have to do is choose one.

You're in the saddle, brud, why don't *you* choose? Jimmy said, so I did.

Hey! One of the big guns! Cherry breathed, kind of chuckling to herself.

Mal, who was on the sidelines at that stage, gave this cheer that set the candle flames dancing again.

Attaboy, Dan, he said. Why mess with tiddlers when there're game fish to be had? I can hardly wait.

Yeah, Jimmy joined in. A few nights from now some fat-cat company director's going to find out what a hot seat really is.

They were all laughing by then, with relief I think, and Mal had gone out into the kitchen where he was groping around in the dark, hunting up some beers so we could celebrate.

I wasn't in the mood for celebrating though, and not just because I don't drink. Partly it was because of what Jimmy had said about the company director. It made me feel I'd come full circle, that I was back in the house above Sugarloaf Bay, standing over my Company man, a lighted match in one hand, a heap of petrol-soaked cloth at my feet.

I knew then, while the others clinked glasses, that for me there's only one way out of the circle. And I didn't have to look over at the candles to be reminded of it. I already had the Buddha quotation going round and round in my head, the one Mal had screamed at us in the pub. 'All things are on fire', that was it.

All things!

Us too, I expect. After this anyway.

Nov 23

Bonny rang last night and asked if I wanted to come over. For some company. It was late, around one, so I knew what she meant, but I turned her down all the same. It was a bad time for me, was all I could say, and she seemed to understand.

Cath must have been woken by the call because she came padding into my room, half asleep, and sat in the chair by the bed. The first three letters of her name really suit her, the way she can curl up in the tiniest space. She has a sixth sense too, especially where I'm concerned.

She gave me this look through a tangle of hair and I guessed what was coming.

You and Mal are up to something, aren't you? she said, her voice still croaky from sleep. So what is it this time?

Don't ask, I said.

Why not?

Because then I won't have to tell you any more lies.

Any *more* lies? she said. Did I hear that part right?

I didn't answer, and she came and sat on the bed and leaned into me. She has this warm smell when she's just woken up, which always makes me think of when we were kids, hiding out together while Dad was on the rampage.

It's all right, she said, feeling me draw back. I'm not going to cuddle you if that's what you're worried about. I know you're too old for that stuff these days.

God, Cath, I said, you don't have to talk this way to me.

But we do have to talk, right?

It depends.

Cath can be as big a liar as I can when it's called for. And in spite of what she'd just said about not cuddling, the next minute she's got one arm around my neck and the other around my shoulder and she's rocking me backwards and forwards and murmuring away as though I really was a kid.

I can't remember everything she said because there was such a lot of it – she must have gone on for ten minutes or more – but what it amounted to was how she's accepted the fact that we can't agree about certain things. Some pretty big things actually. On the other hand she doesn't think of us as being on opposite sides. Never that. Because whatever happens, no matter how bad, she'll be the one person I'll always be able to count on.

You mean like my country right or wrong? I said towards the end, trying to laugh it all off, because it *is* kind of embarrassing having your sister rock and cuddle you.

She didn't get mad, and she didn't let go of me either.

Laugh if you want, she said. You won't make me go away. I can't. You wrote in a letter once how we're tied to each other. We're two sides of the same coin. Wherever you are, I'm there, too. I hope you'll remember that one day, Danny, and be glad.

Maybe I will, one day, but not then. After she'd gone, I lay here in the dark and felt more alone than ever. When I closed my eyes, I couldn't even get a clear picture of her face. The shape of it and her features kept slipping and changing, like when you're out under the stars and you gaze at someone through an open fire.

Nov 25

It was so damned easy, that's the scary part. I was braced for something to go wrong, and nothing did. From the moment we met up at the house, it all went according to plan, just as we'd hoped. Cherry had located the address; Bonny had worked out the route; Mal already had a message written on a pad, for reading over the phone later; and Jimmy was wearing this back-pack full of tools, prepared for anything.

It's up to you now, Danny boy, Mal said as we piled into the VW.

Then we were bowling across the bridge and up onto the North Shore, the roads pretty empty at that time of night.

We'd decided not to check the place earlier in the day, in case someone remembered seeing us there. So the agreement was, we'd go in cold, and if we hit any snags we'd pull out straight away. Except as soon as we turned off the main highway, I had this feeling that the situation was perfect. Nothing *could* go wrong.

For a start, the street itself was really dark. There were only a few street lamps, and they were nearly smothered by all these leafy trees growing along the side of the road, so hardly any light showed through. Then when we came to the house it was set right back, well away from the garage, which faced directly onto the grass verge.

Bloody marvellous, Mal said as we cruised by, which about summed it up.

We parked a couple of streets off, collected up our gear, and backtracked. And that's another amazing thing: not a single dog barked at us all the way there. Mal, he was practically dancing with excitement by then.

God's in His heaven after all, he whispered, kind of giggling the words out as Jimmy set to work on the garage door. The Big Feller's smiling down at us.

The alarm started up the instant the lock gave, but loud as it was we didn't care. We knew we had a minute or two at least, because nobody goes busting out into the dark in the middle of the night, not even to save a big black Merc. Long before any lights could go on in the house, we'd prised open the lid to the locked petrol cap and smashed the cap right off.

The rest was even quicker. I had long strips of cloth all ready, and I threaded them down into the tank and gave them a dousing. A single match was all I needed after that, and we were out of there.

The 'Wump!' of the tank going up sounded before we could reach the end of the street. I felt this shock wave at my back, like someone hitting me between the shoulder blades with the heel of their hand, and Cherry went down, from surprise I expect. We hauled her to her feet, and we were at the corner, the whole street lit up behind us, this big balloon of light rising up into the black from where the garage had been. Then we dashed off to the right and were out into the dark again, with an orange glow showing through the trees overhead.

At the car the rest of us were for heading out straight away, but Mal couldn't contain himself. He did a weird dance right in the middle of the road, like he was at a party, and we had to grab him and force him into the back seat. Even then he kept sort of singing to himself and making these crowing noises.

Shut it! Bonny told him as we threaded our way back to the main road.

For a while, though, he was too far gone. Delirious almost. Thrashing around in the back seat like he was on something.

Did you see it? he kept shouting. Bloody bee-yew-tiful. Bloody-Hiro-bloody-shima! That's what it was! Bloody Krakatoa all over again! Boom, and it wasn't there. That'll show them. It wasn't bloody there any more! So much for their big deal status symbols. Boom!

The rest of us were trying to calm him down, which was difficult because we were pretty high ourselves. Most of the way back I just felt weird, as if I'd stepped through this forbidden door into another place. Somewhere I'd never been before. The place I'd come from still existed, right behind me, but I couldn't see it any more, and I knew there was no going back. Ever! This new world, where cars exploded and streets lit up and the night sky turned orange, this was where I belonged now. It was my new and chosen country, that's probably the best way of putting it. A big roomy space, like the bush out beyond the mountains, with hardly any rules and hardly any people. Just the five of us, surviving as best we could and making up the rules as we went along, which was the weirdest part of all. Kind of unnerving and exhilarating all at the same time.

Maybe that's how Mal felt too. I don't know. He wasn't making much sense most of the way back. He was still carrying on like crazy when we hit the city, and Bonny suggested making the call to the newspapers herself.

That calmed him down, and when we parked up near Central he was more or less under control. Bonny, she still had some doubts, and she nodded for me to go with him to the call box, but as it turned out there was no need.

The fireworks are over, bro, he told me, his voice hard and steady, and he dialled the number. Now let's see what they make of our manifesto.

It took him a few minutes to get through to the newsroom, and after that he didn't bother with the message he'd written out. He just kept it simple and direct – a short description of what had happened, followed by a warning that this was only the start of The Conflicts. He said those two words twice over so they'd sink in. Then he promised there'd be a lot more to come if the mining companies didn't pull in their heads over things like uranium mining and land rights.

You did good, Dan, he said as we walked over to the car, and linked his arm through mine, mates again.

Done, was all he said to the others.

Back at the house no one was in the mood for bed. Not yet. We were still too high. We weren't in the mood for celebrating either. We'd gone beyond that in the long drive down from the North Shore. So we made some tea and lit what was left of the candles and sat around.

The others dropped off one by one, blinking out like the candles, till only Bonny and I were left, with this grey light seeping in through the windows. She'd crawled over and curled up next to me on the couch.

Mmmh, she said, breathing in the petrol smell still on my hands. I simply l-o-v-e your perfume.

Then she was asleep too, and I was alone in that new country I was talking about. It can be creepy there when no one else is around. Not just empty – hollow almost. I kept thinking, what the hell am I doing in this place? What? And there was no answer. I tried holding onto my amulet, for good luck, but that only made me think about Mum, which was too much. I knew I had to get out into the light and air, where I could breathe, so I slid a cushion under Bonny's head and walked back to the flat through the early morning traffic.

I still haven't been asleep. I'm not ready for it yet. Cath's gone off to work and I'm alone again. I don't mind too much because the sun's out and there are cars going by in the street and the sky's a bright blue. Not that I'm fooled by any of it. I've seen how the sky can really look. Wump! And it's a brilliant orange and there are no maps any more, and no rights or wrongs, and no one to tell you how you can or can't ...

But I don't think I'm making too much sense so I'd better stop.

Nov 26

Mal reckons we've been betrayed. He had the papers spread open on the floor and he was yelling so hard there was spit spraying out all over them.

I can't *believe* these journos! he kept saying. I can't bloody believe them!

What'd you expect? I said.

Expect? He looked at me as if *I'd* written the article. I *expect* them to get at least a few details right. Such as what we stand for, and why we did it. But not a word about any of that. Not a solitary bloody word!

Yeah, well you shouldn't have got your hopes up, I said, and tried to walk through to the kitchen, except he moved in my way.

What do you mean by that? he demanded. What's wrong with hoping for a bit of sense and decency for once? Or at least efficiency?

I waited for someone else to answer, but I suppose they'd been getting it in the neck for an hour or more before I arrived and they'd had enough.

Well? he said, glaring at me.

The newspapers don't *have* to treat people like us decently, I told him. From here on we're terrorists as far as they're concerned. We're on the outside. We're mad dogs. That's how they see it.

Come again? he said, and stepped right up to me.

Leave it out, Mal, Bonny warned him, but he only stepped in closer.

I had one last try.

Listen, I said. Things like fairness don't apply to us any more. We're the enemy, for God's sake. The people out there can say what they like about us. And they will, you'll see. It's their news.

He tried to get closer still, crowding my space. I shoved him back onto the couch, but he bounced straight up again, really firing now.

So how come you know so much about it? he shouted. When did you get to be Mr Worldly Wiseman?

When? I repeated. If you must know it was last night, when I lit that match. It happened then. *I* realised what I was getting into even if you didn't.

Oh yeah, and what's that? What exactly *have* we got ourselves into? Can the big oracle tell us that, too?

I could see he wasn't really arguing with me any more. I just happened to be there. He was practically in tears and past caring what he said.

Come on, O wise one, he yelled in my face. Give us the benefit of your supreme wisdom. What is it we've landed ourselves in this time?

I backed over to the door.

A war, I told him, and left, so I don't know how he or any of the others took it.

Mal rang to apologise. He said he doesn't know what got into him and how we mustn't let a bunch of no-hoper journalists drive a wedge between us.

Apart from agreeing, I didn't say an awful lot. Mostly I listened to him complaining about the press, and about how difficult it was to get your point across.

After a while he ground to a halt, and I said: You know what they say, Mal, actions speak louder than words.

There was this long pause.

Pardon? he said.

You heard me.

You mean ... give them another dose? So soon?

Why not?

He started to laugh then, cackling away at the other end of the line.

Christ, Danny boy, what's happened to you?

I'm wondering about that myself, I admitted, as though it was a new idea, whereas in fact it was what I'd been thinking about all day.

I can't say I've been able to come up with any great answers since he rang off. All I know for sure is that once you've crossed over, you've crossed over. It's done.

Well, that's what happened last night, when I struck the match and stepped away, into a new kind of dark. From here on, anything can happen. I have no idea what's waiting out there, but somehow that doesn't really matter, because like I said before, there's no going back. The only way now is forward.

Cath's sixth sense is working again.

You're acting funny, she said, and spent the next hour grilling me.

Bonny turned up in the middle of it. I'd meant to spend the evening alone, trying to get things straight in my head, but by then Cath was on the warpath, so Bonny and I went off together, back to her place.

Later on the situation became a bit heavy with her, too. She kept urging me to stay, and I'm not ready for that yet. Especially now, with all this other stuff going down. I made a feeble excuse in the end and got out.

It was raining, but not hard, and I walked for quite a while, thinking about Mum mostly and what she'd make of all this. I tried imagining what it would be like actually explaining it to her. That was *really* hard and I didn't get very far.

It was Cherry's choice this time.

Directors rule, okay? she said, and chose some big wheel in the chemical and paper-making industries.

No one objected. As we all agreed, people like him have a lot to answer for. A damned sight too much if you ask me.

He has a place up near the northern beaches, and when we located it, after dark, there was this four-car garage right on the street, same as before.

Somebody upstairs still loves us, Mal said, just about dancing already.

But that was nothing to how he performed when we forced open the door and found it packed with cars.

Holocaust time! he crowed, and started twirling around in the open doorway.

The rule is, the one who chooses also gets to set the fire. So once Jimmy had smashed off the petrol cap, the rest of us fell back and left Cherry to it.

From the far side of the road we saw a match flare in the dark, burn for maybe ten seconds, and flutter out.

What's she up to? Jimmy demanded.

Another match flared, held for a while, and also died, and I guessed then what was happening.

Why won't the bloody thing catch? Mal hissed.

I shoved him aside and headed across the road, remembering how it had been for me that day in Sugarloaf Bay. How I'd just stood there, frozen, watching the matches burn down.

When I groped for Cherry in the darkened garage, I found the rags still clutched in her hand. She hadn't even fed them down into the tank. Already there was a dog barking further up the hill. Although I couldn't see out, I could picture all these lights flicking on in the surrounding houses, and I grabbed the rags from Cherry and felt for the opening to the tank.

She didn't run away, I'll give her that.

I'm sorry, Dan, she kept repeating. Honest, I'm sorry.

It's all right, I said, and eased the rags back up.

I didn't strike the match till the petrol smell was really strong. Then I dragged her out of there, the lot of us pelting off down the road.

Mal described it afterwards as a giant fireworks display, but it was much more than that. The first loud 'Wump!' was only the start of it. It was followed by several more heavy explosions as each of the cars went up, this big flaming ball climbing higher and higher into the dark and expanding outwards as it went.

It was the sky I had to stop and look at. An even brighter orange than before. Changed. Like the backdrop in one of those science fiction movies, where you expect to see about three moons and a couple of planets come sailing up over the horizon. Off world, I think that's how they describe it.

The car was already rolling when I got in. I was the last, with Cherry crying quietly to herself on the back seat.

I reached over and rested my hand on her bare neck.

Don't worry about it, I said. It does you credit.

Bonny, who was driving, turned her head for a second and gave me a funny look; and Mal, he kind of snorted through his nose.

Credit? he said, as if he was choking on the word.

What else? I said, and wound down the window, letting the wind blow through the car.

We drove on without talking after that, all the way to the city, where we chose a different phone booth for Mal to make his call from, just in case.

Let's see if they can give us a fair go *this* time, he said as he climbed back in.

Don't hold your breath, I told him, and then I asked Bonny to take me straight round to the flat.

When she dropped me off, she said hopefully: You sure you won't come home with us?

Yeah, positive, I said, and I was glad it was dark so I couldn't see her eyes.

The car revved – that rattly noise VWs make – and Jimmy poked his head out through the window.

Hey, brud, he said softly. I'm proud of you.

Me too, Cherry called.

I'm not, I said, and that was something else I felt really sure about.

You're tired, Mal said. We all are. Get some sleep and you'll feel better.

I wish it was as simple as that.

The papers have got it more or less right this time. The story's splashed right across the front page, which is not surprising considering the size of the explosion. They couldn't exactly ignore it. 'Eco-warriors' they call us. Inside there's this long article about targeted groups in big business and the 'new terrorist threat'.

Mal couldn't be happier.

You see! he said when I went round to the house. I told you we'd get through to them. They're finally giving us a fair go.

Yeah, and they're also calling us terrorists, I pointed out. Or hasn't that sunk in yet?

But he was in one of his you-can't-put-Mal-down moods.

What's in a name? he said, laughing. Eco-warriors? Terrorists? It's all the same. The important thing is that they're listening to us, and after last night they've got no option but to pass on the message.

You could be right, I said. Or maybe for once they thought the truth would make a better story.

He didn't want to hear that.

Whatever way you explain it, we're on a roll, he said, and did one of his funny little dances. The bastards'd better watch their backs because we're coming through.

He calmed down after a couple of beers, and that's when Cherry asked if she could choose again, meaning of course that she wanted to make up for last night.

I wouldn't if I were you, I said.

Why not?

Because you'll only regret it.

Everyone was staring at me, and I could see them wondering.

Do *you* regret it, what you did out there? Bonny asked.

I've already told you, I said. I'm not proud of it.

What about regret? she insisted.

Yeah, I said. That too.

Dec 6

I should never have let Bonny persuade me to stay over. I might have guessed what a mess I'd make of things.

Bonny reckons it's often like that your first time.

It's nerves, she said.

No, it's more than nerves, I told her.

What then? Is it because of me?

No, me, I said. I don't know where I am.

She asked what I meant, but I couldn't explain. When I tried, all I could think of was how the night sky had turned orange.

It's unnatural, I said. The sky shouldn't be that colour. How can anything be normal after that's happened?

Shush, she said, and pulled me back beside her on the bed. Don't say any more. Shush.

Dec 7

I dreamed about the demo on the south coast, and the bull-dozers coming at us out of the mist in the early mornings.

'Dragon dawns', Bonny called them.

I could hear her saying those same words in the dream, and I woke up while it was still dark, gasping for breath and wet through, as though I'd been running.

Dec 10

I wish Cath wasn't so hostile. I sometimes think it would be good to have a real talk with her. To explain.

Except what would I say? Because basically it all comes

down to this: I can't keep going the way I am, and there's no turning back, either. I'm stuck. Or maybe trapped would be a better word.

In any case I know what Cath would advise. She's been preaching her anti-revenge thing ever since we lost Mum. She believes you can just wake up one morning, forget about the past, and start over. Like Mal the other day, telling me I'd feel better after a good sleep.

I wish.

Dec 12

Another dream about the south coast. In this one I was in the timber yard they said I fired, and it really was burning. There were flames all round. Even the ground was on fire.

I could hear Bonny yelling for me to get out, and I ran off through the dark and into our old house, which was the way it used to be.

Mum was kind of waiting for me in there.

Look at the state you're in, she said. You should be ashamed.

When I came closer, she peered at me with this puzzled expression on her face.

Where's my Danny? What have you done with him? she demanded, acting now as though I was a stranger and had spirited the real me away.

I could still hear someone yelling for me to get out, and I woke up, breathless like always, with Bonny leaning over me.

You're back, she whispered, and wrapped both arms around my neck. It's okay, you're back.

She soon drifted off again, but I had the shakes after that and couldn't sleep. Pretty soon it started getting light and there was a currawong calling in the tree outside. That reminded me of when I'd been a kid. Where we'd lived, we'd had lots of currawongs around the house. And I realised then what was wrong about the dream. Why it had *only* been a dream, nothing else, and why I didn't have to take any notice of it. Because in the dream Mum had looked young and healthy, as if nothing bad had ever happened and she had her whole life ahead of her.

Dec 16

Mal reckons I need to *do* something. He says I'm moping too much, whatever that means. So today we went together and checked out Cherry's latest 'choice'.

He has a house out of town, on the southern shore of the Hawkesbury, well away from any other property, which is nothing like as ideal as it sounds. For one thing there's only one road in, and we could easily be spotted. The cops could even close it off if someone sounded the alarm early enough. Also, they have this big guard dog, half Ridgeback, half German Shepherd by the look of it. Luckily it seems to be kept chained up most of the time – after dark anyway, which is when we were there. Even so, it makes a hell of a racket.

When we reported back to the others, Bonny was for calling the raid off. She said it sounded too dangerous.

All the more reason to go ahead with it, Mal argued. It'll show them what we're made of.

You could see Bonny wasn't convinced.

I thought we were trying to get our point across, not pass a test, she said.

All life's a test, Mal came back at her. Remember it's the strongest that survive, not the weakest.

It was the first time we've been split right down the middle, over anything, which is why I suggested an alternative plan of attack. I didn't seriously expect them to agree, it was too crazy for that. I was just keen to break the deadlock without openly opposing Mal. But before I could finish spelling it out, he grabbed at the idea like it was a lifesaver.

Brilliant! he said, all excited. Bloody brilliant!

Jimmy was also nodding away, and when we voted on it, Bonny was the only one who objected. Nobody seemed to notice that I didn't bother to vote.

It's on then, Mal said, and the next thing there was a lot of nervous laughter and they all joined in one of Mal's little dances.

This is a madhouse, I said.

Yeah, Mal agreed, twirling around. You could be right.

Dec 18

We were in too much of a hurry, that was the trouble. We should have cased the place more carefully than we did. If we had, we might have noticed . . .

But I'd better keep things in order and start nearer the beginning.

As planned, we parked on the far shore, put on the lifejackets we'd bought, and roped ourselves loosely together. That was so no one would get carried away by the current. We didn't all need to cross, of course, but we have this one-for-all type pact and we decided to stick to it.

We're pretty good swimmers, but even so I think we were dreading the actual crossing. *I* was. Especially when we climbed down the bank and into the shallows. The water felt so *cold*, and out in the centre it looked so deep and black, with these swirls of current that kind of glittered in the moonlight.

Here goes, Mal said, and led the way.

After the first shock we were more or less okay, at least till we reached the middle. That was the hardest part because the current kept shoving us all over the place, and every time the ropes tightened I'd feel myself being sucked under. Then the ropes would slacken off, I'd bob up, and I'd see someone else struggling further along the line. It felt lonely out there too, even though we were together. With the shore so far off, and nothing but black water and black sky all round, it was like being in outer space, cut off from everyone.

I suppose Jimmy had the worst of it, weighed down by the heavy crowbar strapped on his back. So when he suddenly heaved his shoulders clear and started wading, I knew we'd made it.

We landed about a hundred metres downriver from the house, where we untied the ropes. We were also downwind, which was lucky because it meant the dog didn't get our scent till we emerged from the scrub next to the garage. Once it saw us it really started up, barking like mad to begin with, and then making these choking-cum-howling noises as it strained at its chain.

My job was to go and pacify it. I had these chunks of raw meat in a plastic bag, and I took them out one by one and tossed them over. God, I've never seen meat disappear so fast in my life. The dog swallowed them down without missing a beat, and without getting any friendlier either. Once the last piece had gone, it started rushing its chain so hard I thought the connecting plate would tear out of the wall. And the racket it was making!

I couldn't do any more there so I ran back to the garage where the others were having a few problems of their own. They'd found two cars inside, and they'd forced the petrol cap off one of them. And can you believe it? The tank was empty! They'd fished around with a length of rag and it had come up dry.

Meanwhile the dog was just about having a fit, plus a light

had flashed on in the house. Another one came on, and it was obvious we were seriously out of time.

Let's move! Bonny hissed.

I followed her round the garage and down the bank. I thought the others were right behind us, but I was wrong. I heard this loud clanging above the noise of the dog, and I realised they'd stayed and were attacking the second car. I turned back, and that was when I saw it, the kind of thing we should have taken into account when we first decided to tackle a country property: the long white shape of a gas tank, one of those big ones, set close against the rear wall of the garage.

Bonny had also spotted it.

Jesus! she said, and we raced back up the slope together.

A couple of seconds would have made all the difference. But as Mal had explained right from the start, a petrol-soaked rag is like a fuse, hard to put out. Chancy too. And when we saw those bluish flames licking up round the car's fender, all we could do was yell for them to run.

We'd barely reached the bottom of the bank when the car blew. A second or so later the gas tank went up, too. I can't remember any noise, only a rush of air that knocked me flat on my face in the shallows. I climbed back up, and there wasn't any black sky left. The whole night had caught fire, lit by this weird orange light, and bits of brick and iron roofing and jagged lumps of metal and wood were raining down on us. I could see Mal scrambling away, water streaming off him, but apart from a ringing noise in my ears I couldn't hear a thing.

I really wanted to follow him out into the dark of the river. I knew, though, that I needed to think about something first.

The dog!

I swung around to where it had been chained up, and where there was now just a jagged hole in the side of the building.

Bloody hell!

I didn't hear the actual words, but I saw Bonny mouthing them, right next to me, her hair and face stained the same orange colour as the sky. Then I felt this kind of explosion somewhere in my head, and as I went down I thought, Yeah, this is what we deserve. All of us. This!

They told me afterwards how Jimmy got me back across the river. Our lifejackets were in shreds, and I must outweigh him by at least 15 k, so God knows how he managed, because I was out of it the whole time.

When I came round I was lying flat on my back in the mud on the far shore, with Jimmy sprawled across me. I could feel this hammering against my chest, and it took me a while to realise it was Jimmy's heart, going like the clappers.

Someone hauled him off, and I tried to open my eyes, but there was blood in them. I knew it was blood because when I wiped a hand across my face it came away warm and sticky. I could see now though, and Bonny was crouched next to me, looking worried. Jimmy, on his hands and knees beside her, was still struggling for breath.

Jeez, brud, he wheezed. You weigh a bloody ton, d'you know that?

I reached past Bonny and gave him five.

I owe you, I said.

Yeah, and Cherry owes you, he said, laughing between breaths. It all evens out in the end.

Bonny helped me up, handling me as if I might break, and the three of us stood for a while, watching the fire across the river. It had spread to the house, which was ablaze already, so bright I could have read by it even at that distance. The river, the surrounding bush, our skin and clothes, were all caught in its soft light. That's the thing I noticed most, the softness of it. Watching the flames lick up around the roof, I found it hard to credit what had happened to the dog – or what could easily have happened to the people inside.

We were still standing there, looking on, when Mal's voice drifted down from above.

What the hell's keeping you? You on a bloody sightseeing tour or something?

I called back: This wasn't supposed to happen. It wasn't part of the plan.

I could see him now, peering through the bushes on the lip of the bank. He waved one hand at the blaze.

Think of the house as a bonus, he said.

Was the dog a bonus, too?

Dog? What's he going on about? he said, appealing to Cherry, who must have been standing somewhere behind him.

The one we just killed, I said.

To give him his due, he didn't sound too thrilled.

Oh yeah, sorry about that, Dan. One of war's little casualties. It had to happen sooner or later, you must have realised that.

He was right – I had. So who was I to be standing there arguing with him? It wasn't a good idea anyway, not with the first of the sirens wailing faintly somewhere on the far shore.

Hey! Better wrap this up, Jimmy whispered, and we made tracks downriver to where we'd left the car.

The siren was much closer by then, and we drove off without lights, bumping slowly through the dark until we'd put a few kilometres between us and the fire. Then it was all systems go as we headed for the nearest main road, away and free.

As I remember it, Mal was the only one celebrating. I still felt a bit dizzy, and I used that as an excuse for not saying much. Mainly I didn't want to get into an argument with Mal, not then, so once he'd made his usual call to the papers, I got them to drop me off like before.

Bonny didn't seem too happy about that, because of my

head, but I'd felt the cut with my fingertips and I knew it didn't amount to much.

I'll be okay, I said, acting like I was sleepy more than anything else.

God, doesn't anything get to you, Dan? Mal said.

I think Jimmy was the only one who saw through the act. And Bonny maybe.

Sorry about the dog, brud, he said.

Me too, Bonny agreed.

Yeah, a casualty of war, I said.

I could hear myself sounding bitter, but it didn't matter much any more because they'd already gone.

Dec 19

Mal has what he wanted from the press. There was this huge headline in the paper this morning, **SYDNEY BURNS**, followed by a whole lot more stuff about 'eco-warriors' and their 'campaign of terror' and how an innocent family had been driven from their home.

I was sitting in the kitchen, reading all the lurid details, when Cath appeared, still in her nightie. I thought she was checking up on me at first, but she'd stayed home because of a bad cold.

When she saw the state of my forehead – and it had really swelled up during the night – she gave me this oh-no-not-again look and started in with about a million questions. For a while it was like going ten rounds with some heavyweight champion. What saved me, in a manner of speaking, was the bell.

Phone, I said, relieved, and escaped to the living room.

It was Mal, full of beans after what he called 'our triumph'.

Did you see the write-up? he nearly shouted. We're in the big league now, Danny boy. Just wait till they see what we have in store for them next time. They'll blow a bloody gasket when . . .

I cut straight across him, making the big decision there and then, though without quite knowing why.

There won't be any next time, not for me, I said, and I had this sinking feeling in my gut, like I'd jumped off a cliff.

Hey? Come again?

I'm out, I said, and if I'd really jumped from anywhere, I'd have landed then with a nasty bump.

You're having me on, he said.

'Fraid not, Mal.

I heard him take a long breath, and as he let it out all the excitement seemed to flow out of him, too.

It's because of the dog, isn't it?

You could say that.

Listen, Dan, don't do anything hasty. We're coming round there, all right? We're ...

Don't bother, I said.

Why not?

I've told you, I'm through.

And I put the phone down before I could change my mind – only to discover that Cath had been standing right behind me, listening, the whole time.

You're through with what? she asked, suspicious.

Oh a ... a job I've been doing with Mal, I said, which sounded pretty feeble and didn't fool Cath one little bit.

What about the Bonny girl? she pressed me. You through with her, too?

That was harder to answer, and I gave up pretending and took the plunge.

Yeah, her as well. I think ... at least I *hope* so.

You're not sure?

Look, I'm doing my best, okay? I'm trying to wind the clock back, like you said.

She must have understood, kind of anyway, because she came

at me then, arms open wide and a relieved look on her face.

Jesus, Danny, you have no idea how long I've been waiting to hear you say that. You have no idea!

Hey, what about your cold? I said, trying to fend her off.

Haven't you heard? she said, laughing and holding onto me. Families that cough and sneeze together, stay together.

⊚　⊚　⊚

Later: Bonny came round on her own. As agreed, Cath refused to let her past the front door. I hid in my room, listening, and feeling like a coward.

He's asleep right now, Cath said, her voice nearly as cool as the river last night.

If I could just see him for five minutes, Bonny pleaded, which isn't her style at all.

But as I've said before, Cath can be like Mum when she wants. She won't change her course for a few kind words, or for a few hard ones either.

In my opinion he's been disturbed enough already, she said, and this time there was no mistaking her meaning.

After that it was a straight-out argument. About halfway through, Bonny started to cry, which is really something for her, and from then until the front door slammed I kept my ears blocked.

Cath came into my room as soon as she'd gone.

The things I do for you, she said wearily.

Dec 20

The whole group pitched up on the doorstep first thing this morning. I think they were a bit surprised to find Cath here, the same as I was yesterday. I could hear her telling them to get lost, and then a crash as they forced their way in.

Where I come from, Dan, this isn't how you treat friends, Mal said, barging straight into my room.

The others were behind him.

He's right, brud, Jimmy agreed. You're out of order on this one.

With the doorway blocked, Cath was left standing in the passage, seething.

Who are you to talk of what's right? she shouted. This is *my* flat. You have no right to . . .

Cherry closed the bedroom door in her face, and all four of them found themselves seats around the room as though they planned on staying.

I want to tell you something, Dan, Mal said. This isn't the Boy Scouts that you can quit when you please. There's a question of security at stake here. *Our* security.

Oh, so you're worried I'll dob you in now, are you? I said.

Not exactly.

What then? Is this a threat maybe? Stay with it or else?

Not that either.

We're here to appeal to you, Bonny cut in. As . . . as friends.

I could see how much that cost her – how grouping herself with the rest wasn't easy, not where I was concerned. But round about then the door opened and Cath marched in and plonked herself down on the bed next to me. Like some guardian angel or something.

So what do you call yourselves these days? she said, really sarcastic, and not looking at anyone in particular. Freedom fighters? No, wait a minute, I'm out of date. They had it in the paper only yesterday. *Eco-warriors*, that was it. Yeah, I like it. It's kind of colourful, and a bit over-the-top, but good. Not the sort of thing you're going to forget in a hurry.

Jesus Christ! I heard Mal mutter under his breath.

But I suppose that's the point really, Cath went on. It's like those ads. You know, Louie the fly and stuff. Catchy. It sounds almost noble, too, if you say it quick. Now if the papers had called you, say ... *terrorists*, that would have been a real bummer. Not to mention unfair. After all, you're only blowing up a few cars, and the odd house here and there. What could be more noble than that?

It had taken us until then to get over our surprise.

Your sister's got quite an imagination, Mal said, his voice steady enough, but his face deadly pale.

Yeah, she's seen too many films, Cherry added.

Or read too many comics maybe, Jimmy said, and tried to laugh.

Cath didn't say anything for a while, just looking at them.

You may be good at blowing up cars, she said firmly, but I tell you, you're lousy actors. You should see yourselves. If you were in court right at this minute, it'd be all over. The jury'd *know* you were guilty from your faces.

Now wait a minute! Mal began, but Bonny waved for him to be quiet.

Is it that obvious? she asked.

Cath dropped all the sarcasm and gave her a straight answer.

From where I stand it is.

And where *do* you stand?

That was the big question, for all of us, and Cath gave her another straight answer, but not only in words this time.

Curving an arm around my neck, she pulled me hard against her and said: Big as he is, he's still my brother. Mum asked me to look after him, so there's no way I'm sending him back to Karlin. Or worse.

Thank God for that, Mal breathed.

Cath added: It's your business what you choose to do from here on. All I ask is you leave Danny out of it.

Is that what Danny wants? Bonny said, as if I wasn't even there.

Part of him does, Cath admitted.

It's the other part of him we've come here to talk to, Mal said, looking past Cath to me. You see, he still owes us. Or to be more exact, he owes Jimmy here.

No way! Jimmy protested.

But Mal knows what he's doing. What was said was said, and couldn't be taken back now. He knows me too, the way I feel about paying debts.

How about it then? he asked me direct. Bearing in mind of course that without Jimmy you'd be floating belly-up somewhere in Pittwater by now.

I could sense Cath wanting to jump in and start arguing, but I took her hand to keep her quiet.

What's a fair trade? I said to Mal and Jimmy together.

Two more hits, Mal said. That'll make one for each of us.

I shook my head.

One more then, and it's Jimmy's choice. Come on, Dan, one lousy hit. We'll give it away after that.

What about casualties of war? I asked him, because we both knew that was the sticking-point.

There won't be any, not unless it's one of us. We'll be putting ourselves on the line, no one else. Though while we're on the subject, wasn't your old lady a casualty of war, or is my memory playing tricks on me again?

Cath was already on her feet. Damn you, Mal! she shouted. Then to me. You don't have to do this, Danny.

I'm sorry, Cath, I told her, but I do.

I tried to sound like I was making the hardest decision of my life, whereas in fact I wasn't. The truth? It was actually a relief to be back in the group, if only for another week or so. Destiny's a pretty big word, but right then I felt as if Mal and the group and the hard road we'd chosen, including my doubts and what had happened to the dog, they were my one true destiny. And once we split up ... well, I can't say about that yet. I'll have to decide when the time comes. Something'll turn up, as Dad used to say.

Cath, meanwhile, was still on her feet, yelling at me. You're a traitor, Danny! D'you hear? A lousy traitor!

But a traitor's the one thing I'm not. She knows that better than anyone. So would Mum if she still existed, if her spirit or whatever was still up there and could look down.

Except I can almost hear what Mal would say to that: Welcome to the wonderful world of fairytales, Danny boy.

Dec 21

The cops have paid us a visit. I've learned since that they also dropped in at Mal and Bonny's place. To be honest, I'm surprised they took so long to get round to it. We *are* known firebugs after all, so it's only natural for them to check us out.

Still, it was a shock to answer the door and find them standing there. Not that they were particularly suspicious or anything. It was a routine visit mostly, and of course Cath was great. Miss Innocence herself. You'd have thought telling lies was against her religion. Just watching her in action was enough to give me confidence. Also, I remembered what she'd said yesterday, about how guilty we'd looked, and I made a big effort to act natural.

Everything seemed to go all right anyway. The important part was when they asked where I'd been on the night of the last fire, and Cath sort of gave me a shove and laughed.

Don't ask, she said, as though it was a joke. I really wanted him to watch this video I'd taken out. So what did he do? He fell asleep in front of the TV as usual.

He was here the whole evening? this one cop asked, the younger one of the two.

Yeah, where else? He doesn't get out enough in my opinion. I'm always going on at him about it. He doesn't take after me, that's for sure.

Why, d'you like to party? the cop said, and you could see he fancied her.

Whenever I get the chance, Cath answered, turning on the charm. Whenever someone asks me to.

The cop took the hint: I might do something about that myself one of these nights.

Why not?

And so it went on until Cath saw them out. Though it was a different story once we were on our own.

Now I'm as guilty as you are, she said, standing with her back against the closed door.

I didn't contradict her. Instead, I explained Mal's theory about good and bad lies.

A lie's still a lie, however you describe it, she insisted. It still leaves you feeling grubby.

I could have told her what grubby really feels like. Being shut up in Karlin, for instance, with some egg-head shoving questions in your face. Or how it is when you turn around and see a great big hole where a dog was once standing. But I didn't want her to know about any of that stuff, because then we'd both be in the same fix, and I need her out there just as she is.

You're good enough for me, Cath, was all I said.

Dec 24

We had a meeting in a trendy Glebe pub. (What a way to spend Christmas Eve!) Bonny reckons it's not the kind of place where cops go looking for no-hopers like us. We didn't hang around even so.

The main order of business was whether we should stay with our original plan or maybe lie low for a while. And the general opinion was that we should carry on regardless. As Mal pointed out, the cops won't expect us to do anything rash, not after their recent visit. So another raid within the next few days will make it look as if we're not the guilty party.

Only a fool would rush in now, he said, grinning at us. And you know what they say about fools and wise men.

No, what do they say? Jimmy asked.

Mal went bright pink, caught out for once.

Buggered if I remember, he said, and we all laughed and clinked glasses, clinching the deal.

As a precaution, though, we've decided not to meet up too often, and to be *very* careful what we say on the phone.

If we don't take any chances, Mal warned us at the end, it'll be bloody near impossible for the cops to track us down. Think about it, we're like serial killers, striking at random, and everyone knows how hard *they* are to catch.

Although I didn't much like the killer idea, I could see his point. We all could.

The meeting broke up after that. On the way out Bonny pulled me in behind the door, where the light's dim. It was quite a narrow space, and wedged in there with her, I could smell the warm scent of her body and hair.

I've missed you, she whispered.

She was pressed up against me, and I didn't have to put on an act.

Me too, I said, and she gave me this long slow kiss.

Yeah, she said, licking her lips. The simplest things are the best.

I wish I had something different to write about, but it's happened now, so what's the good of playing make believe? There's another thing, I don't have a lot of time if I'm going to get everything finished up here, including this diary. A few more days at the most, because once they identify what's left of the body ...

But I'd rather not think about that part, never mind put it into words. What a waste! And what rotten luck – no, not luck, not after the way *he* acted. Murder, that's the only word for it. Who did the old fool believe he was anyway, God or someone? Mal should have left him to me. The mood I was in, he wouldn't have walked free. Or were Mal and Bonny maybe right in what they did? It's hard to be sure even now. Which is one good reason for writing down exactly what happened, to try and make sense of it that way. There's nothing much else I can do tonight, because I sure as hell won't be able to sleep.

Here goes then.

Jimmy's choice turned out to be one of those really steep properties up near Palm Beach, with about a million degree view of the Pacific Ocean. It's not far from a lookout point cum nature reserve, and we parked the car well off the road and crept down through the bush to what Mal called Millionaire's Row. It looked it, too. Palms and flowering shrubs everywhere, and all these mansion-type houses either set up on stilts or slotted into the hillside. Standing there in the dark you could almost smell the money, as though it was wafting up out of the shrubs.

The house we were after was a bit closer to the road than most, and still had a light on at an upper window, which wasn't the best. Cherry and I were for holding off for a while, but Mal reckoned we should go straight in. We were still arguing about it, whispering together in the cover of some trees, when the light clicked off and settled the matter.

Right, Mal whispered, making like he was on one of those TV cop shows, Let's do it. And you be careful out there, people.

The thing is, we thought we *were* being careful. We'd done a recce on the place, for instance, and after our last experience we'd made dead sure there was no guard dog on the property. What we *hadn't* checked were the houses all around, because you have to draw the line somewhere. Also, there were things we couldn't check out properly, not just by looking, such as the kind of alarm system we were up against.

Well, we found out about that in a hurry. My job was to lever open the garage door, and the minute I shoved the crowbar into the gap and metal touched metal, this unbelievable clanging noise started up and about ten overhead lights flashed on. It was like standing in the middle of Sydney Cricket Ground on the night of a big match. Dazzling!

Home time, guys! Bonny hissed.

Then Mal, kind of talking over her: Never mind the lights! Just remember what you're here for and do it!

I figured there'd be no bright lights inside the garage, and I kept going. A couple of wrenches with the crowbar, the door buckled and gave, and we were in. But a second or two later, so was this little dog from one of the nearby houses. It wasn't big, some kind of terrier I think, but it came at us like a bullet, snapping and worrying at our ankles.

Get off! Mal yelled.

I began swinging at it with the crowbar, doing my best to keep it clear of Jimmy, who couldn't do much anyway, not till we'd smashed in the petrol cap of the big Merc standing in the shadows.

For maybe half a minute or so there was absolute chaos.

Then I took a wild kick, which somehow connected and sent the dog skidding off down the drive. It was soon back, but wary now, yapping at us more than rushing in – not that you could hear it much above the endless clanging of the alarm – and that gave us time to attack the car.

I can't remember exactly when I decided to cut our losses and run. Jimmy was gouging and smashing at the petrol cap and not getting anywhere, and suddenly I knew it was time to quit.

Come on, brud, I said, and grabbed at his arm, but he pushed me off.

That bastard up there has it coming! he grunted, still hacking away.

I'd heard Jimmy talk earlier about his 'choice' of target – how he was a mining and grazier type who'd pushed through some lousy deals with local Aboriginal people – but I hadn't realised until then how much Jimmy resented him. This was personal payback stuff. You could tell from the way he kept spearing the crowbar into the cap, as if it was alive and fighting back.

Leave it! I said, and tried to haul him off, knowing he'd thank me for it later.

But he just hung onto the crowbar, which he'd jammed in under the cap. We were both heaving at it now, with me straining to pull him free, and it was the extra weight probably which did the trick. Because the next minute the cap shot up towards the roof and we were flat on the floor, all tangled together.

Bonny was in there with us when we scrambled to our feet.

Time's up! she yelled straight into my face. We have to split! Now! This instant!

Yeah, get going, Jimmy agreed, stuffing a length of rag down into the tank. I'll be right behind you.

He was already groping for his lighter when I let Bonny drag me out of there. As we cleared the garage, we collided with someone I thought at first was Mal. Then I saw the gun in his hands, one of those double-barrel shotgun jobs, and this old face, topped with grey hair, glaring into mine. I was too surprised to move, and Bonny shoved at him just as he brought the shotgun up, so it went off while it was still pointing at the sky. There was this loud explosion, deafening, and Bonny and I reeled off down the drive, with all these bits of shredded leaf fluttering down around our heads.

When we looked back from the cover of the trees the old guy had Jimmy bailed up in the garage. What was worse, the rag-fuse had already been lit, these bluish flames licking up around the side of the car.

Mal, Cherry, the lot of us, we all started yelling for Jimmy to get out of there. And I swear he tried to, even though the old guy was bang in the middle of the drive, the gun still trained on him. Jimmy kind of ducked his head, ready to dash off regardless, but then the dog made another run at him and he held back. For a couple of seconds, maybe less, while he kicked the dog away. Long enough, though.

Jimmy! Mal sang out.

And the car, the garage, and everything else went up in a long tongue of flame, Jimmy and the dog included. God, it was horrible! One minute they were there, alive and well, the next they'd vanished. The sky had turned a familiar orange and I was pounding across the road and up the drive as hard as I could go.

The old guy was down on his knees when I reached him, his hair burned away by the blast. Most of his clothes had gone, too. At that range the heat from the fire was terrific, and he was shielding his face with both hands and sort of whimpering.

I have to say he looked in pretty bad nick, but right at that moment it wasn't enough for me. Not after what he'd made happen to Jimmy. I wanted a lot more from him. Everything!

And I started pounding on his back with my bare fists, and then kicking at him as the others dragged me off.

Get a hold! Mal breathed into my ear, his face pressed hard against mine. Don't bloody lose it now! D'you hear?

Bonny was on my other side, not saying a thing, but with her teeth clamped hard on the loose skin of my neck, holding me there.

She didn't slacken her grip till I stopped struggling.

That's better, she whispered. Now stay cool.

I pushed them both off and took a last look at the fire. I really wanted to say something, and more than just goodbye, except it was too soon for words and promises. I knew they'd have to come later. A whole lot of stuff would have to come later, but I couldn't think about any of it yet.

Shock, Mal called it afterwards. We were back in the car by then, though God knows how we got there. The fire was still going strong down below, casting this flickering light up through the trees, and I could see from the streaks on Bonny's cheeks that she'd been crying.

D'you need me to drive? Cherry asked.

It was more than a hurry up. She sounded really concerned. I started yelling again all the same, and Mal had to grab me from behind.

You still owe him, Danny boy, he whispered fiercely. Which means you have to live to fight another day. You got that?

It seemed to make sense at the time, and he sounded so calm, his hands steady on my shoulders as we drove away. I began to think nothing could ever rattle him. Yet when we eventually reached the city and stopped for him to make his call, he lost it worse even than me. You could have heard him yelling into the phone from nearly a block away. Vengeance stuff mainly, about what they could expect from us after this. And he damn near kicked in the side of the phone booth before Cherry and I could haul him out and push him into the car.

For the rest of the way back he kept muttering things like: They want war, they'll bloody get it! They won't forget Jimmy in a hurry!

Shut it! Bonny told him, but it didn't make any difference.

I think we were all glad when the journey was over, even Mal, who was having a hard time keeping back the tears.

We stuck to our original plan and parked the car in a back street about halfway between both our places. That was in case there were any nosy-parker cops looking out for us. The idea was for the others to bunk over their back fence and pretend they'd never been out, and it was easy for me to do more or less the same at the flat.

Just as we were about to split up, Mal wrapped his arms around me and hung on, his face buried in my shoulder, like he was expecting me to run off for ever.

Keep the faith, Dan, he said, his voice more of a groan than anything else. Whatever you do, keep the faith.

I will, I promised, and at the time it really was a promise.

I was back here and ready to start writing this down before the truth finally hit me.

After Jimmy, what *is* the faith?

Dec 29

I've told Cath the whole story, and we agree about one thing at least. I need to clear out fast, because sooner or later they'll find out who Jimmy was, and after that they'll be onto us.

Cath reckons I should lie low for a while, and then make a quiet life for myself somewhere. I'm half inclined to agree. Or am I chickening out again? It's hard to know what to do when something like this happens. I'm not sure why, but the death of someone close to you always seems to change the rules. It's so final, like a knife coming down and cutting you off. You don't know where you are after that.

Cath says the trick at a time like this is not to come to any sudden decisions. To sit still and ride out the storm. But how can you do that when the storm's inside you? I said as much and she had no answer.

Apart from what I might do next, her main worry is how we'll manage to stay in touch. I should be able to contact her easily enough, through a post office we've agreed on out in the burbs. It's the other way round we can't work out, at least until I settle somewhere.

And if I don't settle? Well, that's her other big worry. Mine too. Though compared with what happened to Jimmy . . .

No, I mustn't think about that. *Mustn't.*

◉   ◉   ◉

Later: I was just packing some things in a bag when Mal rang. Although he was being careful on the phone, he still sounded upset.

We need to talk about our outstanding debt to . . . to Jimmy, he said, and I could hear how difficult it was for him to say the name.

What's there to discuss? I said.

Don't play the hard man with me, Danny boy, he shouted, nearly losing it again. I *know* you! I know what you're feeling right now.

There was no point in denying it. I could feel this hard knot rising from the bottom of my gut, and I put the phone down before I made a spectacle of myself.

It's odd how we can't seem to share some things. Grief's

one of them. It belongs to each of us alone. That's how I see it anyway. Which is an excellent reason for clearing out before he or Bonny get it into their heads to pay me a . . .

Dec 30

It's broad day, there's nothing but trees all around, and I'm writing this in a lay-by near . . . never mind about that. Let's just say I'm in the country and on my way to somewhere. Mal reckons it's dangerous to be more exact. He also objects to this whole diary thing.

Think what'd happen if it fell into the wrong hands, he warned, wagging a finger at me.

I pointed out that it's no more risky than stealing a car, which I wasn't *at all* happy about, but as usual he had his arguments lined up and ready. The VW is registered in Bonny's name and could be used to trace us; stolen cars probably don't get entered into the cops' national network for at least twenty-four hours; and even when this one is found, there's no way of knowing who took it. So effectively we vanish.

I couldn't really argue with any of that, nor with his point about the diary, which means I'll probably make this the last entry for a while. He'd prefer me not even to make this one, but I told him: I hate leaving things in the middle. And he saw straight away what I was getting at.

Good one, Danny, he said. Go for it.

He and Bonny are over by the car now, waiting for me to finish, with that blank look on their faces which always comes with sunbaking.

What a change a few hours can make!

They both looked a lot different last night. Upset and sad, but also determined. They turned up just before I was due to leave, and it was no good trying to keep them out.

Going on holiday? Mal said, nodding towards my packed case.

Holiday's not a word I'd use, I answered.

Yeah, Mal agreed, and wrinkled up his lips like he had a bad taste in his mouth. Maybe broken promise would be a better way of describing it.

Amen, Bonny muttered.

Cath had decided to stay quiet, just watching us. Everyone waiting for what I'd have to say for myself. And really, when it came to the point, there was only one thing I *could* say.

I never ran out on him, I protested. None of us did. Not while he was alive. We stayed with him till the end.

The end? Mal seemed to consider the idea. Tell me, Dan, when does the end come exactly? When a person breathes their last?

I could already see the trap he was setting, but somehow I couldn't avoid it.

When else? I said.

So your old lady, for instance, Mal went on, your dear departed mum. According to you she's over and done with. We added the last full stop to her story quite a while back, right?

Wrong, I said.

Bonny moved up alongside Mal, the two of them facing me together.

How is Jimmy any different then? she said.

And put like that, what else could I do?

7 What the
Papers Say

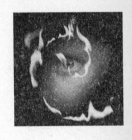

FIRE-BOMBER IDENTIFIED

It was revealed today that the police have finally established the identity of the body found at the recent fire-bombing in Palm Beach. He was James Campbell, aged twenty, of Sydney. Although he was burned beyond recognition, it appears that his dental remains match perfectly with records held at Karlin Detention Centre, a low-security prison for young offenders in New South Wales. 'There's no longer any doubt about the bomber's identity,' a police spokesman claimed. 'People's teeth are like their fingerprints. No two sets are the same.'

'James Campbell was a known offender,' the same spokesman said. 'He had been in trouble with the law since the age of fourteen, and it came as no great surprise that he was involved in this recent spate of terrorist activity.'

Police are now searching for possible accomplices. In particular, they would like to speak to Malcolm Arden, Beatrice ('Bonny') Stewart, Daniel Fenton and Clarice ('Cherry') Morrel. Anyone knowing of their whereabouts is asked to contact the authorities.

'It is too early yet to say whether they are directly involved,' the police spokesman said, 'but they were known associates of James Campbell and we'd like to interview them.' He went on to emphasise, however, that the general public should be wary of approaching these or any other suspects. 'We're dealing here with international-style terrorism,' he said, 'and we mustn't under-estimate what such people are capable of. The public at large, like the police themselves, would do well to tread carefully.'

Asked whether the death of James Campbell would spell the end of the terrorist activity, the police were non-committal. 'It's far too early to tell,' their spokesman said. 'James Campbell was known as something of a ringleader, and prior to his time in Karlin he'd been deeply involved with Aboriginal action groups. On the other hand, his involvement in this series of fire-bombings is of another order of magnitude, and there's no saying at this stage whether he actually masterminded the attacks.'

The police were less non-committal on the question of whether the bombings were racially motivated. 'Beyond the fact that James Campbell was of Aboriginal descent,' they said, 'we've encountered no evidence to support such a claim.'

They further warned against jumping to hasty conclusions. 'In the three phone calls which the terrorist group has allegedly made to the press,' the police spokesman pointed out, 'the emphasis has been upon their resentment of big business. On the evidence of those calls, we have every reason to believe that the group's main aim is the overthrow of Australia's current mining and forestry policies. If the Aboriginal question does feature in their agenda, it is merely part of a larger series of concerns.'

In a closing statement the police strongly advised both press and public alike not to romanticise the bombers and their aims. 'These are dangerous and destructive people,' they said. 'They are fanatics by anybody's standards and there is nothing heroic about what they're doing. Calling them eco-warriors, or comparing them with Ned Kelly, will only make our task more difficult and encourage them to continue on their chosen path of blackmail and threat.'

True Life   *Jan 6*

ONE DOWN, FOUR TO GO

So Australia's very own dead terrorist turned out to be a known criminal. Hardly a great surprise. Our readers might also be interested to learn that he was only free to walk the streets because he had been paroled early. Not much of a surprise there, either. What would astonish decent Australians is an official policy which saw to it that dangerous maniacs like James Campbell are kept safely behind bars where they belong. Or better still, eliminated like the mad dogs they truly are.

One of them has been eliminated, no thanks to the police or prison authorities, but we're told there are still more of them out there. Think about it: four possible fanatics wandering our streets. And guess what? Yes, you're right! It turns out that they're all known criminals, too. And yes, you're right again! They were also paroled early.

The big question is this: How on earth can we keep our streets free of human garbage while government departments are run by do-gooders who have forgotten what prisons are really for? Here's another question: How many bombs have to go off before we learn to keep our prison doors locked?

Mindless criminals like James Campbell and his fire-bombing friends don't deserve our sympathy. They don't even understand it, so why waste it on them?

Nation   *Jan 20*

TERROR CAMPAIGN SHIFTS TO MELBOURNE

Shortly before 11 p.m. last night, a Toorak mansion belonging to prominent Melbourne businessman, Sir Garth Earlwood, was shattered by a huge explosion and subsequently gutted by fire. As yet the police are unsure of the actual cause of the explosion, but they have no doubt it was the work of the same terrorist group that carried through a series of fire-bombings in Sydney recently.

According to Inspector Michael Hart, a spokesman for the police investigative team, this latest attack has all the hallmarks of the gang's handiwork. 'It was unprovoked,' he said, 'it was aimed at a leading businessman, and typically it was followed by a phone call to a major newspaper.' The phone call, we understand, threatened further such attacks unless there is an immediate move, nationwide, to stop all wood-chipping.

Speaking to reporters in the early hours of the morning, Inspector Hart said, 'We can only be thankful that Sir Garth's house was empty at the time of the explosion. Had any of the family been at home, I doubt whether they would have survived.'

Close neighbours, Clara and Ian Rhymer, reported being woken by what they called 'a thunderclap of noise', and by a blast which smashed several windows in their bedroom. 'We were terrified,' Ian Rhymer said. 'We thought at first we were the ones under attack. Then we went out onto the terrace and saw the Earlwoods' place. It looked as though it had been hit by a hurricane. The whole front of the house had literally been blown off. God knows what kind of explosive was used, but it was something really powerful. No petrol bomb could have done that.'

The police agree that they're dealing with more than a petrol bomb in this case. 'The gang seem to have moved on to bigger things,' Inspector Hart admitted. 'That's probably the most worrying feature of this attack. I'd like to tell you we know exactly what we're up against here, but we don't, not yet. Not until our technical people have had time to carry out all the necessary tests.'

Police experts are currently combing through the remains of the Earlwood mansion, trying to establish what kind of explosive was used. 'Different explosives tell us different things,'

Inspector Hart pointed out. 'Depending on where this variety comes from, it will indicate whether or not our terrorist group has an international connection.'

True Life   *Jan 21*

AUSTRALIA UNDER SIEGE

Some experts believe our bombing war is Libyan inspired. Others are talking about Iraq. Others again are of the opinion that we're dealing with a home-grown variety of terrorist.

What we would like to ask is, what difference does it make? A maniac is a maniac wherever he comes from. And this particular pack of madmen has us under siege, as the Melbourne bomb makes clear. Those are the facts that count. Those are the facts we have to deal with.

The so-called experts would do well to bear that in mind, and not waste their time wondering what lies behind the bombings. We can tell them that already. James Campbell and his crazed followers are inspired by a desire to destroy. They may give you other reasons, but that's their real motive. It always is with avowed terrorists. They want to burn down a world they don't understand.

Our world!

GAS THE CULPRIT IN TERRORIST ACTION

In a surprise announcement, the police revealed late last night that the Earlwood mansion was destroyed not by a conventional bomb, as was first believed, but by a gas explosion. Unlike most gas explosions, however, this one was not sparked off by accident. It was deliberately engineered, police claimed, and proved no less lethal than any other form of manufactured bomb.

Inspector Hart, again fronting the investigative team, highlighted the dangerous simplicity of the terrorist attack by outlining the probable course of events. 'One or more people broke into the house while it was empty,' he explained, 'and turned on all the gas outlets in the kitchen. Before leaving they also set up a detonating device in a room near the front of the house.'

Asked what device they had used, Inspector Hart declined to answer on the grounds that it might produce copy-cat behaviour. 'Let's just say it was a common household item, and leave it at that,' he said.

'It would have taken some time for the gas to drift from the back rooms to the front,' he went on, 'and by then the gas build-up would have been considerable. In effect the whole house became a potential bomb. The resulting fireball tore the walls apart.'

Responding to questions, Inspector Hart conceded that in the light of these latest findings, it is less likely that Australia is the object of international terrorist activity. At the same time he wished to make it clear that this in no way lessened the nature of the threat.

'Australian citizens are under attack,' he said. 'The lives and property of innocent people are seriously at risk. There's no other way of putting it.'

PM PLEDGES MONEY AND TASK FORCE IN DEFENCE OF NATION

The terrorist threat dominated Question Time in Parliament yesterday. In answer to a suggestion by the Opposition that he had done nothing to allay the growing fears of ordinary people, the Prime Minister lashed out at what he called 'fifth column elements' and 'the traitors within our ranks'.

He said that he, like all decent Australians, was appalled by the recent series of unprovoked attacks and he called on law enforcement authorities to redouble their efforts. The Government for its part, he said, would set up a national task force to coordinate regional investigations. He also pledged a 'fighting fund' to help local police meet the challenge posed by 'these new-found enemies of the state'. 'Those who believe they can change society by force', he said, 'will be sadly disappointed.'

The Attorney General later assured Parliament that he would personally oversee the distribution of the PM's fighting fund. 'There's no place in our society for mad dogs,' he said. 'We must hunt them down at whatever cost.'

The Courier   *Jan 26*

NATIONWIDE HUNT FOR TERRORIST SUSPECTS

In an unprecedented move, all major newspapers across the nation have today featured photographs and detailed descriptions of the four suspects wanted for questioning in connection with the fire-bombing terror campaign.

This follows an appeal by the leader of the National Task Force 'to make Australia an unsafe place for those who would live by violence and threat'. 'We must see to it', he added, 'that there is no corner of this vast country in which they can hide or hope to find sanctuary.'

The Victorian and New South Wales police chiefs have also issued a joint statement urging all readers to study the printed photographs of the four suspects. 'Pin them up on the living room wall if that will help you remember them better,' one high-ranking officer was reported as saying. 'Make a rogues' gallery of them, and report any possible sightings in your area. The only way we'll rid Australia of these unhealthy elements is through nationwide vigilance.'

Feb 9

Dear Cath,

I'm just hoping you sometimes check at the post office and that this eventually reaches you. If it does, don't take too much notice of the postmark on the envelope. I'm not that dumb. These days we go to quite a bit of trouble to cover our tracks, as you can imagine.

I suppose my main reason for writing is to stay in touch. It's a way of keeping you close to me, especially when things get tough, and I don't mind admitting they've been extra-tough recently. We're all finding it *really* difficult having the whole country against us. Before, we could at least walk down the street in broad daylight like everyone else. We could pretend, and it was only inside ourselves that we felt different. But since they published our pictures everywhere, we daren't go out until after dark, and we have to be careful even then. It's like being a leper, or something worse, because you know there are weirdos out there who'd shoot you on sight and then be treated as national heroes for cleaning up the streets.

Most people would say that's no more than we deserve, and maybe in a way they're right. I don't expect everyone to agree with where we're at, it's too extreme. What gets me, though, is how the papers and the TV and the Government keep calling us maniacs and mad dogs and traitors and all the rest of it, and how there's hardly a word about *why* we're doing all this stuff. You'd think that printing our point of view even once would contaminate their newspapers or whatever.

Mal reckons they won't give us a fair go because they don't want people to know what we stand for. They're scared shitless that if they printed our side of things, the whole country might start talking about the things that really count. Like how we're messing up our forests and our farming lands, or how we're contaminating our rivers and coastline, and even the air we breathe. Then there's our undeclared war on Australia's plant species and animals, not to mention how we rip off any human beings who happen to get in our way, including most of the original inhabitants.

What's a bomb or two compared with that lot? It's no more than a puff of smoke. Ask any native animal or tree what they'd rather have: us and our bombs, or business as usual? If they could talk, they'd soon tell you. And they deserve a voice too, never mind what the Prime Minister or anyone else has to say.

There, I really am starting to sound like a certain person we both know! I can hear it. If you're still with me so far, I'm sorry.

No, on second thoughts, maybe I'm not. Otherwise I'd give up, wouldn't I? And I can't, because in my heart I know we're at least partly right, if not in what we're doing, then in what we believe. Someone has to stand up and be counted, so why not us? It's a hell of a lot better than fighting in some useless war, like that Vietnam thing years back.

Not that I enjoy being an outcast. It's awful. I can't describe how lonely it gets, even with friends around. You feel you're nobody. It's like living on the moon and looking down on an Earth where people can't be bothered to lift their heads and see you there, waving and trying to get their attention. As far as they're concerned you're no more than a bad dream, and all they want is to wake up and forget you ever existed.

But the worst would be if you turned against me, too. That's *my* bad dream. So hang in there if you can, Cath. I need to know there's at least one person who doesn't think of me as a mad dog. Sometimes at night, when I can't sleep, I wonder what would happen if you weren't around, and I get to thinking how I'd soon become as bad as they say I am. Which kind of makes you my lifeline. I'm not just talking about the fact that we're related – all human beings belong to one big family when you come to think about it. What I'm on about here is memory, and how you're the one who connects me to happier times and better people, meaning our early days and Mum of course.

Mal's been taking a peek at this over my shoulder. He says I sound pathetic, and I probably do. The thing is, I can't really give you any of our day-to-day news – where we're living and what we're doing for money and stuff – so it's hard to know what to write. As I said at the beginning, the main thing for me is to make contact. And I've done that, so I'd better think about signing off.

I won't ask you not to worry. Considering what's going on around here, that *would* be stupid. Try not to worry too much, that's all. I know it must sound freaky, but I have this idea that nothing very bad is ever going to happen to me again. I've reached a stage where – and don't laugh! – I'm sort of fireproof. When I look at the others I don't see it, not even in Mal, but when I look inside myself I feel safe somehow. It's like I've been through the fire and it can't burn me any more.

Bonny reckons that's a fancy way of saying I'm up myself. But God knows, Cath, I'm not proud of what's been going down. Nor ashamed either. All I'm trying to say is how I feel in my bones that I won't be hurt ever again, not like I was before. I've stepped through the flame and emerged on the other side, into a place where they can't touch me.

I wish you were here all the same. Bonny's become a really dear friend, if you see what I mean, and I like her a lot, but I'll never get as close to her as I am to you. I can feel that in my bones, too. You and me, Cath, we might have been twins, hatched from the same egg. Somewhere back there we learned about each other's minds and how they fitted together, like those yin and yang signs you can buy in markets.

But I've come round to my lifeline thing again!

I needn't remind you to do an Inspector Gadget on this letter. You know, the old message-destruct-mechanism. Pouf! And it's gone, and all that's left are the voices in our heads, which are what really count. Don't stop listening to them, Cath.

Much love,
Danny

@ @ @

SECOND TOORAK BOMBING

In a continuation of the ongoing terror campaign, a second Toorak mansion, this one belonging to the eminent financier, Sir Benedict Caulfield, was blown up in the early hours of the morning. There were no casualties. Like the previous bombing, this one occurred while the house was empty.

The police have made no formal statement as yet, but sources close to the Commissioner told reporters that all the early indications suggest another gas-fuelled explosion.

An eyewitness account bears this out. A resident of the area, Harold Croft, was driving by at the time and was forced off the road by the blast. 'There was a brilliant flash,' he said, 'and the whole house seemed to erupt.'

It is understood that this explosion, like the last, was followed by a threatening phone call, demanding reforms in the areas of mining and forestry.

Informed of events by phone, Sir Benedict responded angrily. 'I refuse to dignify their absurd demands with an answer,' he said. 'And I would urge the press not to afford them the free publicity they crave. Their unsavoury activities tell us all we need to know about such people.'

POLICE RAID BOMBER SUSPECTS' HOUSE

Following a positive sighting of Malcolm Arden, one of the alleged bombers, police raided a house in Fitzroy yesterday afternoon, but found it empty.

'There's no doubt they were here,' a senior officer said. 'Judging by the belongings they left behind, I'd say they got out in a hurry. We couldn't have missed them by much.'

The same officer admitted to finding cartons of electrical goods in one of the abandoned rooms. 'If it's all stolen, as we suspect,' he said, 'then at least we know how Arden and his mates are financing their little war.'

Asked about a lapse in time between the reported sighting and the actual raid, police refused to comment. An informed source, however, spoke of a 'four hour delay', and of a 'breakdown in communications between State and Federal authorities'.

The Victorian Premier has called for a full report on the matter.

BOMBER SUSPECTS IN HIJACK DRAMA

In a dramatic series of events, the unexpected sighting of the alleged bombers turned into a nightmare for Charles Drake of Sydney.

Driving home from Canberra in the late afternoon, he was overcome by tiredness and pulled into a lay-by to sleep. 'It looked at first as though I had the rest area to myself,' he said, speaking to a crowded press gallery. 'Then I noticed a Kombie van nestled in under the trees, sort of hidden away, and that made me curious.'

Charles Drake's curiosity led him to leave his own car and investigate.

Referring to the four suspects he said: 'They were sitting together in the shade. When I recognised them I should have walked back to the car. I realise now how stupid I was to run. All I did was give myself away.'

It appears that Daniel Fenton was the one who chased him. 'I didn't realise how big he is,' Drake admitted. 'Once he caught up with me I didn't have a chance.'

In the company of the whole group, Drake was then bundled into his own car and taken on what he described as 'a terror ride into the bush'.

'I thought they were going to kill me,' he said, 'the way they just sat there not saying a word. I tried reasoning with them, but they wouldn't listen. They wouldn't even answer.'

Drake's 'terror ride' ended in an area of deserted woodland about fifteen kilometres north of the Hume Highway, when the car suddenly stopped and he was pushed out.

'They were whispering together over by the car,' he said. 'It sounded like an argument. After that they gagged me and tied me to a tree.'

As far as he remembers, Malcolm Arden was the only one who spoke to him directly.

'Tell them this is just a taster,' he said, and they drove off.

A subsequent phone call informed the local police of Drake's whereabouts, and he was rescued an hour later.

'I was lucky,' he said at the press interview. 'They could easily have hurt me. I think some of them wanted to. That's probably what they were arguing about.'

In a further phone call to this newspaper, a man claiming to be one of the bombers spoke of the hijacking and issued a series of now familiar demands.

For the full story, see inside pages.

The Tribune   *March 12*

NO BARGAINS SAYS PM

In Question Time today the Prime Minister dismissed any suggestion that the terrorists' demands should be taken seriously.

'Nobody bargains with the Devil,' he told Parliament, 'because we all know he's a lost cause. It's the same with these people. The very fact that they've resorted to bombings and hijacking means they're losers, and we'd be losers too if we started listening to them.'

Later in the same speech he referred to 'the long slippery slope that awaits those who respond to blackmail. You give in once and you've created a dangerous precedent. From then on it's downhill all the way.'

⊚   ⊚   ⊚

Published extract from a television interview with Catherine Fenton, the sister of bomber suspect, Daniel Fenton (Interviewer: Dave Scott)

Dave Scott: What do you have to say to the people out there who are living in fear of what your brother and his cronies might decide to do next?

Catherine Fenton: I wouldn't say anybody's living in fear exactly. All that's . . .

DS: Hold on, hold on. Are you telling me people aren't scared for their lives after what he's done?

CF: Not particularly. Not if they've got any sense.

DS: I just don't see how you can sit there and . . .

CF: People aren't scared for their lives every time they get into a car, for instance, yet we all know what can happen on the roads.

DS: And we also know what can happen when your brother's around. He's like a car out of control, you can't deny that surely. He's dangerous.

CF: Only to property. No one's been hurt by him.

DS: What about the man he tied to a tree in the middle of a forest? Would you call that a friendly act?

CF: No, all I'm saying is that he didn't actually harm the man.

DS:	I can hear what you're saying. I'm finding it hard to understand, that's all. I mean, this man was snatched in broad daylight, dragged off to God knows where, and tied to a tree and left. What's more, on his own admission he thought he was going to die at any minute. And you seriously want us to believe he wasn't harmed?
CF:	Not in a physical sense. Danny wouldn't kill or injure anyone. He's not like that.
DS:	What *is* he like, Miss Fenton?
CF:	At heart he's gentle. He's one of the most caring people I know.
DS:	(*Laughs*) You could have fooled me, and most of the viewers out there, I expect.
CF:	It's true all the same. He's only carrying out these raids to make the rest of Australia sit up and take notice. He ...
DS:	He's succeeded in that all right.
CF:	If you'll let me finish, he wants us to realise ...
DS:	I'd like to let you finish, Miss Fenton, I really would. But you see, I have a problem here.
CF:	What kind of problem?
DS:	Well, whenever I ask you to admit what's obvious to everyone else, you deny it. I point out that your brother's scaring the life out of people, and you tell me he's not. I say he's dangerous, and you start quibbling about the meaning of the word harm. And so it goes on. We're just not getting anywhere.
CF:	That's because you won't let me explain things properly. You keep twisting everything around.

DS:	I'd say the boot's on the other foot. *You* won't even admit to what we've all been reading in the newspapers, day after day. Or are they slanted too?
CF:	Some of them are. They leave too much out.
DS:	Oh, I see. So there's a country-wide conspiracy at work here. Your brother's really innocent, and we're all trying to put him down. *We're* the problem, not him.
CF:	There you go, twisting things around again.
DS:	Is it twisting things around to assert that he's a public enemy? A danger to the community? A time-bomb waiting to go off?
CF:	In a way, yes.
DS:	(*Looks helplessly at camera*) Then frankly, Miss Fenton, I wonder why we're bothering with this interview. What exactly did you hope to achieve by coming into the studio today?
CF:	I wanted to explain about Danny, about why he's doing all these things.
DS:	But that's precisely my difficulty. How *can* you explain away fire bombings?
CF:	I said explain, not explain away. I'm here to give his point of view.
DS:	He's doing a pretty good job of that himself.
CF:	No, I mean the reason for the bombings.
DS:	Can there be a reason for an unreasonable act? Does a mad dog have a reason for biting you?
CF:	(*Angrily*) Danny's not a mad dog! He's not any of the things the newspapers say he is!
DS:	We're back to the biased press, I see.

CF:	(*Still angry*) No, listen for once! He's only where he is today because he got hurt. When he was still just a kid he ...
DS:	We all get hurt at some time or other, Miss Fenton. That's how life unfolds for most of us. It's not a good enough reason for declaring war on society. Or are you perhaps suggesting it is?
DS:	You see! There you go again, turning things around.
DS:	Plenty of our viewers might disagree. They might even think that I'm putting a perfectly acceptable question to you. So let me repeat it. Are you of the opinion that your brother's childhood pain – whatever its cause – is somehow reason enough for his ... his ... let's be kind and call it his unruly behaviour?
CF:	Yes, to some extent that is my opinion, all right?
DS:	Aah, then ...
CF:	Wait a minute, wait a minute! You're only getting part of the picture. He's also trying to make the world a better place. You have to take that part into account as well.
DS:	How does burning the world to the ground make it better?
CF:	The bombing itself isn't what he's on about. You're missing the point. He wants you to look past all that, to what's making him act the way he does.
DS:	*Making* him? Did I hear you correctly?

CF: He's drawing attention to all the greed and pollution. To the plight of our soils and forests. To what happens to animals and rivers and ordinary people when they get in the way of certain kinds of big business. *Those* are the sorts of things he wants you to think about.

DS: I'm still finding it hard to see the connection. What does fire bombing have to do with improving the world? It sounds more of the same to me.

CF: I'm not just talking about improving it. I ...

DS: Precisely.

CF: I was about to say that the bombs are his way of telling us to stop. To turn around. To *think*. The improvement will come later, once we've begun to ...

DS: I'm sorry to interrupt, Miss Fenton, but something's worrying me here. To my ears at least, you sound as though you've come here to plead his cause. As though you *agree* with him. Do you?

CF: Not completely.

DS: Ah, so you *partially* agree with throwing bombs. Have I got that right?

CF: No, you've got it wrong again.

DS: Mmh, surprising, because you seem to have a lot of sympathy for his extremist views. In fact you sound a lot like him to me.

CF: To you, maybe.

DS: But you honestly do.

CF: (*Stands up*) One thing's for sure. I'd rather sound like Danny than someone like you.

DS: (*Smiles at camera*) There's clearly nothing more for us to say, Miss Fenton. Thank you for your time.

⊚　⊚　⊚

BOMBERS KIDNAP TV STAR

In the latest terrorist outrage, well-known television presenter, Dave Scott, was kidnapped from outside his Castlecrag home soon after dark last night.

A tear-stained Eileen Scott described how she watched helplessly as her husband was strong-armed into a waiting van by a group of masked figures. 'I tried to stop them,' she said, 'but there was nothing I could do on my own.'

In a further shock revelation, she insisted that more than four people were involved in the abduction. 'I'm sure of it,' she said. 'I counted at least five, and that didn't include the driver.'

'I couldn't see any of their faces,' she went on. 'It was dark, and they were all wearing balaclavas. So I have no idea whether or not they were the bombers. Maybe it was someone else. I'm not accusing anybody. All I want is my husband back and for no one to hurt him.'

The police, meanwhile, are convinced that they are dealing with the same terrorist group. 'Everything points in that direction,' a police spokesman said, 'right down to the threatening phone call.'

Asked to explain the reason for the kidnapping, he admitted

that it wasn't altogether clear at this stage. 'We know only that they mean to hold Dave Scott until certain conditions are met. What those conditions are, we have yet to find out.'

'We might well be dealing with an act of reprisal here,' he added. 'Dave Scott recently conducted a nationwide interview with the sister of one of the bombers. From their standpoint, he gave her a hard time. This could be their method of hitting back.'

Commenting on the present size of the gang, he had this to say: 'Of course we haven't ruled out the possibility that they've picked up new recruits. On the other hand we're far from convinced. Without wishing to undermine Eileen Scott in any way, we think it far more likely that she overestimated their numbers. That's easy enough to do when you're alone in the dark and feeling threatened by people as ruthless as this.'

He said the police have no intention of sitting still and waiting for the kidnappers to clarify their demands. Short of endangering Dave Scott's life, they were doing everything in their power to trace his present whereabouts.

8 The Journal

(The Hunt Begins)

I've decided to start this up again. Mal's not happy about it, but that's bad luck. Without Cath around to talk to, this is the next best thing.

Well, we've done it, we've picked up that Scott creep. And he *is* a creep. All the TV stuff was a mistake, he tells us now. It was the producer, not him, who wanted the show slanted against us. He's all for putting on another programme, one that'll give us a fair go. He says he's even been working behind the scenes to get it up and running.

Yeah, and pigs are about to take off and head out across Sydney, winging their way into the sunset!

I wish we didn't have to deal with people like him, but as Mal keeps reminding us, he's a popular figure. People will do a lot to get him back. With luck we can swap him for some good coverage on that rubbish programme of his. Mal says that if we work on him while he's with us, we might even be able to win him over, but that sounds like pie-in-the-sky stuff to me. I can just about hear those pigs taking off again!

Anyway, the plan is to lie low in Sydney for a day or two, until the row over the kidnapping dies down a bit, and then go bush. Mick's offered us the use of his place out near Mudgee; and Fay and Kris have come good for us here in the city.

The idea wasn't really to drag them into all this. What we were looking for was a helping hand, and after that to be on our way. But the minute we contacted them, they were on side. I kind of half expected Fay and Kris to jump in, because they're old-style rads who want a part of anything that might 'rescue the planet', as they put it. Mick was the surprise. Since we last met, the welfare people have taken Zizi off his hands, and it's changed him. He's a hard man these days, with nothing much more to lose.

So here we all are jammed into Kris's beaten-up little terrace in Redfern. The joke is, Dave Scott's the only one with his own room.

The bloody cellar'd be too good for the bastard, Mick argued when we first got him here, still blindfolded and trussed up.

Except there aren't any cellars in these old places, and the upstairs back room is the closest thing we have to secure space. With the window boarded up and an old mattress nailed against it, it's pretty sound-proof. And if he somehow managed to get loose, he'd still have to creep right through the house and past all of us to reach the street. In any case someone's in there watching him most of the time.

Which reminds me, it's my watch in about four hours from now so I'd better get some sleep.

Sydney
March 30

I've just done my stint with Scott. I didn't want to talk, but it's nearly impossible to shut him up. As Bonny says, running off at the mouth is the only thing he knows. It's what he gets paid hundreds of thousands of dollars for every year.

From the minute I walked into the room he really gave me the treatment, the full benefit of his TV smile and his I-love-you-man TV manner. He must think I'm an idiot or something.

Listen, I told him, my sister was the one you worked over on your programme, so don't make like I'm your greatest friend in the world.

But it made no difference at all. He just motored on, telling me how we'd completely changed his attitude to friendship, and how he could see now that we were the best friends he'd ever had, because we'd opened his eyes to the state the planet's in.

If I'm ever lucky enough to get a second chance, he

promised, I'll turn the whole television industry around on this one. I'll personally see to it that green issues are given the prime time they deserve.

So he went on, piling up the bullshit. I had to cut across him just to get a word in.

Hold on, I said, it sounds to me as if you've seen the light and changed sides. In which case here's the good news: you get to lead our next raid. It's a privilege we reserve for new recruits.

That set him back a bit, and before he could rev up again I tore off a length of gaffer tape and pasted it across his mouth.

Most of the time he's pretty good at hiding his feelings, but for a second or two, while I was smoothing the tape against his cheeks, he let the real Dave Scott show through. In his eyes mostly. I swear he'd have killed me if he'd had the chance.

I can't say I cared too much. In fact it was a relief somehow to know he has some genuine feelings – that he isn't just a talking dummy, the sort I couldn't even be bothered to hate. And before I could stop myself the words slipped out.

D'you know what? I whispered, leaning in close. You remind me of a businessman I knew once. He didn't like me much either.

Maybe it was my tone of voice, but he looked really scared then, reminding me of my Company man more than ever, and I wondered whether I'd needed the gaffer tape after all.

Mudgee
April 2

This is a great place, well away from the road, and with a permanent creek just down the hill.

When we arrived in the dark early this morning, our head-lights picked out a couple of wallabies grazing on the slope.

They sat up and stared at us as though we were invaders from Mars, which is about how I feel while we have Dave Scott in tow. I couldn't help laughing, the way they went bounding off the moment we dragged him out of the car.

See that, Dave? Bonny said, pointing. They must be friends of yours.

She calls him the man without a soul, which is pretty right. But that's enough about him.

This place, as I say, is fantastic. It's so grown in, it kind of merges with the surrounding bush. There are possums in the roof, vines pushing through the window spaces, and a thick stand of tea-tree pressing right up against the back walls. At night, with the creek gurgling away in the background and the tea-tree rustling, it's easy to forget you're in a house. You could be out there amongst it all, sleeping rough, as much a part of the whole wild scene as anything else.

The only thing about the place that gets to me is the old built-in veranda where Bonny and I spent what was left of the night. It faces east, more or less, and when I woke up an hour or two after dawn, there was this swarm of dust motes dancing in the sunlight above my head, exactly as if I'd stepped back in time.

Bonny woke up too after a bit.

What is it? she said, holding onto me. What's the matter?

I tried to tell her, but it wouldn't come out right.

April 4

We had the radio on all day, until the batteries started to cark it. (No working radio in the cars, unfortunately.) Still not any real news. Just the usual stuff about the police continuing with their investigations.

This evening, after we'd listened to the last bulletin, Mal had an absolute rave.

Wait and see, they'll cave in, he shouted, waving his arms around. They'd bloody better if they want him back alive.

Dave Scott sat in the corner, at the edge of the lamplight, listening. He isn't smiling any more.

I can't help feeling sorry for him.

April 5

We had to heat the batteries in the old wood range to get them to work. They still weren't marvellous, but by nursing them we managed to pick up most of the news. The part that counted anyway.

It came through early this evening. And it's official, not just some commentator's opinion. Both the head of the TV station and the Minister have announced there's to be no deal.

This Government will not compromise itself by bargaining with traitors and rebels, the Minister said.

Dave Scott heard it all, like the rest of us, and he had this stricken look on his face.

So what happens now? he said in a scared voice.

I say we call their bluff, Mal announced, and what worried me most was how calm he sounded.

You mean waste the bastard? Mick asked.

What else?

No way! I said, and some of the others backed me. Not all, but some.

I've never seen Mal come on as heavy as he did then. He was standing directly under the lamp, his face streaked with shadows so he didn't look like himself any more. Or at least not like the way I've come to think of him.

Didn't I warn you this was the big league? he whispered, talking as if we were alone and nobody else mattered. You see, Dan, we're eco-warriors now, caught up in a guerilla war, and you must know what that means. We can't afford to take prisoners.

Let him go then, I said.

Mal shook his head, like he was dealing with a kid who has to be reasoned with.

We can't afford to do that either, Dan. We're the same as the Minister you've just heard, we daren't compromise our standards. If we go soft now, that'll be the end of us. We'll have zilch bargaining power.

It'll be the end of us if we start acting like some weirdo army, I countered. We'll have lost touch with who we are and what we believe in. We'll be just another bunch of crazies.

Danny, Danny, he said, shaking his head. Where did you leave your brains this morning? On the pillow? Stop a minute and think. We *are* crazies as far as that lot out there are concerned. It's what we have going for us. They believe we're capable of anything. So let's prove it to them. Let's dispose of this piece of human garbage. He's a very small price to pay, Dan, and they'll think twice about not dealing with us next time.

I didn't turn around, but I could hear Dave Scott blubbing to himself in the corner.

Then we'll be worse than crazies, I said. We'll be monsters. Is that what you want?

No, it's what *they* want, Fay answered, chiming in on Mal's side.

She's right, Mal said. They're the ones paying the piper.

Yeah, but we still don't have to dance to their tune, Bonny said.

Mal didn't even blink, and he was looking straight at me, so I might have guessed what he'd come out with next.

I need to get this clear in my head, he said in the same whisper as before. If I've heard you right, you're saying there are *two* sets of rules here, and what's okay for them, the people out there, isn't necessarily okay for us.

Enough, Mal, Bonny murmured, except he wasn't hearing anybody but himself now.

Two sets of rules, Danny boy, he repeated. One says it's okay for them to waste your old lady, and the other says it's wrong for us to return the compliment. Now is that fair? I ask you.

I can't remember what I shouted back at him. Things would have really fallen apart if Bonny and Mick hadn't pushed between us.

That'll do, Mick said, hauling me off. Let's sleep on this, all right? It'll look a lot simpler in the morning.

But I'm not sure it will. And as for sleeping . . . I gave up on that ages ago.

It's late already and I'm out on the veranda, writing this by candlelight. Bonny's lying beside me, but I can tell from her breathing that she's not asleep either.

Ten minutes or so ago she asked what we're going to do. I haven't answered her yet. I probably don't need to. I think we both realise what must happen next. Mal hasn't left us any other option.

April 6

Mick was on watch when we went in to get Scott, everyone else asleep.

I'm not certain how I feel about this, Mick whispered.

Well, make up your mind, Bonny said. D'you plan to stop us or help us?

He turned up the lamp to get a good look at our faces. Whatever he saw seemed to convince him.

Mal will go spare, he warned us. And I'll be the one who'll have to do the explaining.

Not if you pretend you dozed off, I replied, and I reached past and cut through the rope attaching Scott to the ring-bolt we'd anchored in the wall.

Scott was so scared he couldn't stop shaking, and he clung to me all the way to the door.

Hey! Mick called in a whisper. You coming back afterwards or what?

We're faithful types, Bonny said, following me out. Just try and keep us away.

Of the two four-wheel drives we'd picked up in Sydney, we chose the smaller one and pushed it about two hundred metres along the track before starting it up. Scott's a real office athlete, so he was gasping for breath by the time I bundled him into the back seat.

Where are you taking me? he wheezed.

Home, I told him.

The next best thing to home anyway, Bonny said. This is your lucky night, Scottie boy.

He didn't answer and I think we both took it for granted he believed us. We didn't realise until later how scared he must have been down there behind the front seat, and I'm sorry about that. He'd been through enough already.

Bonny did the driving, heading south along the back roads as far as Lithgow, and then cutting up into the mountains along the Bells Line of Road, which we had almost to ourselves at that time of night. By about three o'clock we were close to the Mount Wilson turnoff, and the night mist was really thickening up, rolling out of the trees and across the road like big whirls of grey-black fairy floss.

The break in the mist and the gap in the trees both happened together.

This'll do, Bonny said, and we swung through the gap and bumped down the slope to where the trees started again.

It wasn't until she turned off the engine that we heard this choking noise from the back seat.

Oh God! Bonny groaned. He thinks we're going to kill him.

Except for the car lights, it was pitch-dark outside, and the mist had rolled back even thicker than before. I suppose from his point of view it must have looked pretty hellish, because as soon as I pulled him out of the car he flopped down onto his knees and started pleading with us.

You're free, I told him, but nothing was getting through. He just went on sobbing and choking and begging for mercy.

Why don't you listen for once in your stupid life? Bonny shouted. We're letting you go. Understand? It's all over.

He looked up at her then, his face wet with tears, these long strands of spit dangling from his mouth.

We're leaving you here for the time being, she explained. Mount Wilson's not too far away. You can make your way there as soon as it's light.

And that was the worst part of all, how he snatched at her hands and tried to kiss them; and how, when she pulled free, he snatched at my hands instead.

Get off! I shouted, and shoved him down into the damp leaf litter. I couldn't help myself.

Bonny draped a blanket across his shoulders before we left, to keep out the worst of the cold. Anyone would have thought she'd handed him the crown jewels.

You're so kind to me, he sobbed. So very kind.

He was still on his knees amongst the leaf litter when we finally drove off.

I'll never forget this, he called after us. Never!

It was all too depressing for words, which is maybe why we got so careless a bit later and stayed on the main drag after skirting Lithgow, instead of sneaking off through the back roads like before. It didn't seem much of a risk at the time.

The roads were still empty, and we really wanted to get home.

Then out of the blue, or the black rather, a car comes gunning along behind us. We could have done lots of things – slowed down, pulled over and let it pass, or even turned off onto a side road. But no, we had to go and speed up, and the next minute there's this blue light flashing and this siren wailing, and the cop driver's damn near nudging our back bumper.

Christ! Bonny said, and didn't hesitate. She just swung the wheel, and we careered off the road, crashed through a wooden fence and a line of bushes, and half slithered, half nosed our way down a steep slope.

The cop car stayed with us for a while, but then we hit the creek and lost it, with water drumming underneath us and spraying out everywhere. As we lurched clear on the other side I looked back and saw the cop car's white outline, tail up, marooned at the edge of the far bank, its lights kind of dimmed from where its nose was underwater. Then we were in amongst the trees, swinging from side to side like we were in one of those slalom races.

Slow down! I yelled, but if anything Bonny only seemed to speed up.

She told me once how she spent her early teens on a big property out near Moree, and God, you can tell once you let her behind a wheel. She really knows what she's doing when it comes to four-wheel driving. The best I could do was hold on as we churned across a couple of open paddocks, dodged through a mini forest, crashed another fence, and finally dropped down onto a back road. And I mean dropped! The crunch when we hit the gravel would have broken up any ordinary car.

We're going the wrong way, I said, because we were heading south, the sky all switched around from how it had been before.

Who cares? she answered, and we swung off into the bush

again, with the car going like the clappers and just about shaking itself to bits.

Because of the noise it was impossible to talk until we reached the next road, which wasn't much more than a track really, with bare-looking hills on either side.

Where're we making for? I asked.

Who cares? she said again, and shrugged. Those cops will have put out a general alert by now. What's important is to clock up some distance between us and them.

And after that?

After that we find somewhere to hide for a day or so.

I could see what she meant. It was already starting to get light, and we hadn't a hope of reaching Mudgee by sunrise. From then on the roads would be swarming with cops, all on the lookout for us. The only thing left was to hole up for a while and wait.

Which is what we've done. We're hiding in a thick stand of trees on top of a hill, so we can see all around. The car's camouflaged with branches, and we've made a branch shelter near the edge of the trees where we can sit and watch.

I was worried about how we'd survive without food and drink, but there's a dam right below us, and Bonny found a plastic ice-cream carton in the back of the car and went down there. I thought she'd gone for water, but from where I was sitting I could see her creeping around after a bunch of cows. When she came back half an hour later, she had white stains down her front and a carton nearly full of milk. The creamiest I've ever tasted.

Once a farm girl, always a farm girl, she said, grinning at me.

⊚　　⊚　　⊚

Later: Lots of cop activity out there on the roads. Blue lights flashing most of the afternoon, which means they must have picked up Dave Scott and put two and two together. They don't need to be geniuses to work out who we are, especially if those cops managed to take down the number of our car. They'll have realised by now it was pinched only a couple of hours before Dave Scott disappeared.

Anyway, Bonny thinks we should play it safe and wait another day, and I agree. Milk's not the most interesting diet in the world, but it'll get us by.

What I'd like to have is a radio, to find out what's going on. I'd also like to contact the others, to let them know we're okay. If they've got any sense they'll sit tight and wait, the same as us, but with cops swarming everywhere they might decide to head out to someplace safer. And if that happens we'll have to fall back on what Mal calls Plan B.

If it happens, it happens. We'll link up either way. It's just that I'm not much good at waiting. It makes me feel jumpy. I don't know what I'd do if I didn't have this journal to keep me busy.

Bonny asked me about it this afternoon.

How come you always carry it with you? she said.

It's kind of like a close friend, I told her, and I saw her face fall.

I thought that was me, she said.

Yeah, you too, I added quickly, but not quick enough.

She came over and squatted next to me in the shade.

D'you know the difference between a loner and someone who's lonely? she said, and then, before I could answer: I'll tell you, there's no difference. They're the same. Try sharing that with your book.

April 8

God! What a time! And we're still not sure where we stand. Even so, I'd better try and keep these entries up to date, or this will get out of hand too.

As planned, we stayed on our hilltop for another night and a day, until I felt I'd be sick if someone so much as mentioned the word milk. All I could think of was solid food, like bread and vegetables and stuff.

Some guerilla fighter you turned out to be, Bonny said, making fun of me. Haven't you heard? People like us are supposed to live off the land.

She's good that way, Bonny, you can't beat her down. The tougher life becomes, the tougher she gets. If we're ever in a really tight spot, I hope she's there next to me.

On second thoughts that's a dumb thing to write, because we were in a tight enough spot when that cop car was on our tail, and we aren't exactly in a Club Med-type hideaway right at this minute. If the situation gets any tighter than it is now, I hope *neither* of us happens to be around.

This time last night, though, things looked a lot different. We'd decided to leave late, so the roads would be clear, and we didn't take any chances. The least sign of headlights, and we were off the road like a shot. Wherever possible we kept to bush tracks and shallow creek beds, working our way steadily north. It all took time, but it was better than being chased and having to hide out again.

Bonny, as usual, was great behind the wheel. She never bogged us, not once, even though we went through some pretty rough country, and by about three in the morning we were nearly home.

Nearly, that's the word which counts here, because with only a few kilometres to go we spotted our first cop car, over on the main highway. A few minutes later, from the cover of some trees, we saw two more.

D'you think they know we're around? I said.

It could be worse than that, Bonny answered, and with the lights doused we drove on.

Not as far as our place. When we reached the edge of the neighbouring property, we turned off, bumped down through a boulder-strewn paddock, and followed the line of the creek till we were fairly close to where it curved round below the house.

We guessed straight away that something was wrong. There were too many lights for a start, and when we crept up through the bush we could see people moving around outside.

I was all for leaving it at that, but Bonny wanted a closer look, so we crept on. Until we could just make out something sort of vibrating in the breeze. I felt this hollow space in my stomach as I recognised what it was. Police tape! The kind they use to mark off a crime scene. I'd seen it lots of times on television. It was stretched right across the front of the house.

The bastards have killed them! I whispered, and the hollow in my gut had turned into a sick feeling.

I don't know why, but I was remembering the time Mal had walked out of Long Bay and kissed me on the cheek, like he thought I was his long-lost brother or something. And I could hear myself muttering things, threats mainly, and couldn't seem to stop.

Bonny, meanwhile, was wrestling with me there in the dark, trying to shut me up. She was also doing her best to drag me back down the hill, and I was digging in my heels, don't ask me why.

You've got to help me, Dan, she kept whispering. You've *got* to!

We were nearly to the creek before I could slow my breathing and regain control.

If they've hurt Mal ... I began, and she cut me short.

No personal vendettas, okay? That was *Mal's* rule, remember. We'll do what we have to, nothing more.

Yeah, what we have to, I agreed, and for maybe the first time in my life I felt I didn't have a doubt in the world.

With so many police around, we didn't dare chance the roads. We kept to the bush tracks and the creeks again, which was slow work, making ten kilometres or so before dawn broke. That's not as far as we would have liked, but as Bonny pointed out, it's a big enough buffer if we're careful.

We've hidden the car this time in an old shearing shed that's well away from any farmhouse and looks as if it isn't used much any more. To be on the safe side, we're camped in a clump of trees further up the hill, where we've built another branch shelter. From here we have a good view of the surrounding country, the same as before, and can easily get away if someone comes nosing around the shed.

Now it's a case of sitting still all over again, at least until after dark. Then we switch to Plan B and head north to the emergency rendezvous point just outside Coonabarabran.

It was hard enough waiting before, but not knowing what's happened to the others – whether they're still alive even – only makes it worse. For once Bonny's almost as edgy as I am. About ten minutes ago she announced that she was off to look for some cattle.

Not more milk, I groaned.

You should be so lucky, she said, and somehow managed a smile.

God knows, we need some lightening up around here.

⊚   ⊚   ⊚

Later: We're both feeling a lot better. There're some shearers' quarters at one end of the shed, and when we broke in we found an old radio. Most of what comes out of the speaker is static – snap, crackle and pop, Bonny calls it – but after a lot of fiddling we eventually coaxed it onto a local station. And the news is, the others got away.

The cops aren't giving out too much information. They rarely do when there's egg on their face. It seems pretty clear, though, that the Mudgee place was empty when they arrived there.

I'm only guessing now, but I'd say the others probably took our disappearance as a danger signal. Either that, or they assumed we'd already switched to Plan B, and they pulled out anyway.

Which leaves a single question outstanding. A really big one. How did the cops trace us even as far as Mudgee?

April 9

Things are looking up. We arrived at the crossroads outside Coonabarabran about an hour before dawn, flashed our lights once, and there they were, waiting for us under some trees further up the road. We had just enough of the night left to head west and set up this camp in a hilly, well-timbered part of the national park.

I'm glad to say there have been no recriminations since our arrival. Only a lot of hugging and back-slapping.

Ah, I thought I'd lost you, Danny boy, Mal said, and I swear I could see tears in his eyes.

I tried explaining then about Dave Scott, and why we'd run off the way we had, but he wouldn't hear any of it.

The world's full of Dave Scotts, he said. Stuff them. There are only a few of us, and we stick together never mind what.

That's the weird part about all this, we really are sticking together. As Bonny put it, when the pressure's on, the glue either melts and runs, or it bonds stronger than ever.

Well, we've bonded. There's no doubt about that. I could feel it, like something in the air all around us, when we sat down this afternoon for a council of war.

It was one of those perfect days you sometimes get out west, still and warm and smelling of eucalypt. The sky was clear, the ground speckled with sun and shadow, and wherever we looked there were these bush-covered hills closing us in. Sitting in a circle in the middle of it all, we felt so peaceful and safe. I know I did. Too safe maybe, because it came as a kind of shock when Mal reminded us what we were there for.

Okay, he said, we've won ourselves a breathing space. Let's put it to good use. So, problem number one: how did the cops find out about the Mudgee house?

There was a lot of discussion about that, and we finally decided how they probably traced us through Pete, who's still in gaol. Once he'd told them about my involvement in the animal rights group, all the cops had to do was investigate the other people. The trail would have led them first to the Redfern house, and then on to Mudgee. The good part about that explanation is how it puts us in the clear, because after Mudgee the trail would have stopped dead.

Right, it looks as though we're safe enough for the time being, Mal said, hurrying us on. Problem number two then: where do we head for next? If we have to get out of here in a hurry, for instance, how do we go about it?

That proved easier to deal with. Bonny and Cherry both know something about the country to the north. They explained how it isn't far to the Moonbi Range, which would offer us some cover; and from there we could make a quick dash across the Tablelands to the wild gorge country that leads down into the Macleay Valley.

Our third problem was the really difficult one – our lack of supplies. We have hardly any food, and both cars are low on petrol.

Why not live off the land? Mick suggested, and Kris backed him up, waving her arms around in that vague way she has.

But after a couple of days on milk, Bonny and I stood out against them.

Fay pointed out next that guerillas are supposed to win the support of the people.

What we need to do, she said, is make friends with some of the property owners around here.

How the hell do we manage that? Mal objected. This is the Aussie heartland. These are conservative people mostly. You try telling them how you want to change their world, and you'd better get moving, because more than likely there'll be a couple of rounds of twelve gauge humming past your ears.

From there the discussion became pretty heated in a friendly kind of way, with everyone dumping on everyone else's ideas. In the end only one idea was left standing – to make a raid on a local store and service station.

It's risky, but the general feeling was that if we leave a lot of mess behind, and make it look as if a bunch of kids have vandalised the place, we might get away with it. After all, there must be plenty of break-ins every day in New South Wales, so the cops shouldn't automatically think this one's down to us.

That's the theory anyway. The plan is for Mal and Cherry to test it out tomorrow night. Too many people would slow the whole action down, Mal argued. He and Cherry can be in and out fast.

Well, here's hoping. Though what keeps nagging at me is the business of having to pinch petrol. Would kids do that? Mick and Fay both think petrol-heads might, but I don't know. Right near the end of the meeting I had this feeling that we were making a wrong move, and I said so.

We have no other choice, Mal insisted.

There's always another choice, I said, and I could hear how boring and dogged I was sounding.

Oh yeah? Mal said, and ruffled my hair. Give us a for instance.

He wasn't being aggressive, in fact he was hardly like the old Mal, and yet I still couldn't come up with an answer. Not a real one. I could only repeat what I'd said before, about this particular raid being a wrong move.

I thought I'd made a fool of myself. Even after the meeting broke up I could feel Bonny sort of looking at me from the corner of her eye. Except it turned out she wasn't thinking bad stuff.

You and Mal, she said, you kind of dance together. D'you know that?

Dance? How do you mean?

She waved a hand in the air, nearly as vague as Kris.

It's the only word I can think of. He leads and you follow, like in a dance. At least that's how it used to be, back at the beginning, but not any more. Now it's all starting to turn around.

I don't know about dancing, I said, but Mal's still the leader, say what you like. You saw him today.

Yeah, and I saw you too, she said, and gave me the same sideways look as before.

Time to draw a line under all this. The light's failing, and Bonny and I need to get up the hill for the first watch.

April 11

Mal and Cherry are back with a carload of food and petrol, and so far the signs are good. No one disturbed them while they were in the store, Mal says, and he's certain no one followed them afterwards. He reckons the Phantom couldn't have done a better job, and he'll get no argument from me. Everyone was so elated that we chanced a small fire and cooked up the best meal we've had in days.

But that's only half the good news. They brought a newspaper back from town, and inside there's an article about Dave Scott, and how he's used his TV programme to come down on our side. I could hardly believe what I was reading! It only goes to show you can never tell with people. There I was thinking we'd need about a million years to get through to the likes of him, and all along he was taking on board every word we said. It's there in the paper, in black and white. 'Young people with consciences', he calls us. And a bit later:

These are the embattled few who are prepared to stand up for what they believe. We may not approve of their methods, but we ignore their message at our peril. Our forests and shorelines *are* under terrible pressure; the poor and the powerless *are* still with us; the creatures we share this land with, the very land itself, *are* being abused. This is the message of these young people. The bombs are merely their blunt and unlovely means of gaining our attention. Long after the bombs have stopped – and stop they must – their message will remain. I hope we as a nation have enough heart and courage to act upon it and so protect our precious heritage. For then and only then, in my opinion, will these young folk step free of the darkness into which they have wandered.

When I finished reading that aloud, there was a general cheer and plenty of high fives. Mal was the only one who didn't really join in, but not out of spite or anything.

Hey, Dan, he said, and tucked an arm through mine. There you were in the big league all along, and I never realised.

That was Mal's way of admitting he'd been wrong back in Mudgee. He said it so softly I didn't think anyone else had heard, but straight away Bonny began whirling around like those old fashioned dancers you see on TV. Before I could get clear she danced right up to me.

You to lead, she said, laughing.

April 12

It looks as though we started celebrating too soon. Around eleven this morning a police helicopter came buzzing overhead, searching. Luckily we had the cars and our gear well hidden. It gave us a scare all the same. Mainly it reminded us that Dave Scott is just one small voice, and nothing much has changed. The cops are still scouring the country, and what nearly everyone wants is for them to catch us. And also to string us up, according to Mal.

Later: We're now double sure there was nothing routine about that patrol. They're onto us all right because two more heli-copters have shown since then. When the third one flew over we were already loading up the cars, getting ready to clear out as soon as it's dark. From the cover of the trees we could see the big blades whirling and this cop in a crash helmet and dark glasses checking the ground below.

Right again, Danny boy, Mal said, looking up. The kids around here *don't* pinch petrol. It was that busted pump must have given us away.

April 13

We've had a hell of a night, but at least we've made it as far as the Moonbi hills. Don't ask me how. There were so many big rigs around! We spent half the night dodging on and off the road, trying to avoid them, and the other half beating our way across country. Without any headlights it was really hard, and the cars have taken a battering. I don't think they can stand much more of this. Nor can we. The others are already asleep, dead tired, and I'm sitting here writing because it's my watch and I have to stay awake somehow.

We're camped at the head of a gully in some pretty thick bush. I'd feel reasonably safe except for one thing. Around dawn, just before we left the road for the last time, this big truck caught us unawares. We came around a corner and there it was, headlights blazing. The driver must have had a good look at us, he couldn't help himself. Whether he realised who we were of course ... that's another matter.

I just wish I had a crystal ball ...

April 16

Things have been frantic over the past few days, but I don't want this to slip too far behind or I'll never catch up.

The mad scramble began three days ago when we were woken late in the afternoon by the sound of helicopters, two of them working backwards and forwards across the lower slopes. They weren't out for a joy ride, you could see that much. The pilots knew we were in the hills somewhere, they just weren't sure of the exact spot.

We didn't wait around. The minute they dropped below the line of the ridge, we jumped into the cars and made off. Although the sun was still up, down in the gullies it was pretty shadowy so there wasn't much chance of being sighted.

By dusk we were deep in the hills, but at the same time not far from the road; and round about dark we rejoined the highway and gunned north across the Tablelands.

The idea was to drive to Armidale, where we'd head east into the gorge country, and for a while it looked as though we'd do it easily. Then north of Uralla we ran into a police road-block. Plenty of cars and trucks had stopped ahead of us, luckily, all waiting to get through, which gave us time to peel off onto a side road and sneak back into Uralla.

We still weren't trapped because of the Oxley Highway branching away to the east. We managed to cut through to that, and again we had a clear run, at least as far as Walcha. But the cops had set up a road-block there too, on the other side of town. We'd have driven slap-bang into it if Cherry hadn't glimpsed a blue light off in the distance.

Cops! she yelled, and Bonny did the same rally-driver thing she'd done the night we dumped Dave Scott. She just swung the wheel, crashed a fence, and hared off across country, with the other car following as best it could.

There's not much real bush around Walcha. Mostly it's open paddocks, so we made good time. We knew the cops had prob-ably seen us, but with the edge of the escarpment not far off, that didn't seem to matter very much. We'd have made it easily if it hadn't been for the helicopter.

We were bumping down the last long slope. In the head-lights we could see an untidy heap of boulders and what looked like thick bush beyond. Another minute and we'd have been safe. But as we slowed, searching for a gap between the boulders, a dazzling light seemed to zoom down from above and the whole night filled up with this deafening clack-clack-clack and the sound of someone yelling at us through a loudhailer.

Bastard! Bonny yelled back, because the light was blinding her. If they'd given her time, I think she might even have stopped. Except they had to start firing, didn't they? They couldn't wait a few more seconds.

We didn't actually hear the shots, there was too much noise. The first we knew of what was going on was when the windscreen shattered and blew in on us. Little bits of glass went flying everywhere, and I reckon anyone but Bonny would have given up. Instead, she did the very opposite: she floored the accelerator. I could see vague shapes of boulders through the light, and then the boulders were behind us and the car was kind of flying.

We hit the lower slope with a crunch I'll never forget. I expected the car to break up, but somehow it survived. So did the other one. I looked back, and I could see its lights weaving between the trees behind us. Then a few hundred metres further on the lights seemed to go out, or disappear or something, because suddenly they weren't there any more.

Bonny didn't need any warning from me and Cherry. She'd already slammed on the brakes, and soon all three of us were running back up the slope.

We found the other car jammed between two trees, a total write-off. Even worse, Kris had busted her leg. We didn't realise what was wrong until we tried getting her out. She gave a terrible scream, and in the light from the dash we saw this piece of shin-bone sticking through the skin, a whitish-looking thing in amongst all the blood.

Christ almighty! Mal muttered. What the hell happens now?

Kris herself was tops. She must have been in awful pain, but that made no difference.

Get out while you can, she said.

And leave you here alone?

Not alone, Fay cut in. I'm staying with her.

Don't talk crap! Mal shouted. The cops'll bloody get you both!

Okay, so they'll get us, Kris said, real calm.

And Fay, standing right next to her: The rest of you split before it's too late.

We could hear the helicopter somewhere above the trees, and already these thin spears of light were pushing down through the canopy quite close to the wrecked car. Further up the slope a whole lot more lights had appeared, bobbing around like fireflies, from where the cops had begun searching the dark on foot.

What are you waiting for? Kris said in a tired voice. Christmas?

Yeah, or Batman maybe, Fay added, and that did it.

Take care, you two, Bonny said in this choked-up voice, and took off.

She was right. It wasn't the time or place for big farewell scenes, not with the cops getting steadily closer and the tops of the trees churning in the helicopter's downdraught. The best we could do was give the girls a quick hug and make for the remaining car.

Just as we drove off, Bonny did something great. Risky, but great all the same. She hit the horn three times, as a kind of thank you and goodbye all wrapped up together. Seconds later she doused the headlights, and we crawled away between the shadowy shapes of trees and rocks, with the car continually crunching into things we couldn't even see. Sometimes we'd bounce off or forge on through; sometimes we stalled altogether and had to back up and try another route. Every now and then Bonny would use the headlights in a short burst, but only when she had no alternative. It was too chancy otherwise, because of the helicopter which was still up there, searching for gaps in the canopy.

I'm not sure we'd have got clear if we hadn't been lucky enough to stumble on the creek. The car nosed down suddenly, slithered sideways, and we were in it, surrounded by a rush of shallow water. From there all we had to do was follow the stream downwards, bumping slowly across rocky beds and picking up speed a bit when we reached sandy stretches. But fast or slow, we didn't need the lights after that because there were no trees to worry about. Not until we were deep in the valley, where the creek sort of petered out, and by then the cops were miles behind.

When we stopped and listened, the noise of the helicopter had dropped to a low murmur, like some nasty little insect somewhere off in the dark. It sounded so far away in fact that we chanced the headlights again. Only in short bursts like before, but that was enough to get us through the worst places, where the trees grew thickest or the level ground gave way to long stony ridges.

We trundled on like that for a few hours. Then some time after midnight, when we'd stalled about three times in a row, Bonny killed the lights and flopped back in her seat.

I'm finished, she said.

We all were, and we curled up on the spot and went to sleep. The three in the back couldn't have had much room, but I don't think they cared. We were too worn out from the constant jolting, not to mention all the drama back there on the edge of the escarpment.

I didn't just sleep. I seemed to topple into the dark, and it was a hell of a long way down. When I finally floated back up to the surface it was broad day, and my body ached from where I hadn't so much as twitched for hours. I also felt hot, from the sun flooding in on us through the windscreen space.

The sun!

I was really slow in working that one out, I admit it. If I'd sat forward and looked up, I'd have *seen* the gap in the canopy right above us, but I was still dopey from sleep, and I only realised the danger we were in when I heard the helicopter.

But my watch is nearly over, and it's time we moved on. I'd better give this a break for a while.

It's after dark and the others are asleep again. A fire would be too big a risk, but we have some candles from the raid in Coonabarabran, and I'm using one of those. It's been a long day, though, so I'll keep the rest of this short.

Now where was I? Oh yeah, back in the car, trying to wake Bonny, with the helicopter hovering somewhere above us. She came to with a rush and soon got the car under cover, but for once she wasn't quick enough because the cops were onto us again.

That more or less set up the pattern for the rest of the day. We'd lose the cops for anything up to an hour, and then we'd run into a thin part of the forest and they'd be back. We just couldn't manage to shake them off.

We had the same trouble the next day, by which time we were hopelessly lost. We could have been driving round in circles for all I know. We were also seriously tired, which was probably how we came to wreck the car.

If we'd been more alert we would never have tackled that last hill. We'd have realised it was too steep and shaly, and how it fell away too much on either side. But like I said, we were whacked, kind of numb, and the car never really had a chance. It started to slide and that was that, it just kept going until it hit something and rolled, and rolled again, and finished up with its wheels in the air and the five of us in a heap on the inside of the roof.

We hadn't been going fast enough for anyone to be badly hurt. We were a bit scratched and scraped around was all. And depressed, that more than anything. I won't go on about what we said and did when we crawled out of the wreck. All I'll say is that there were quite a few tears and slanging matches, and a lot of regret. For about an hour, until the helicopter re-appeared, we weren't what I'd call a pretty sight, in any sense.

If the cops had been able to peer in on us, they'd have thought we were falling apart, and there'd have been no point in denying it.

Here's the funny thing though, the helicopter was what steadied us, the noise it made as it swooped overhead. I won't say we changed back into the tight group we'd been before. We were too filthy and beaten up for that, and way too many bad things had been said, but we did drop all the arguments and the hysterics, and start collecting some gear together. We had to, with the helicopter working that part of the valley and refusing to go away.

Within ten minutes we'd rigged up makeshift packs and were walking out of there. We've been on foot ever since, and I can't pretend we're in great nick. Our shoes are caving in for one thing – they're not meant for this kind of country. And mentally we're also beginning to cave in, as a group anyway. I can feel it in Cherry and Mick especially. When we stopped this evening, for instance, they just flopped down and stared into space, really miserable. We couldn't even persuade them to help set up a basic camp.

What's the use? Cherry said. It's all over, isn't it?

No, it's not bloody over, Mal told her, but without his usual confidence, so the fix we're in is getting to him, too.

Not that it's surprising. We've never really recovered from what happened to Fay and Kris. And being lost like this rattles you after a while. We know we're somewhere in the Macleay Valley, but what's in a name? After days of slogging up and down hills that all look alike, we could easily be on the moon. Except there'd be no cops there.

Mind you, that's one good thing so far: we haven't been bothered by the cops since early this morning. We've heard the helicopter way off somewhere, but it hasn't been near us. They obviously think we're in one of the neighbouring valleys.

I said so to Mal, but even that didn't seem to cheer him up.

They'll probably be back, he answered gloomily.

Bonny's the one who's bearing up best. This evening, before I began writing, she came and sat close beside me, as though she wanted to keep well away from the gloom of the others.

We're going to make it, Danny, she whispered. We're not giving in now.

I have no idea why I answered her the way I did.

Yeah, I agreed. This is only the beginning.

Once I'd said that, it felt kind of true. No, I *knew* it was true. Everything starts here, it always has, in an unspoiled forest like this one, where there are no asbestos mines, and no hospitals, and no businessmen in suits. Only the sound of the wind through the canopy

April 18

We woke to a very different sound this morning. The clack of helicopters. Three of them working this area, maybe more beyond. And the worst news is, they belong to the army.

Cherry was close to tears again.

They're going to shoot us down like dogs, she said.

They don't call the army out against dogs, Bonny pointed out.

They have to find us first anyway, I said.

I was hoping for some support from Mal, but he's pretty glum most of the time and doesn't say much any more. As for Mick, he's crumbling the same as Cherry, you can see it in his face.

I say we surrender while we're still in one piece, he suggested.

And I say you shut your mouth, Bonny came back at him, so fierce that no one said much more, and we set out.

Our one chance is to reach the coast, pick up another car, and disappear. That's easily said. Doing it is another matter. These ridge-type hills seem to go on for ever, some of them too steep to climb so it's impossible to stay on an easterly course. Then there's the forest itself, the way the canopy blocks out the sky most of the time, making it harder still to navigate.

This afternoon Mal started ranting against forests generally, yelling on about how he hated the bloody places and how all these trees were stifling him.

I sat him on his bum in the end, and reminded him that without the trees to shield us, we'd soon be in an army-style paddy wagon.

He soon cooled down, but from then on things were fairly tense. And they didn't improve later in the day when we *might* have been spotted.

Again it was a case of being over-tired. We'd just slogged our way up a hill topped by a big slab of rock. It was a rare break in the canopy, and after a long day we were so glad to see the sky that we stepped into the open without thinking. There was no sign of helicopters, no sound of them either, but only because of the swell of the hillside. The next minute this gush of noise hit us in the face, and as we scrambled for cover one of those big combat craft rose into view.

Did they see us? Hard to say. But that didn't stop everyone arguing again.

Cherry's main complaint was that Mal had led us all on. Everything was his fault.

You and your crazy schemes, she yelled at him. You sounded so plausible, and look at us now. Just look! We're being hunted down by the bloody armed forces. We're *at war*, for God's sake!

I kept out of it until Mick joined in.

Listen, I said, pushing between them. If you want to make

like the army and fight amongst yourselves, that's your business. Me and Bonny, we're heading for the coast.

They all followed us, like I knew they would, but no one's
happy, and there's no real group left. We're a bunch of people
on the run, nothing else. And now even Bonny's beginning to
lose heart.

I can't really blame her. For instance, it's been three or four
hours since we stopped for the night, and yet the helicopters
are still whirring away in the dark. I can hear them somewhere
down near the bottom of this valley where we're camped.

What are they *doing* out there? Bonny asked me a while
back, and I could hear a sort of crack in her voice, like she's
not sure of herself any more.

I told her: I haven't a clue.

I also tried telling her we'd get away just the same, but
although that's something I'm certain of inside myself – more
and more certain all the time in fact – I found it harder to put
into words.

This is our place, not theirs, I said. They're the outsiders
here. The forest will see us through.

Yeah, and God's in His heaven I suppose, she said bitterly,
and turned away to sleep.

April 19

The mystery of last night's helicopter flights has been solved.
I almost wish it was still a mystery, because it turns out they
were ferrying in troops. Soldiers for God's sake! There are
dozens of them, stationed along the ridges and blocking off
both ends of the valley.

We didn't realise they were there until we tried to walk out,
early this morning. We were about halfway up the side of the
nearest ridge when someone called for us to stand still; and

when we backed off there was a burst of automatic fire that ripped through the canopy overhead and brought hundreds of bits of leaf cascading down. The noise alone left us feeling stunned for a minute. Then Mick began grovelling in the leaf litter as though he wanted to dig himself in; and Cherry sank to her knees muttering Mother of God, Mother of God, over and over again.

I knew we'd lost the two of them right there. Scared as we all were – and I mean scared – I guessed that for Mick and Cherry it was over. We almost had to carry them back to the camp, they were in such a state. And I have to say the rest of us weren't much better off. The whole thing had turned into a lousy mess.

As soon as he found his voice, Mick declared he was giving himself up. He wasn't going to die for us or anyone. Cherry, she just went and stood next to him, the two of them more like a couple of dirty, feral kids than the full-on terrorists they were supposed to be.

Mal was still pretty trembly, but not ready to chuck it in yet.

There'll be no bloody deserters here, he insisted. All for one and one for all, that's what we decided.

Except everything had changed since then, us included.

You can't keep people against their will, Mal, I said.

And Bonny gave me a despairing look, thinking I was giving up, too.

Jesus, Danny!

No, listen, I said. We let them go, but on one condition. They tell the big brass out there we've got guns. That way the army won't come busting in on us. They'll hold off long enough for us to think what to do next.

Good one, Danny boy, Mal said, trying to grin.

Then to Mick and Cherry: You got that?

They nodded and were gone, scuttling away between the trees.

There was hardly any wind in the valley, and we heard the challenge from the ridge a few minutes later. This time there were no shots, just a long silence, and we knew they'd been taken.

It wasn't our greatest moment, but we didn't want to waste it all the same, and while the troops were busy with Cherry and Mick on the south ridge, we took off to the north. Where we ran into the same trouble as before – a challenge followed by a burst of automatic fire that tore the canopy to shreds.

We tried both ends of the valley after that, and met with the same result. Except maybe the last lot of gunfire was a bit lower, slamming into the trunks above our heads and spraying us with bark.

Holy Christ! Mal muttered as we stumbled back towards camp. They've got us in a cage. A bloody cage!

And that started me thinking, but I don't want to write any more until I've worked it all out in my head.

◎　　◎　　◎

Later: Two things have happened.

The first is that someone's called to us through a loudhailer. He told us what we knew already: that we're trapped and can't get out and might as well give ourselves up. There was no mention of the soldiers coming in, not yet, so we probably have a day or two before the action starts, perhaps longer.

The other thing is that we held a council of war, and Mal and Bonny are both for hanging on as long as they can.

We make them play it out, Mal said. We go right to the wire.

It sounded like a kind of surrender to me, but he denied it.

You've got me wrong, Danny boy. What I'm saying is that we sit tight. We keep our pride. We force the bastards to come in and take us.

What about breaking out? I asked him.

Get real, Dan, Bonny said. This is it. All that matters now is how we bring it to an end.

We haven't talked much since. Right now they're putting up a leaf shelter for tonight, leaving me free to do what Bonny calls my scribbling. But mostly I've been thinking, and I've more or less decided where I stand.

I'm not with Mal and Bonny any more, which is really sad, but that's the way it is. Because I can't stop now, and I can't stand the thought of going back into a real cage, of being poked and pried at by the press like I was a dancing bear or something. Which means that when the time comes, I'll either get out or I won't. That, I admit, is a pretty scary idea, but also the way it is.

One thing's for sure: the days and hours I have left here are precious. Far too precious to waste, and I plan to use them getting everything in order, just in case. I'd hate to disappear for ever, the way Mum did, and not leave behind my side of the story. Part of it is written down in this diary, but there are other bits and pieces I have no record of. Like what I got into with Pete after they let me out of Karlin; and what set me on this course in the first place, long ago when I was a kid and Mum was still with us. If I'm not going to be around much longer, I at least want Cath to know as much of the truth about me as possible.

So, I'd better get started.

April 22

I've filled in as many of the blanks as I can. I would have liked to write something about Karlin too, how it felt to be in there, but I've run out of those precious hours and days I was talking about. Or very nearly. They called to us from up on the ridge earlier this evening, and dawn tomorrow is their final deadline.

It's really late now and the others are sleeping. Their faces look sort of bruised in the candlelight, but that's only because of the dirt and the dried sweat. They also look surprisingly young, which isn't how I've come to think of them. Or of myself. If I reach out I can touch Bonny's lips with my fingertips. She stirs when I do it, and I'd prefer her to go on sleeping. I've always hated goodbyes, ever since those last terrible days in the hospital.

Up there through the trees I can already see what could be a tinge of grey. The day can't be far off. Soon the birds will start singing, the sun will rise ...

And then?

But before I finish up and leave, there's just one more thing I have to say. It's an admission really, the biggest of all. Last night I took off my amulet and buried it under the leaf-mould at the base of a tree, one of those forest giants that look as though they'll last for ever. It's where Mum belongs. If she lived and died for anything at all, it was for a forest like this one. For all this clean earth and sky and everything in between. As far as I'm concerned this is the only kind of place that makes sense of who we are. We begin and end here, all of us, her included. That's what I've come to believe. It's also why I've done what I've done. And although most people won't approve, they can't call me a liar or a hypocrite. They can disagree, that's all.

9 Report

(The Hunt Ends)

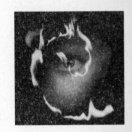

Extract from Confidential Report on Anti-Terrorist Action in Macleay Valley
Reporting Officer: Major Kevin Lofstock

On the morning in question, all troops were in position and all were fully briefed. To the best of my knowledge there had been no attempt to break through the military cordon during the previous twenty-four hours. Nor had there been any response to our final plea.

Accordingly, we went in shortly before sunrise, as planned. Accompanied by a squad of hand-picked men, I led the first probe in person, proceeding straight up the valley floor in a westerly direction. Contrary to expectations, we met with no initial sniper fire nor any other form of resistance.

We came upon the terrorist camp approximately halfway up the valley. It proved to be rudimentary, consisting of a humpy made of cut boughs and a circle of firestones. A lookout platform had been constructed in the fork of a neighbouring tree, but was unoccupied. Moreover, no sentry had been posted.

When we stormed the humpy, we found only two of the terrorists there, Malcolm Arden and Beatrice Stewart, both of them unarmed, both of them dirty, undernourished, and in poor physical condition. We surprised them while they were still asleep, so they were easily overpowered.

Questioned as to the whereabouts of their companion, Daniel Fenton, they failed to tell us anything of substance. Whether they even knew of his exact whereabouts remains problematical. In the course of the interrogation, for example, Beatrice Stewart suddenly broke off and shouted words of encouragement out into the surrounding forest. They were obviously intended for Fenton. Thereafter, she and Arden refused to say any more. Neither would tell us when they had last seen Fenton or whether he was armed.

Before the questioning was complete, I received an urgent message on the field radio, informing me that one of my men positioned on the north ridge had been reported missing. Minutes later the message was amended and I learned that he had been discovered, bound and unconscious, a short distance from the ridge. His rifle had been taken.

I immediately deployed my accompanying squad in a defensive configuration and proceeded to escort the two captive terrorists back down the valley. Those men remaining on the north ridge were also ordered to withdraw, both to cover our retreat and for their own security.

I do not concede that their withdrawal was a tactical error. They were seriously at risk, as the disarming of one of their number had shown, and in the event they incurred no further losses.

We came under attack in the lower part of the valley, in a sparsely treed area of rocky outcrops. As we entered this area there was a single burst of sustained fire from the north ridge, in our general direction, but high. Whether it was intentionally high, I cannot say. We suffered only one slight casualty, as a consequence of a severed tree limb falling on one of my men. Although we returned the enemy fire, as did the troops on the south ridge, there was no answering attack.

At my explicit command we retook the north ridge soon thereafter, but could find little sign of the enemy. A brief foray into the adjoining valley met with the same result.

In the opinion of our two captives, the attack was intended only as a warning. Beatrice Stewart, in particular, was of the view that Fenton was telling us, in her words, 'to back off'. While this is a possible explanation, I proceeded on the assumption that his action conveyed a more deadly intent, and took every precaution throughout the remainder of our retreat. This consisted of keeping my men in a tight defensive pattern and making every effort to secure my existing prisoners. I believed then, and I believe still, that my primary directive at that point was to deliver those prisoners to the relevant authorities. Not until I had reached base camp and placed them under heavy guard, prior to their being flown out, did I give my full attention to Daniel Fenton.

Again I deny that this was a tactical error. Had I pressed home our counter-attack prior to securing my prisoners, I might well have placed our action in jeopardy. Fenton was armed, he had proved himself to be both capable and dangerous, and in the past he has shown friends a high degree of loyalty. It would not have been beyond his capacity to mount a rescue attempt had I sustained the offensive and spread my forces more thinly than I did.

Once at base camp, I resumed my interrogation of the prisoners. Despite my best efforts I was able to find out nothing about Fenton's plans or probable destination. Beatrice Stewart summed up the spirit of that session when she spat in the face of Sergeant Spillane. Towards the end, Malcolm Arden became violent and had to be physically restrained. I deny the charge, widely circulated in the press, that I or my men abused the prisoners in any way, either before, during, or after the interrogation.

Meanwhile, I had divided the balance of my forces into two search parties, and in conjunction with air support they began combing the forest to the north. There were no positive sightings of Fenton throughout that first day, but late in the afternoon one of the two parties found the rifle he had stolen, wedged under some rocks. It had been smashed repeatedly against the rocks and was unfit for further use. Fenton also appears to have discarded the remaining ammunition, which was found scattered in the undergrowth.

We have yet to account for this last piece of destructive

behaviour. One theory is that the rifle jammed and was of no more use to him, though this cannot be proven as the breach and firing mechanism are now too badly damaged. Another possibility is that he merely gave way to his notoriously destructive impulses, and of the two theories I consider this the more likely.

On a positive note, the finding of the rifle did give us a definite bearing, and from that I was able to calculate his flight trajectory, which gave me every hope of overtaking him within the next twenty-four hours. Unfortunately, however, the weather closed in on us during the night. By morning there was widespread rain and heavy mist at ground level. These conditions persisted for the next three days, and although we continued with our search, we were hampered by poor visibility and appalling conditions.

At no time during this period did any of my men give less than their best. And after being fired on by Fenton, they had an added motive for tracking him down. That they failed to do so is not a reflection on them, and nor does it imply any superiority on Fenton's part. In such wild country, a force ten times larger than mine would have been hard pressed to find him. If my men were defeated at all, it wasn't by Fenton, but by a combination of weather, terrain, and the ever-present tyranny of distance.

10 A Meeting

She hadn't heard from him for two years when she made her periodic visit to the post office and found his letter waiting for her. As before, it was addressed to Ms A Grien, and it contained a plain sheet of paper listing a date, a place, and clear directions on how to get there.

A week later she took a roundabout route out of Sydney, and then drove north along the Pacific Highway. Several times in the course of her long journey she detoured onto side roads, to make sure she was still alone; and once she even doubled back briefly, on the lookout for familiar cars. That night she spent in a lay-by just south of Nambucca where she slept uneasily, starting awake at every noise.

By dawn she was travelling north again, but only as far as a small resort between Nambucca and Sawtell. The sun was rising over the ocean when she parked her car and walked onto the beach, which she had mainly to herself at that time of the morning. Only a few hardy surfers and swimmers were there before her, and she soon left them behind, wandering slowly along the sand with a towel and costume draped casually over one shoulder.

The beach itself stretched on for several kilometres and was flanked by dune growth and by the duller greens of the encroaching bush. About halfway to the distant headland she came to a small brackish lagoon, and it was there that she found him.

Her first impression was that he had changed dramatically in the intervening years. She barely recognised him. He seemed to have grown so much older, harder, leaner. Then he breathed her name once, and as they hugged each other in the warm sunlight, she found again the brother she had lost, recalling the childlike smell of his body all those years before.

'Don't cry, Cath,' he kept murmuring. 'Don't cry.'

But she believed ever after that her tears served a purpose.

They washed her eyes clean and enabled her to see him as he really was, unchanged in spite of all that had happened. He looked older, yes, but that was all. His face retained its original openness, its freshness, and that air of vulnerability which had always made her think of him as special, as one of the truly chosen.

'You're the same!' she said, laughing through her tears.

'What else?' he said, laughing back at her, glad just to have her there.

Arm in arm they walked around the lagoon to where the sand gave way to low dune scrub. The whole area appeared lifeless to her at first, but once again, as her eyes grew accustomed to the scene, she saw it anew: the tiny wax-eyes darting through the undergrowth; the even tinier crabs emerging jerkily onto the hard-packed sand; the endless play of hovering insect life, close to the water's edge.

'It's beautiful,' she said.

'It's what we're fighting for,' he answered simply.

'We?'

He shrugged and glanced away. 'I can only do it because I know people like you are out there, Cath.'

'I have to tell you, Danny,' she said. 'I still don't approve. I never will.'

He shrugged again. 'It doesn't make any difference, not to me. You're real, you exist, that's what matters.'

She was silent for a while, waiting and hoping for words of reassurance which she sensed now he would never offer her.

'So you didn't bring me here to tell me you're giving up,' she said at last.

He shook his head. 'I just needed to see you. It's been too long.'

'But haven't you done enough?' she persisted. 'Bonny and Mal say they wouldn't go on even if they were released tomorrow.'

'That's for them to decide,' he said.

'And for you. Why do you have to be different? Your name's in the papers nearly every month. You never seem to stop.'

'How can I?' he said. 'There's still so much to do, and no one's really listening yet. They say they are, but all they want is for everything to carry on the same.'

She nodded, half ashamed of the settled world she came from.

'They'll catch up with you in the end,' she pointed out sadly.

'I don't think so. I'm more careful these days. I learned a lot from my time with Mal and Bonny.'

After years of anxious waiting, she couldn't bring herself to share his easy confidence. Yet she hadn't travelled all that way merely to argue with him. She had more important things to discuss, things that had been preying on her mind ever since a certain morning, years earlier, when she had read aloud a letter from someone she had never heard of before.

'What do you think started you on all this?' she asked in a hesitant voice.

'We both know the answer to that, Cath,' he said softly.

'No, I'm not sure I do,' she confessed. 'Sometimes I think it was because of me. How I didn't do anything after we heard from the Company lawyer. I was the eldest, after all. Mum was sick, Dad useless, and I . . .'

'It wasn't your fault,' he broke in.

'Whose then?'

'Not yours.'

'You aren't answering my question, Danny.'

'Theirs,' he said uneasily.

'Who are ''they'' supposed to be?'

'People with money and power who should know better.'

She took several long breaths, readying herself for what she had to tell him next.

'It may be their fault,' she said, 'but they're not the ones you blame. Not *only* them, anyway.'

'Who else is there?'

'I can't make up my mind,' she admitted. 'There are times when I think you blame yourself.'

'And at other times?' he prompted her.

For her this was the most difficult part of all.

'I think perhaps you blame Mum. You can't forgive her for dying the way she did. All this eco-warrior stuff, it's to show her how different you are. It's to put her in the wrong.'

'From where I stand she *was* wrong, Cath, she should never have died without a fight. She gave up far too easily! Though that doesn't mean I didn't love her.'

She winced and felt her eyes prickle with tears again.

'Christ, Danny! D'you think I don't realise that much?'

'I'm telling you is all.'

'And I'm telling you you've never been able to see her straight. She didn't believe in fighting. It wasn't her way. Why can't you accept her for what she was? Why can't you forgive her? Or better still, forgive yourself?'

He picked up a piece of twig and scrawled two intertwining letters in the sand.

'I don't know if I can explain,' he began, 'but Mum and I . . . we're kind of knotted together. That's the only way I can put it. And somehow, over the years, the knot's pulled itself so tight I can't seem to get it undone.'

'Let me try and undo it for you,' she offered.

'You can't. Nobody can.'

'So you'll keep on like this for the rest of your life,' she said indignantly, daring him to contradict her. 'You'll never stop showing Mum what she should have done, what you've decided to do in her name.'

'No, not in her name. In mine.'

'You know what I mean, Danny.'

'Okay,' he conceded, 'but that's only one way of looking at the issue.'

'Is there any other?'

'Yeah, as a matter of fact there is. Towards the end Mum actually taught me something, the way she lay there in hospital and never complained. I didn't agree with her, but even so she showed me you have to be who you are. Well, here I am being who I am.'

'And who's that?'

He answered with an assurance that surprised her.

'My version of a loving son.'

'Aah, Danny.' She leaned her face against him, blotting out the sunlight. 'What does that make me?'

'More or less the same. A loving daughter.'

'Even though we're so different?'

He pondered his answer for a moment.

'Look at it this way,' he said. 'If Mum posed the question, then you and I, Cath, we're the two possible answers. And like you said before, one of them isn't necessarily right and the other wrong. They just are.'

'You make it sound as though there's an unbridgeable gulf between us,' she said unhappily.

'No, not a gulf,' he corrected her. 'We're knotted together, too. As I wrote and told you long ago, we're two halves of a whole. Like it or not, we need each other.'

She had accepted that idea once, but now she shied away from it instinctively.

'Are you saying I *need* all those things you're doing? The awful things I read about in the papers month after month? All the fire-bombing and tree-spiking and God knows what else?'

'As the world stands you do.'

'No!' she said, and rose hastily to her feet. 'I can't go along with that, Danny. I never will. If you must know, I feel wrong just being here, talking like this.'

She began dusting the sand from her skirt, making ready to leave.

'Not yet,' he pleaded, tugging at her hand. 'Stay a while longer.'

'What for?' she asked hopelessly, but she sank down beside him just the same, unable to break the bond that held them to each other.

'I feel so peaceful with you here,' he said, and rested his head on her shoulder as if they were children again.

She didn't answer – she was no longer sure how to – the two of them sitting with the vague mass of the land at their backs, their arms entwined, gazing out at the ocean.

About the Author

With a host of award-winning novels to his credit, Victor Kelleher remains one of Australia's most celebrated writers for both adults and children. Born in London, he lived in Africa for twenty years before moving to New Zealand, where he began to write, prompted by homesickness for Africa. He moved to Australia in 1976. His novels have received many awards and commendations, including the Australian Children's Book of the Year Award and the Australian Science Fiction Achievement Award. Formerly an associate professor of literature, Victor now writes full time.